TRAMP

B S BHAMRA

Published in 2019 by FeedARead.com Publishing I

A CIP catalogue record for this title is available from the British Library.

Chapter One

As I sat down on my big sofa slowly putting the extremely large cup of coffee a choca moca double chocolate down on it's place amoust the ciggerettes obviously smoked and used, by me with the sound of traffic that I could hear in the disrtance as my window was open and I could clearly hear the argumenyt which was going on in the car park next to my pad built supidly. As a bad piece of arcutecture by all accounts. It was me that stupidly decided to buy the house that had be built for the sheer reason, the purpose of knowing that it was a place for trghe perfect argument. The house was reasonable new and modern I did not like old houses especially the ones in the country side which was why I built this one, only to change my mind a few weeks after later. I had moved in although it was equipped with everything that I could of possible fitted in it and that it was modern including hi- tec sound systems and other machines. You could call me a city boy as most of my family came from the country.
It was reasonably quiet at first but as time went by and time moved quickly as it seemed things especially my surroundings were changing fast.
For the first instance I thought it was my imagination but infact it was true. For example the chip shop which I had personally would not eat in had become a pub the traffic around the place had changed. It had become noisy and there was ofen traffic driving past most of the time, the school was to close and there was the constant noise of children playing I was close enough to hear them. Why I told myself, I did not notice this when I first got here that was a gfood question why I might add it was cosure when I brought it. I thought taking in to account what I have just said. My name is Benjamin

and my girl friend is called Lucy we are going to get married. I am a lawer and my girl friend, well she is my girl friend. She is my girl friend, what, I did not want to tell you is that she is unemployed. Lucy does things that I cannot really discuss with you just yet.

As we both sat down to eat some proper food a conversation started it began it started as I was half way through my half cooked meal one of many I have to remind myself one of many to this day I had not mentioned it. point why? It was because it would cause an argument or it would rain on the relationship a good relationship or maybe it was because I was scared of my girlfriend. Lucy had not caught on and she must of and something wrong with her taste buds because the food was absolutely disgusting. I was quite lucky that we had a dog. Benjamin thinks that Lucy had caught on and knew about benjamins distaste for her food and benjmain in front of her often gave the dog quite a considersable amount of the food that was on his plate under the table. Lucy did not mind she knew not to say anything benjamin knowing with the look on her face that she was upset it was like Lucy was looking at Benjamin with her head on side ways. Lucy still did not make a comment. As Benjamin looked at her he could see that Lucy was going to crack for the first time she was looking really upset. A small conversation started which tuened in to a bigger one it went on all night.
Lucy: " Do you like my cooking."
Benjamin lowers the book that he is reading. He pauses as he speaks to the dog totally pretending that he did not heard her and practically ignoring her blatantly. Still pretending after a nudge, he was obviously else where occupied by the dog.

Lucy throws her napkin down, not angerly but upset enough to leave the table. Upset enough to send a message to Benjamin that she was hurt. Benjmain continued to play with the dog, The dogs name was theo. Lucy wanted to leave the table after sitting back down She had finished. Benjamin did not look up as Lucy's expression on her face was changing especially the colour of her face she was turning red.
Lucy was getting angry for the first time in a few years of there relationship. As benjmain gets up and plays with the dog he is walking around behind Lucy who is sitting down benjmain still playing with the dog as he does grabbing Lucy's attention Benjamin answers the question.
Benjamin:" The food you said what is wrong with it."
There is a long pause as they both look at each other. Lucy looks harder than Benjamin waiting for answers. There is a long silence then Benjamin speaks.
Benjamin:" Oh the food it was good, it was good I enjoyed it."
Lucy: " Is that why you gave it to our dog."

Benjamin continues answering her questions and tells her no it was just scraps he continued.
Benjamin: " Come on darling it was left overs it was what I had left on my plate."
Lucy: " it was more than that it was half of your plate Benjmain."
Benjmain:" prove it go on prove it."
Lucy: " come on im not going to fall for that one the dog has already eaten it there is no evidence left is there."
Benjamin did not know what to say and Lucy had actually started an argument for the first time in there relationship. In a mood with a smile on her face Lucy had finished, they both leave the table taking the plates off the table. In the kitchen while they both do the washing up, Lucy is still angry and contin ues to wash the dishes Benjmain leaves her side Lucy is left talking to her self as she wahes up.
Lucy:" My food I would like to see you cook better, I mean."
Lucy shouts out towards Benjamin who is at the other end of the house,
Lucy: " you know what Benjamin you are really bad company."
Lucy was trying to start an argument.
Lucy: " when lunch is around."
Lucy knew that Benjamin would not hear her clearly so she starts to joke telling benjmain as she acts like he is in front of her.
Lucy: " That was totally rubbish and everything else that goes with those words."
As Benjamin takes a seat as he pours himself out a drink, totally forgetting his cigar and as he gets up to go and find one getting off the bar stool by his personal bar goes behind the bar to find one.

Eventually Benjamin starts to settle down his mood was changing as he picks up his lighter and lites the large cigar only to spill the drink that he poured down himself forcing another change in his mind. He speaks to himself as Lucy was not there.
Benjamin: " Bloody seat."
As he gets up drinking what is left of what was in the glass. The tumbler was empty, half drunk as Benjmain begins to feel drunk he goes of to find himself another drink. As he pours himself another drink he is looking over his shoulder like he was trying to hind the fact that he was drinking like it was a secret or some thing like he had a guilty conscious. He notices that the curtains needed drawing there was a slow welcoming breeze it hits him and he then notices that the window was open as well he chooses to ignore it. he continues to pour the drink in to his glass. He finishes the drink where he is standing as he walks to the other side of his study he closes the window cutting off the fresh air turning a nice brightful room in to a deep dark pace it was a heavenly place Benjamin finally sits down in the dark as he picks up his cigar and continues to puff on the end where he had left it. As Benjamin puffs he is believing and thinking that his marriage is coming to the end and with it's fears he trys to thinks about how it is going to happen. He sits gripping the chair, his grip hard enough to make an impression Benjamin was no longer a happy person. As all the thoughts of how he met Lucy and the outcome of their relationship was coming to an end all around them.

As Benjamin comes to the end of his cigar, he was deciding weather he ejoyed them as much as he used to. On this particular occasion he thought that the smoke was a little bit too strong. He knew that they had been a gift from one of his work mates he thought only to remember that he actually brought them when he was aboard. In fact he recalled that he brought them from some place near America. He was smoking them at the time because he thought that it was fashionable, stupid really. As he takes another dreag on the end inhales with a deep breath noticing that the tip was dreached with his saliver takes another deep breath in pain as it was a really strong cigar as they were quite strong. Infact they were way to strong for his taste at this time it was to much for Benjamin And he knows and tells himself not to do that to himself again simply as he could not handle the strength.

Benjamin finally puts the cigar out now feeling the end of the kick his drink had given him which was joining the whisky that he had drunk, as he previously downed making the feeling twice as bad.

As Benjamin is wanting to change the taste in his mouth he pulls a packet of cigarettes out of his pocket he found them by luck as he just assumed that they were there and they were. They were in his jacket pocket outside in the hall way they were in the in side pocket of the smart leather jacket as he opens the packet pulling a cigarette out of the packet and cooly lights it up. It was very unusual that Benjamin would behave like this this and it was really unusual that Benjamin would even smoke. It was obvious that Benjamin was trying to man up simply as his relationship was going downwards and he found the taste of that unbarable, the cigars and cigarettes did not help.

Benjamin stays put and is waiting for Lucy to call him up stairs to bed.
To Benjamin surprise on that particular evening Benjamin was not called to his bedroom benjmain woke up in the middle of the night on his sofa. As he slowly makes his way up stairs not realizing where he was as he is used to being called by Lucy as he moves up the stairs form his study to his bedroom.
Still feeling the effects from the headache that he had required from the whisky smiling half sobre he stubbles abit and climbs onto the bed Lucy is fast a sleep and benjamin was left beside her grumbling about how and why he wass not called.
The mornning came to quickly in Benjamin s eyes as for having not been called to his room only to find that he had lost his sleep leading Benjamin in to a bad mood for the rest of the day.
Lucy was busy trying to avoid Benjamin she did not want to talk to him they had bumped in to each ogther in the kitchen. As Lucy was preparing herself and not Benjamin some breakfast. There was a long silence between them nobody was talking and none of them would care to break the silence a good start to the day there was nothing like early mornning respect.

Lucy walks out exactly two minutes after Benjamin in neither of them spoke benjmain is left sitting down hands on his head in disbelief.
Benjamin thinks that she either knows that she is playing hard to get, Benjaman realizies that he is going to have tell her and goes after her but by the time that Benjamin was ready it was to late she was already in the car. By the time he reaches her she is pulling in to the main road.
Benjamin questions himself adding up the pros and cons of what had just happened. As he tells himself it was not normal but in his case not. Benjamin is looking down at his watch now realizing the time is late for work, also realizing that Lucy had taken the car. Benjamin thinks for a second knowing that Lucy had no job and she could not drive had taken the car out for a spin. He looks at his watch again believing that Lucy had gone to the gym. He tells himself as he rushes back in to his house as he strips off the clothes that he slept in the previous night jeans, t-shirt. Leaving the clothes on the floor in a different parts of house as he he stripped he jumps in to the shower as he turns on the water waiting expecting the nice hot soothing warm water to appear he receives a shock as he jumps out in fright as the water was cold Lucy had used up all the hot water. he turns on the taps again in a hurry double checking on what the situation in all the frustration he climbs back in to the bath tub telling himself as he does that he was getting to old for things like this as he jumps out for the second time. Thinking quickly he turns to his bathroom sink a strip wash benjmain continues that it could not be that bad as he used to have them all the time as a child he runs the sink taps and there is hot water he washes quickly Benjamin

shouts as he washes that he would be barking down Lucy's neck the next time they meet.

Benjamin picks up his clothes the same way he took them off. He was already late and even more so when he realizes that lucy had taken the car again she would normally take her bike which was left by the side of the house. Benjamin looks around trying to think where her bike was when he looked at the side of the house it was gone his first thought ws that it had been stolen. Benjmain is not that stupid as he checks again double checking believing that he might be seeing things benjmain them clicks as he looks a bit further as he looks in there garage it was not there at first but then he looks closely and finds the bike under some other stuff clearly hidden by Lucy, Benjmain smiles although it was hardly the most manly bike that benjamin had ever seen not only this Benjamin was going to have ride it. as Benjamin takes the clutter off the bike he is speaking to himself.

Benjamin:" So be it."

Benjmain gets the bike out he pushes it to the edge of his drive as he gets on it he gets a few funny looks from passer bys he continues.

Benjamin: " Do not worry I am not a crazy person I have lent the car to the misses."

Benjamin: " bitch."

Benjmain cycles off to work two hours late. Benjamin was not the kind of person to get upset infact it was totally out of character. He would never get upset over silly things small things or anything in that a matter of fact. He was normally normal he was a happy person. He was always complimented and complimentary he was always smiling mind you if you had seen his posrture he looked like from the outside to be rather trim there was a possible cause that he was not on his way to work he was off to the gym.

Benjamin hurry's along like a school boy on is way to school and to make things worse the bell on his bike had broken and the roads were packed and filled with car as and buses and children all walking making his journey practically impossible it seemed like a dream it seemd at that moment at least ahundread people all in the same place walking all moving in the same direction. It was like a zoo Benjamin gets off the bike a few people noticed and they noticed as he did that he was the only person pushing the bike making it arcward for Benjamin to get past and move through on coming people. Even though he made that journey everyday he was feeling out of place. And he was sure that Lucy had made him look like an idiot. As for the looks that he was getting did not make him feel any better. Benjamin was shocked as for the amount of people how busy it actually was in the morning. This gave Benjamin the impressin that that he was one of them one of the zoo, a life everyday life does not change the same routeen everyday up at eight, by work by the time meeting people clients in the same place, meeting the same people day in and day out, twenty years I have just noticed that nothing has changed as I gotv ij to the office it had happened again this time I thought that I was going to pass out. The words good journey came to mind as I met the mail lady and the tea boy. As they said there good mornings and it was mr and misses beaty.

Misses beaty was a funny old lady and had been in the company her whole life. I used to think that she was a spy, the way she looked at you and she would appear out of knowhere then disappear the same for her husband. They both would dress smartly, the thing that I found funny was that they dressed the same way everyday. They looked exactly the same I often thought

that one of them must have had plastic sugery, they looked alike so much. Maybe they were twins, I had that thought too but they were not. They were the same apart from there clothes. They were often mistaken for each other and were often judge mental people would say that I would not trust them to make us cups of tea not in a million years. I would not trust him to make my tea. Her husband seemed to follow her around do you think that he is blind simply because he would say I cannot see that is that your name as he handed out the mail off his trolly and if you did not answer him he would raise his voice like a school teacher and ask again. Is this your mail he never made any mistakes it was the usual person not looking at the at the persons actual name on the envelope.
I suppose in a sense they were good enjoying people and also guess that this office cannot be the only office on the planet that an old person an old biddy that does not know how to make a cup of tea and deliver a letter by a man who is half blind
As the day went on Benjamin is behind his desk minding his own business it was coincidence that he was looking outside his office windoiw when he thinks that he sees Lucy. The first thought oh what have I done there was not a second trhought as Lucy had just walked in to his work place to reteive her bike. Benjamin knew that she ment trouble and knew that he would have to esplain to his boss about her visting the offices.
Lucy gives Benjamin the finger as she notices him surprisingly looking surprised that she was there. his words straight afterwards was the same Benjamin signs and finishes and leans back away from his window. Before Benjamin can finish the conversation with Lucy the old lady was talking to him taking his attention

away from lucy. He just tells her he would have a tea except thee was no tea as benjmain contin ues a tea the lady was looking at him stragely as she was not the tea lady she was holding his mail. As he contin ues to tellher to hurry up trfyiong to keep one eye on Lucy. Making sure that he does not start a converstion with the old lady did not occur so he could get on with his day. As he drops his head and speaks quietly the word and it was only one came to mind.
Benjmain:" Bitch."
The tea lady looks up at him.
Benjami. : " Oh no."
Benjamin apologises.
Benjmain:" It is not you I mean the wife."
The tea lady misses beaty looks at benjamin she points her finger to her name and taps it twice walking off after giving Benjmaina wink after turning away and walking off completely.
Benjamin was confused by her actions. Benjamin thought that his secret was being kept a secret the old lady who was at least twenty away speaks out.
Old lady: " women trouble uh."
Everybody in the office heard. The lady spoke very loudly Benjamin was in shock, she had told the whole office, as he leaps off his office chair just about to shout as he knocks over his cup of tea over his computer and on the his paper work and on to the floor. As benjmain shouts in pain not of the point of spilling the tea down himself also but for mrs beaty. Benjmain had scolded himself down his arm, hand and wrist he sits at hiome waiting for the return of Lucy. She had left a message on the fridge door that she would be at the gym and that dinner was in the oven Benjamin had quite a lot to say to Lucy except she was never there to receive it so it may seem not that benjmain was looking for an

argument she was never there when there relationship goes wrong. Lucy gets back late.
Lucy: " Hello."
Finally she speaks.
Lucy: " How has your day been."
Lucy looks at Benjamin and sees that his hand and arm are in bandages she continues.
Lucy;" Erm uh erm".
Looking arcwardly at Benjamin then continues.
Lucy:" Have you had an accident at work."
Benjamin: " Yeah I was busy slagging you off and bumped in to my desk and knock over my coffee, tea."
Whilst the tea lady was having a boast about what chocolate bar she was going to sell me."
Benjamin nearly in tears continues,
Benjamin: " I only wanted to buy her tea to stop her telling me her life story and I was just about to call you a bitch."
Lucy:" Then it serves you right."
Lucy smiles then laughs as she canot drop the thought for a minute benjmain insists that it was not that funny.
Lucy sits down next to Benjamin with the ruc sack that she places in front of him.
Benjamin: " Whats this been to the gym."
Lucy: " Yes that is why I am nice and sweaty."
Benjamin:" that's why you smell nice and sweaty."
Lucy:" No I do not I have taken a shower."
Benjamin: " you do not smell like you have just taken a shower."
It was clear Benjamin had started and had said something funny as Lucy had a smile on his face.
Benjamin:" My God are you thick Lucy."
Lucy:" what."
Benjamin:" you smell you really do."
Lucy stands up looking at Benjamin.

I asure you that when I had finished my work out I am nice and showered and deoderantised theres some thing wrong with your nose if you think that I smell."
Lucy knew that Benjamin was just playing around with the converstion not realizing that he ment it he was being serious. The converstion ends with Lucy leaving the room and going back up stairs, Benjamin is left alone he falls asleep on the sofa in front of the tv. Only to be woken by the claws of his cat early in the morning. As he lays there on the sofa half asleep trying to fight the cat off him at he same time. The cat wanted feeding. Finally Benjmain gives up and pushes the cat off himself. Speaking out half consciously half asleep.
Benjamin:" Lucy get off, Lucy go away."
The cat continues until Benjamin feels his fur and not his claws. This time Benjamin jumps pushing the cat off himself.
Benjamin:" Ah it is you. I know you you need feading."
The cat still half politly looking at Benjamin as soon as Benjamin had finished talking to the cat they both walk to the kitchen the cat leads the way.
Benjamin feeds the cat and leaves him to eat, as he puts the plate down the smell of the fish in the food makes Benjamin think whats in it instead of reading what is on the packet he refers to the cat that it gets a better meal than him and continues to tell the cat that Lucy cannot cook. He strokes the cat and goes upstairs to bed. Lucy is asleep. When Benjamin awake this time he is on time he gets washed and dressed, this time leaving Lucy asleep as he goes off to find his car keys. He leaves Lucy asleep an heads off to work.

As benjamin starts his journey it begins to rain, Benjamin could see clearly that it was going to be one of those days. Benjamin had missed his breakfast he could feel the effect of not having his morning coffee which Lucy would normally prepare. As he looked upwards the clouds were changing and Benjamin was beginning to enjoy himself he really in joyed the elements and if therfe was going to be a storm he would be the first in it. he could see the storm above him as he watches the clouds darken and the daylight disappear it was close to an eclipse but not quite there as he pulls hisb car over and takes some pictures it started with his route that he was on and ended with did you see that obviously the lightening from the storm which had arose within a few minutes not forgetting the thunder it was loud. Benjamin knew it was the perfect weather for his fravorite hobbie he leaves his car parked by the side of the road away from trees and pilons and goes off in to a large field knowing that he would be late for work he sits himself down in the field and takes some photographs of the storm. He did not care if he was late for work Benjamin was looking for the perfect photograph. He was going to write about his pictures and send them to the local press. He would write the story when he gets to work, hopefully nobody would notice. He sits down crossed legged and takes the pictures. There was all kinds of tthings happening in the skys above him. As he clicks taking picture after picture as he changes his posture as the clouds around him change.

Out of twenty three pictures that Benjamin had taken Benjmain had three reasonabvle good photographs. The ones that he really liked were the ones with the lightening in. After getting a second opinion he taped the photographs to his desk in front of him was a picture of Lucy carelessly he removes the picture tears it up and throws it away with out a thought only to realize later what he had actually done. Benjamin had hurt himself not realizing the picture was a good one it was one of the photographs of when they had first met. Benjami needed to change his attitude. By the end of the day Benjamin did not have to much to do and finding the storm earlier in the morning gave him a lift although it had made him late for work and a small minor grilling by his boss. The second time this week due to girl friend relationship problems. As the clock ticked Benjamin was waiting for the last few minutes as he tidied his desk. It did not matter to much he got up from his desk and picked up hus jacket leaving he building aas he gave his good byes. As Benjmain neared the door hoping for another storm but denied as it looked ok outside and Benjamin was a littke bit disappointed with the weather he was hoping that there would be another storm. He said to himself that lightening always looked better in the evening, the nighttime in the darkness of the skys. It seemed to be correct from his point of view it looked better and felt a little more exciting. He tidys his desk once more and and prepares himself to leave five fifteen just a minute and he would be on his way.

Benjamin is watching the time he leaves the building via a lift the lift was on the other side of the room and it gave the office it's status he steps in side pressing the button ton be taken down to the bottom and then he walks to the front door of the building.

Benjamin walks in through th door Lucy is watching tv she had the sound up loud it was loud enough to been herd from the front door Benjamin has to ask her why was it so loud.. before this converstion Benjamin walks in quietly standing behind Lucy watching the programme over her shoulder after a minute he interrupts her with a hello. Lucy jumps and continues to watch the tv then tells Benjamin not to do that which was standing behind her and not telling her.
Lucy:" do not do that you scared the life out of me."
She continues.
Lucy:" Your dinner is in the oven."
Benjamin turns around putting his bag down onto the floor his bag has his coat in it he takes his coat out of the bag throwing over the sofa, not the sofa that Lucy was sitting on he undoes his tie and walks to the kitchen.
Benjamin:" where is the food darling."
Lucy:" it is in the oven."
Benjamin is looking and finds nothing.
Benjamin:" where I cannot find anything."
Lucy:" Er have a look in the fridge."
As Benjamin moves around the kitchen from his cooker to his fridge he asks Lucy what it is, there is no answer from Lucy.
Benjamin:" may I ask what it is, no wait I know I have to guess."
Benjamin was less impressed that it was a saladas he continues as he was hoping for something a little more Monday. He takes te plate of food in to the living room with the plate on his lap he falls asleep in front of the tv.

With Benjamin out cold after his un eaten dinner Lucy goes up stairs for a shower. Benjamin does not awake until late into the evening and when he does he awakes all grumpy as for the salad on his lap it had moved from his lap on to the floor. He was feeling like he had not slept and was acting like he was in the office. He takes himself upstairs he undresses and gets in to bed. Lucy was else where until she joins him. Lucy throws her arm around him only for Benjmain to throw it off him this happens twice during the evening. Benjamin must of been working hard and with Lucy with out a job she was beginning to get jealous. As Benjamin sleeps like a baby Lucy is awake summing things up. As she ways up the pros and cons of getting her own back. She was thinking that in the morning she would start to look for a job and keep it a surprise and if she gets one and tell Benjamin later it would be a surprise for Benjamin and her self. Benjamin awakes as usual late as he struggles to find a clean shirt and looking everywhere for his smart trousers as he hps across his bedroom putting on his socks, and with falling over. As he dresses he stops and asks Lucy to fix his tie she does before he forgets then remembering where he had left the keys to the car. He leaves the house after stealing Lucys breakfast from her hand as he leaves the house he slams the door shut forgetting to say good bye thinking that it would be ok and Lucy would be cool with it.

Lucy goes straight up stairs to her lap top and starts a job search. Lucy was not hinck as such infact she wass quite talented I suppose you could call it left sided the more creative person on the creative side of things rather than right sided which would be the opposite. This continued for about a week each time she hunted she was getting closer to Benjamin not knowing that in the end she would find a job that she wanted except it was in the same place as Benjamin. When Lucy gets a phone call from Benjamin's boss she is delighted knowing that Lucy and Benjamin were going to be house mates team mates best friendsas they are working side by side.

All Lucy had to do was to break the news to Benjamin. Only to the fact that Benjamin went to work to get away from her only now she had the chance to be his partner not in crime but in work. The interview was in a week and it gave Lucy some time to break the news to Benjamin, Who was in control of the relationship at that moment. They were going to sit down and decuss it in a professional manner the in's and out's of Lucy's behaviour. Benjamin was being cool and Lucy was hoping that it would surprise him, Lucy was hoping hat her new boss had not told Benjamin the truth before she did. As Lucy through Benjamin gets the job in the same company as Benjamin he is happy Lucy was now thinking on the same level as him. Lucy was surprised as she thought that benjamin would flip in fact it was the opposite. And Lucy was impressed and surprised that he said nothing and welcomed her.

To lucy it seemed out of character for Benjamin to agree with out an argument some where maybe Lucy was dreaming it seemed so weird that Benjamin had not complained maybe she thought Benjamin was waiting for her to fall thinking hat she would not be able to hold her new job down. Maybe he was just welcoming her because he had no choice. Again when the subject came up in conversation there was no doubt in him for her, Lucy was being paranoid. For the next couple of weeks Lucy was by Benjamin side. Benjamin was now her mentor and also a work mate and a team they were doing everything together at that point they were looking indistructable. Whilst Benjmain continued to introduce her to his team the old ladys the boss and others benjmain could do nothing but watch as he guilds her gently occasionally Lucy looked like she was loving everything about her new job. She was settling down quite quickly. Time to was moving quickly for Lucy as Benjamin's desk job as a desk job Lucy's on the other hand was unusually is asked out on photo shoots, Benjamin was jelious and was keeping a low profile. Lucy could not see the jeliously that she was creating Lucy could not see Benjamin's state of mind and Benjamin could see clearly that it looked like she was going to get him fired and take his place amongst the vips of the company. She could not see the damage that sshe was doing and it was not just at work, Benjamin could see what she was doing. And when he finally flipped with the over thinking of the whole situation he made sure that she was on the receiving end. Benjamin told her while at home that he would take the settee and not his usual place beside her in bed. Lucy did not think anything of it and thought that he hust needed some space. Benjamin jeliously was getting worst he made it unclear why he was sleeping down stairs he continued to take the sofa. Benjamin did not want to speak to Lucy. Until Lucy breaks his silence Lucy had brought it up and Benjamin was itching for an excuse to start an argument over the position she was holding within the company.

Which was now better than his. After a week Benjamin finally gives in and climbs back into bed his word to Lucy were of the sofa was doing my back in. Lucy says nothing as she was aleep with her work on top of her. Benjamin starts to talk.
Benjamin:" Hay."
There is no answer from Lucy. Lucy stays silent fighting the thought as she wakes she answes him with a hay.
Lucy:" have a change of heart uh."
Benjamin:" I could not sleep on that sofa anymore."
Lucy reaches over to him and touches his shoulder.
Benjamin:" What do have have there."
Lucy:" oh nothing some kind of report I cannot get my head around it, it is extremely confusing I do not think it is real."
Lucy continues after a short silence.
Lucy:" It is a report."
Benjamin :" Ok I know you just told me. What report arrh."
Benjamin jumps up right.
Lucy;" yeah a report. I think tht is what it is called where have you been the last six weeks everybody is talking about this article come on you cannot tell me you did not know about it."
Benjamin is gob smacked.
Benjamin:" how did you get that article."
Lucy:" It was given to me buy the boss."
Benjamin says nothing Lucy had chosen to pick and right the article on one of the biggest companys in the world with the business men to go with it. Benjamin continued.
Benjamin:" You have to be seriously good or seriously stupid to except a job like that. I mean to take on hat

kind of responsibility. It is a job that would break you and not make you."
Lucy shuffles up she is now awake sand listening.
Lucy:" What."
Benjamin:" if I could see you coming I'm sure that they would too."
Lucy is quizzed benjmain continues.
Benjamin:" They trying to cut you loose as soon a that article is written they will have you fired as soon as it is printed. "
Lucy: " On what grounds."
Lucy was now getting upset almost instantainously she puts the paper down she is surprised that Benjmain knew simply the fact she had not discussed her job with Benjamin before.
Benjamin|:" I am not saying do not take the job what I am saying is be careful and be craefull of what you right.
Lucy sighs and leans over on to her side she thanks Benjamin. Lucy trhen continues.
Lucy:" Your jelious it is written all over your face."
Benjamin:" No im not I'm just looking over you like I should."
Lucy get even more upset,
Lucy:" Look Benjamin I can look after myself at home, outside, and at work. I know you do not think I am capable but right now more than you. I am ugly enough to look after my self. And in future stay out of my business."
Benjamin butts in.
Benjamin:" Your business I like the way you said that now look I'm just warning you ok look here is a bit of advice drop the story it would be the best thing you could do in your position. If you want to keep your job. There I said it."

Lucy puts the paper down again leaning away from Benjamin. As benjmain suffles down and a little bit closer Lucy turna of the table light ignoring Benjamin. As he suffles closer lucy this time turns her lights back on.

Lucy:" What,"

She turns over forcing Benjamin away, Benjamin says nothing she turns back with her back against Benjamin she turns her light off. Benjamin stays awake with his side table light on. Lucy tells him to turn it off Benjmain does as he is asked he stays put on his side of the bed he lays in the darkness awake.

Lucy:" You know it would be nice if we could fall in love again."

Benjamin:" Again."

Benjamin pretends that he does not know what he is talking about although he shuffles down further in to his duvet there is silence and a long pause lucy is upset as for Benjamin not answering her with a compliment she sits upwards joining Benjamin who ahd moved back out from under the duvet back in to the previous position. As benjamin is struggling to get comfortable he leans a little bit to far falling out of the bed on to the floor. Benjamin falls with a pillow and as he gets up to walk out he takes the pillow with him down stairs. He is on the sofa. Lucy calls to him there is no answer from Benjamin, He picks up the remote control and turns on the tv and falls a sleep. When the morning arrives Benjamin wakes up with a jump automatically checking the time as if it was by habit. Lucy is walking past nice and dressed and ready to leave. In a rush and asks her why did she not wake him Lucys reply that she did not his shudule as she walks out of the room and out of the front door.

Lucy:" ive got the carkeys you've got five minutes to in here I am not going to wait, it is your own fault as you over slept."
Benjmain was in slow motion if that was not enough it was an excuse for another argument if he did not know what was.
Benjamin continues.
Benjamin:" do not worry you can go ill take the bike."
Lucy could see himfrom the car he was by the window looking for a shirt from his closet Lucy calls out to him again a huge below.
Lucy:" You have got five minutes and I am going I am not being late on your account."
Benjamin:" Ok ok look just go I will take the bike."
Lucy:" Ok it is your dession."
Lucy lowers her voice as Benjamin does the same, as Lcuy drive off Benjamin is left talking to himself.
Benjamin:" I will take the bike."
Lucy is also talking to her self.
Lucy:" Good I will see you at the office."
Lucy finishes her toast and does the rest of her make up as she enters the building her work place. She sits down close to her desk and waits. Benjamin is quick to get ready as he tells himself that he has been late again he could not afford to be late again. Lucy steps outside for a moment te plan was to wait for Benjamin and rub it in. Lucy still outside waiting adding un needed pressure. Benjamin slips outside once he has prepared to leave and takes the bike from the ally way by the side of the house heads off to work. Not knowing that Lucy was waiting to greet him knowing that Lucy had taken the car, Benjamin rides in right past her pretending not to notice her and totally ignore her as she called his name making believe that he did not hear her. Lucy catches on believing that Benjamin had given up on her

completely. Realizing the time this time she drives off in a bad mood as she thinks that Benjamin has made her late by not appearing on purpose benjmain was half an hour into his journey to work. Believing that Lucy was already there out of knowhere her car appears driving fast cutting Benjamin up just for the pleasure she did not stop and Benjamin was else where as he did not even notice his own car. Benjamin thinks that he was seeing things and speaks to himself his words were.
Benjamin:" I am sure that wass my car."
There is a pause then Benjamin continues
Benjamin:" Lucy."
His second thought was if that is who I think that was that means Lucy must of waited a nd he did not see her he continued as he watched his car with her in the driving seat as he pulls over on the bike to watch her disappear in to the distance. He tells himself again this time the opposite it was not his car even though he knew that it was. Knowing that it was his car he hurrys to work following as close as possible until they both turn into the work place they are in the car park, they both stop. Benjamin is taking his socks down removing the bycle clips from himself as he puts them both in to his works bag. Lucy on the other hand is still parking he car they both arrive at he same time to the doorway benjamins reminds her that she has no licence and tells her again that the car that she is driving is his he ends that converstion quick by telling her to go first he belived that the term was lady's first. Lucy walks in Benjamin follows, Lucy does not think of the thought of saying thank you. Benjamin is already in a mood they both walks in to the office and sit themselves down on the desks opposite each other who ever chose the desks was playing a dangeroius game and Benjamin was soon to complain leaving Lucy out of the picture

there was no harm done infact Lucy was as happy about it as as was Benjamin a small change of scenary the boss said and Lucy and Benjamin agreed Lucy was now even further up and across the office. It seemed that everybody was getting on Benjmain he was out of the office and Lucy was finishing her article, and wasmakin friends quickly infact she had invited a couple of her work friends back home for a dinner party and totally forgotabout it including Benjamin. On top of that totally forgot Benjamin's feelings. Either way it loked like Benjamin this weekend had company. He was on his best behaviour.

The week ends quickly and Friday nights has arrived. Lucy is getting nervous and showing her nerves. Benjamin is in the kitchen cooking and half way through the conversation which would turn in to an argument.

Benjamin:" You could of told me."

Lucy:" I did not want to reuion the surprise."

Benjamin:" well I was hoping well it certainly has I was hoping for a night in tv and bed that kind of thing."

Lucy:" I thought it would be good you know make some friends that kind of thing."

Benjamin:" you know Lucy you have totally the wrong attitude. It is totally different to mine."

Lucy had forgotten to remind Benjamin of her plans. Benjmain was expecting a nice quiet night in. Lucy smiles and Benjamin was quick to wipe it of her face

Benjamin:" No Lucy it is not ok it is not funny you live in a dream."

Lucy stops laughing as benjamin drops the food that he is chopping up on to his chopping board.

Lucy:" what, what did you just say."

Benjamin knows that he has said something that he should not of said turning the argument in to Lucy's favour.
Lucy:" what did you just say."
Lucy aproches Benjamin looking like she was about to busrt out in anger.
Benjamin:" It was nothing."
Benjamin could clearly see that Lucy had lost her temper. She walks towards him clenching her hand.
Lucy:" You are very lucky that we have got company this evening I will not forget what you implied I will get my own back."
Benjmain smiles knowing that she took the insult lightly.

As benjmain prepares the food Lucy is up stairs getting ready but instead she is having a bottle of wine. As she checks the time she knocks back another glass of wine. Benjmain is now dressed and looking smart casual he too is looking for a drink Lucy had already taken his, Benjamin calls to her from the bottom of theb stairs. Lucy answers knowing already what he wanted,
Lucy:" there are a few more down in the cellar no wait in the cubboard."
Benjamin:" You read my mind."
Lucy downs the rest of her glass and is quickly down stairs to help Benjamin with his. As Benjamin open and pours himself and then lucy a glass of wine Benjamin asks Lucy what time are they expecting there guests. Lucy tells Benjamin about half past eight, Benjamin looks at the clock good Benjamin thought he would have some time to get drunk.
As there four guest turn up two at a time Benjmain is nicly drunk as so is Lucy. The first two guest are quick to compliment Benjamin's home the home was particulary the hall way a popular subject as it had some seriously funky art streamed across its walls. It was the first topic of the converstion at the dinning table. Before the other couple had turned up.
Lucy: Oh hi we did not think that you were going to make it. let me take your coats."
As Benjamin takes them straight to his bar for a drink which was a ritual on arrival. Letting them know that they had not missed much just a small converstion about art. And a couple of drinks, they both join in the converstion. And they all continued the conversation about the art in the hall way. Lucy was in the kitchen busy thinking tht talking about art was not so disiable and wanted to change the subject she was getting upset

as it was her dinner party and Benjmain was getting all the attention. Lucy continued to check the food it was nearly ready.
Micheal:" So how is Lucy setting in."
Benjamin:" She is as she is what you see now it is her all the way. I will stop you there she is in the kitchen if you want to talk to her."
Micheal:" Oh sorry."
Theres a pause
Benjamin: " Hay gotcha." Benjmain and micheal laugh. She is doing fine.
Micheal:" She must have a hard punch she looks like she going to the top. She is shinning all the way through. Her lastest story." Theres another pause from Benjamin he was not really listening Benjamin calls to Lucy she is in a converstion.
Lucy:" hold on te boys ar calling keep an eye on that I won't be a second."
Lucy leaves her guest and her drink.
Lucy: " what."
Benjamin:" Lucy darling micheal has something to say to you."
Micheal catches on and tells Lucy how good her articles are. Lucy smiles after a quick compliment and walks back to her guest, picking up her glass of wine. As the conversations in the room change going from how smart micheals wife is to how cool Lucy was the boys were having a laugh. Lucy and Micheal get stuck in to a long conversation benjmain reminds them that they are out of work hours and should not be talking about work they were hear to get away from that. Benjamin continues that they should drop the conversation and start partying. They all agree and micheals appogises again. Once they are half sobre and seated at the oak dinning table the first couses is served

David the third guest in athe party of four and monica the second lady in the party of four the second pair of guests although that they were all working in the same office lucy only knew them this pair from them walking past each other in the office. They wer not familiar with each other yet. Monica was the youngest in the room Lucy was surprised and David was a few good years older than her he was stern, polite and held a rugged he had a half shaven beard and he looked like a boxer rather than a journalist. Whilst Monica looked fit any bloke in cluding Benjamin would turn there head. She knew that she had it. she clamied tat she wa a bunet but preferred to be blond simply because she wanted more men to look at her. In noticing this Benjamin woundered if he was in a strong enough relationship he was to ask. Michal was older than everybody two years older than Benjamin and two years qualified more than Benjamin. Benjamin had no choice but to look up to him it was qiute imbaressing Benjamin felt. Having to dip his head everytime they met and speaking nicely just to please him because he was older.

They all seemed to have there own personal problems Benjamin had to laugh as for Micheals hair.

Benjamin serves the meal Lucy poured the drinks and everybody started to drink and eat there were lots of nods as the guests tucked in and even more compliments when lucy was mistaken for the chief Lucy finally bowed out of the converstion telling the truth that it was benjamin that had prepared the meal. Benjmain did not take all te credit still he claims Lucy was involved his words it took everybody as he rasised his glass saying thankyou and downing his wine only to pour himself another.

od hour desert was served nobody noticed the t have been a good dinner party. Nobody ..iat Benjmain had missed the starter it was reintroduced by Benjamin at the end of the meal with the after eights and irish coffee. It was getting late and they were still talking. At the end of the evening Benjmain had to try extremely hard to stop the conversations aad throw everybody out. In a sense he was glad it was over and a smaller converstion started as they both cleared up the wine glasses and plates. The guest insisted that they would help but Lucy's stubbornness convinced them that the eve ning was over. Compliments from Lucy about how Micheal refused to stop complimenting Lucy's work of course Benjmain knew Micheals real intentions he was trying to pull his bird. Lucy thought nothing of it as she could not yet see. it was a man thing he was clearly showing off benjamin was pushing the thought behind him pushing the thought a side he thought again telling Lucy that is what dinner party are for and told her he felt fine over the situation however he said if it had happened in the work place he would of acted a little differently lucy appoligises to Benjamin he tells her it was not her fault. Benjamin continued that it was a dinner party and they should drop the converstaion par say he adds when they entertain again that they would be a little more professional on both sides. Going back to Benjamins little conversation Lucy was quite lucky that Benjamin had taken her behaviour litly she knew that she had broken the rules and she realizes that she had over spoken to her guests, and onve settled she apologises again this time bejamin is not so forgiving he walks out of the kitchen and busrts in to anger shouting at Lucy from a short distance telling her that the subject and coverstation had gone far enough and that she was supid to even to think about bringing it back up. Benjamin yells asking her if she is looking for an argument she had already disturbed the whole evening. Benjmain is now talking gto himself and he was asking himself if he thought that alucy was doing this on purpose was she trying to reuion the relationship on purpose benjmain conti ues to talk walking forwards in to one room and then back in to another. There was no answers from Lucy and she could not see the damage that she had done. Benjamin is sitting down as lucy walks in she is standing up Benjamin was not happy Lucy could see that what had she done she was now having a go at Benjamin blaming him like it was his fault for her actions and that he was to blame her words to him was that he was over sensitive. Benjamin could clearly see that Lucy was going to give Benjmain a piece of her mind. It was supposed to be that way but the other way around.

When they are finished he sits down in a mood Lucy was shortly behind him she puts her arm up and over then around him. Getting snug there is a long slence in the room. Benjmain is still up set as the silence continued an hour in to the evening Lucy is itching for another converstion with fighting knowing that it would probably turn in to an argument. As Lucy was going to speak benjmain buts in telling her not to, his words were don't. She attempts to rty again to break the ice. Benjamin gets up and leaves the room he says nothing not even a good night night only to return a minute later whith a duvet and a pillow he throws it on to the floor and tells Lucy to have a good night she was getting the sofa. Lucy looks up baffled. As he leaves to go back upstairs leaving Lucy looking like a child. Before Benjmain goes to bed he looks in the mirror looking directly at his face it was one of disgrace he did not look to happy. He could clearly understand Lucy and he did not want to talk, to talk to anybody at that point. Lucy could not believe it and now she was thinking about benjmains feeling like she should be knowing that Benjmain was upset. Lucy on the other hand was nice and happy and she was thunking that she was happy benjmain should be happy too. Lucy thinks Benjamin was putting his mood on he was acting looking for sympathy. It was only a thought.

Benjamin finds the staircase, he climbs to the top of it was harder than he thought and when he got to the top he could feel himself say to himself that the climb wass hard work. For the first time benjamin for the first time actually believed that he was getting old. Which was on top of the conversations at work the next day. He had his teamof work mates laughing for hours joke after joke. It continued all day people he didn't even no walked past him complimenting him it must have been funny he thought. Lucy joined in and he welcomed her she was a little bit comical her self and probably more of a comedian herself. And as they joked it took a lot of pressure of the both of them in the work place. It looked like there relationship was off the rocks for a while. At the end of the day benjmain was looking more like a boyd-friend again and Lucy was finally acting like a girlfriend and not a room mate in arented house doing a house share.

Benjamin could not of done any better he could not of complimented Lucy any further. He continues to praise her performance all the way home. Lucy had to in the end tell Benjamin to shut his mouth. And continued to joke. And reminded him that they were just jokes and yeah he said sometime they hurt. Or the other way around Benjamin said they can make you laugh. Benjamin interupted her and said yeah but just the good jokes as he continued to praise her up until they reached the front door of Benjamin's house.
Finally Benjamin calms himself down by taking deep breaths as he reaches out holding Lucy and comtinues that he was fine Lucy was thinking that they would have to talk about that experience Benjamin knew she ment it a s a metafore. He told Lucy that he would never forget about what she had said. And thinks that his and her works mates would be talking about that conversation for a long time he tells Lucy that he diod not know that she could act like that. He conti ues again that she was incredible. Lucy smiles leaning over towards him kissing him on the cheek. Benjamin was surprised and jumps as he does he speeks telling Lucy that her approach was a nice one. Lucy parks up the car, Benjamin has already removed himself from the car and is busy getting in to the house as lucy parks the car in his parking space. Lucy looks upward and notices the clouds were dark and there was a storm beginning.

Benjamin disappears and Lucy is trying to find him he is in the shower and using the hot water before alaucy uses it all he can hear her calkling him but is to absorbed and ignores her. As the water cascades down benjmain is finally relaxing. He dips his head under the water listening to his mind and the powerful, water as it hits his face softly then hard as he turns up the power of the machine that is in control not hard or hot enough to harm him as the drops hit the bottom of the bath tub after hitting his face the fifteen minute of repentance begins. The water is hot against his body and Benjamin looks up the bath room door opens and Lucy is there standing watching him.

Lucy:" oh nice there you are I was looking for you."

Benjamin:" well you have found me what up."

As Lucy picks up Benjamins towel Benjamin reaches out for it as he climbs out of the shower leaving it running asks Lucy for the towel as he stretches out his arm to receive it. they continue to talk the subject that was on Lucy's mind the question that lucy was so rushed to ask Benjamin was what would he like for dinner Benjamin thought she was going to ask him for or discuss a subject as the way that she appproched made out in benjamin's mind that it was something important.

Benjamin:" Er what ever you like. There was a pause for a moment then Benjamin comtinued." infact im going to pass if that's ok. I'm not hat hungry."

Lucy:" fine."

Benjamin:" What are we watching this evening on the tv."

Lucy:" I have not decided yet."

As Benjmain drys himself and talks theyb starta discussion about the tv progrmmes Benjmain wasbusy slagging every programme that Lucy conciders to watch off. And with constant disagreements over what they would watch. Benjamin really tried to convince her that tv in the modern world was all fake Lucy really believed that what she was watching was really real. Benjamin was explaining for the hundrethed time that it was all made up, still Lucy did not by it and insists that it is real. They sits down together with a bottle of wine. The bottle of wine did not pursaude Lucy and she walks off in a huff she was thinking that benjamin was wasting her kind thoughts as she hands hima glass Benjmain shouts to her as she returns to the kitchen only because she had forgotten her glass that they could do both.

Lucy out of the room shouts back giving Benjamin answer. He walks back in with a beter look on her face.

Lucy:" What kind."

Benjamin looks confused

Benjamin:" What kind of what. What kind of wine. Oh any."

He says picking up the conversation again after forgeting it straight afterwards. For a while everything seemed to be fine Lucy was a rocket at work and she was always being complimented benjamin could see her progress she was making it up the ladder. One evening Benjamin wanted to question her to find out what was really making her tick. She was doing really good she was a hard worker everybody could see that and it was not the first time that she had been told about working to hard. Benjmains timing was right on the spot as he approaches her in the evening after work whilst wielding a glass of wine, it was good timing she was half drunk leaving herself open for any kind of conversation benjmain used it to his advantage she would have forgotten by the morning it would be like the conversation had never happened. Lucy had not caught on, Benjmain was now looking for nsa good hour of converstion the interagation had started. As he begins to question her. Whilst he denines to join her as she hits the bottle as he dienies to share a glass of wine with her so he could remember everything. As Benjamin had asked her question after question Lucy had not realized that she had drunk so much, even though all of her answers were near perfect and spoken butifully as a narrator Benjamin worked his questioning perfectly they were not working Lucy seemed to have an answer for everything after bringing her down a peg or to it seemd to Benjamin that his little game was not working she was gaining comfidents and giving her self a chance to have a long drunken boast. Benjamin could see that Lucy was disalusioned some of the hings that she was saying ment nothing total rubbish, others made sense right to the point. Benjamin was trying really hard to understand her Lucy seemed to have more reasonable answers and it had been fifty fifty all the way right up until the end of the conversation.

Lucy:" another bottle of wine please."

Benjmain looks at her then tells if that what you need. Lucy says to Benjmain half drunk benjamin did not decline in fact he was delighted with her surgestion he gets up looking really hard at Lucy she does not notice as he cheekly and suoprisingly gets up and goes to the kitchen. As he was hiding the fact that he was not acting like a friend. At that moment more like a doctor questioning his patence. Benjmain returns with another bottle opening it before he gives it to her. As she pours the red wine in to her glass which benjamin also brought her and handed it to her after she had opened the bottle. He conti ues to question her it was now a game it was all in his mind. Lucy basically told Benjamin everything except that she had been flurting with his boss. Benjamin knew he thought it was normal he also knew that it works both ways their were so many women in that building it was not surprising that she would have a flurt. He did but on a level. In that sense benjmain was cool and Lucy had said enough to keep his mind busy with the thought of her recent behaviour. And knowing that Lucy felt flurtaious Benjmain knows he was going to have a hard time keeping an eye on her. Straight afterwards for a while things were running smoothly for them.

The next evening Benjamin has a day off Lucy was at work Lucy did not know that Benjmain had a day off and benjamin lays asleep until Lucy awakes early forgetting the fact that he had a day off infact she had no idea and prompts benjmain to wake. Benjamin says nothing as she prods him he lays in his bed not saying a word. Lucy shouts pulling the beding off him. Benjmain is not happy and shouts back as lucy shouts telling him that he should wait he will make them both late as benjmain shouts back it was his day off.

Benjamin:" What are you doing, get off."

Lucy:" come on I'm late already your getting the bike if you do not move your ass."

Benjamin:" It is five oclock in the morning it is my day off."

Lucy:" Oh I'm sorry I did not know."

Benjamin:" We will talk about it later."

Lucy apologises as Benjmain pulls the duvet back over him self putting back the pillows that came off the bed as lucy removed the duvet. Lucy leaves the room quietly. As she nears the door down stairs she hears Benjamin shouts again.

Benjamin:" It is my day off."

Lucy leaves the building and closes the door behind herself as Benjamin is left half a sleep and not able to get back to sleep. Benjamin would not forget and believes that Lucy had woken him up on purpose. As benjmain tosses and turns desperate to get back to sleep the shouting and cussing Lucy did not make him feel any better. Eventually Benjmain gives up unprepared for the early mornning goes to his toilet and throws up. After he was done he makes it to his kitchen as he fills the kettle eventually he wakes up completely he looks in the cupboard which was placed high srewed in to the wall, which was painted roughly. As he reaches in grabbing the cereal boxes without a thinking but thinking of what he was doing and pouring the cereal missing his bowl completely again Benjamin was out of luck and in thinking that wondering when things would go right for him. the cereal box was empty. Benjamin stops thinking that Lucy was up to old tricks again. As he walks out side not thinking about changing his clothes jumps on to her bike and goes to his work place. On the way stopping at the local shop he is no better mood as when he was awoken by Lucy. He was saying as he came out of the shop with a box of ceral that Lucy would not get one over him, he thinks that it was Lucy who had taken all the cereal and had woken him up on his day off. As he nears the counter to pay for his goods. Which was milk,coffeeand cereal. As he leaves the shop and gets on the bike as he rides he slows down getting off the bike putting the bike neatly against another shop window, there were bike racks there but the mood that Benjamin was in he just did not bother Benjamin was going to leave the bike there just to release the anger that he was in or more so the bad mood that he was in. He pays the man who is polite the man asks him if there anything else. Benjamin does not amswer and walks out.

Noticing also that he had come out with his pyjamias on forcing him to retake the bike and take it back home. before he does he goes back to the shop leaving his bike in the same place he had forgotten hus smokes after approaching the shop assistant again he startsv a conversation which he would never forget as he finished theb conversation he goes outside only to realize that his bike had been stolen. Benjamin cannot believe it he goes back in to the store.

Assistant:" what the problem my man."

Benjamin: " My bike it has been stolen."

Assistant:" well that does not surprise me. Was it locked up."

Benjamin:" No I was only going to be a minute, bloody hell, dam, it was not mine."

Asssiatnt: " well you have nothing to worrie about."

Benjamin looks at him funnily and walks out of the shop.

The assistant leaning backwards over his head produces a business as he hands it to Benjmain and tells him to ring them. Benjamin asks him who is it the assistant tells benjamin that it was a taxi rank. The shop assistant helps him further as benjamin did not have his phone on him and kindly tells benjamin that he could use his. The shop assistant is smiling he obviously found benjamins predictament funny. Benjamin calls for a taxi and within fifteen minutes is back at home. he gets out of the taxi just outside of his home he pays the taxi and thanks the driver leaving no tip. Benjamin walks to his door as he puts the key in turning it around puching the door to open it it did not open benjmain trys again and again it does not open. He trys another key and the same happen's again. It was the wrong keys both of

them. benjmain drops his bags down he checks all of his pockets starting with the pyjams top left, but nothing. Benjamin was finding that he hads locked himself out he double checks and again nothing. He triple checks again until he finaly gives in and agrees to himself that he was locked out.
Benjmain s main concern was that if he wanted to get back in he would have to break back in, either that he would have to wait for Lucy to come home. As he looked around his garden then the outside of the house hoping that he might of left a window open. Another option would be that he could just break a window in that was close what he could not do was ring the lock smith as he had no phone that would be the normal way, Benjamin thinks. Mind you he thought that would cost him money. The only two other options were to as he tells himself one would to be go to work and fetch the keys himself the second would be that is to wait outside until lucy get back he had about five minutes to make a decision as there was astorm coming and the weather was changing for the worst.
Benjamin sits down outside on his door step the cold concret door step was giving Benjamin some trouble he had arse ache and the cold wind which was heading over in his direction was a complete surprise as for the elements as the wind, the stone cold floor as the wind picks up he makes it across his ground to a small doorway that was locked it just covered his head so eben in the cold he ws proteceted by from the rain. It was approximately fifty meters from where Benjamin was to where he wanted to be at his front door. He has to move again this time it ws around the fromt of theb building he could be seen there and Lucy would not miss him not tat it made any difference. As the storm continues he moves again this time back around th back

in the garden it was a little bit more sheltered and a little shelterd from the wind and a little bit more sheltered from the rain. Benjamin had no keys to get in to the house he had no cover from the storm he was really wishing that Lucy would appear. As Benjamin watches the coulds they move quickly followed by a massive crashing sound and finally thunder the clouds were moving fast and Benjamin looks upwards in to the dstance a short distance he could see the clouds clearly amongst the clour of the b sky which had become a dark grey. Ass te sky's contiued to change from a light white godly picture to a dark grey fearsome thundering he was beginning to enjoy himself, not on purpose as th skys changed again the thunderstorm that had been brewing had finally started. Benjamin checks his pyjamas again he ws looking for his phone as there were some good pictures that he could of taken. The phone was not there on this occasion he would have to miss out. He looks through his living room window from the outside he can clearly see his phone on the dinning table.

As the storm begins to rage Benjamin is missing the point all he wanted to do now was to watch the rain and the things that came with it. all he wanted to do was to take pictures of the lightening about fifteen minutes in to the storm Lucy arrives home walking in through the front door as quiet as a mouse and parking her car in the drive way with out a sound around the front not thinking about where Benjamin was and it took him over ahour to realize that she was at home. when he finally gets in after not realizing that she was in. Benjamin before he realizes that Lucy was home goes off for a walk thinking about Lucy's safety. As he cannot walk on the paths as they were to slippery and decides to walk in the middle of the road. After about an hour Benjamin is fully soaked there was darkness everywhere and Benjmain would not walk on the paths that were there, but insisted to himself that he would walk down the middle of the road, after about a mile and a really good soaking, he turns around and heads home and he now wants to return back to his house as he nears his house he can see that the lights were on and he could clearly see Lucy from a distance. The lights were on he was happy now he could get back into the warm. Benjamin knows that he would of stayed out side all night until she appeared. Benjamin walks towards the door as he close he stops by some hedges he stops he can see lucy clearly he was spying on her. Lucy not knowing that she was being watched was acting in front of the tv. As Benjamin really wishes that he had ahd his phone to some pictures. Finally Lucy catches on as she sees him through a reflextion through the living room window. She stops but not before she pretends to be a cowboy blowing on her fingers like a gun Benjamin looks confused it was just Lucy making a joke. Before confronting him at the front door.

Lucy:" What are you doing. And why are you in your pyjamas."

Benjamin:" Where have you beeni am soaked how long have you been here."

Lucy: " Er I got back about half five. Have you been there all this time. There are such things as door bells."

Benjamin:" You did not even notice that I was out side."

Lucy:" you were outside."

Benjamin:" yes . I have been locked out it is a long story. First I lose your bike , after I ahd brought my ceral because you eat the last of this mornings."

Lucy:" Now hold on what has cereal got to do with it you can not blame it on me because you missed your breakfast. Oh I am sorry about that."
Benjamin:" Then I found out that I have left my key on the dinning room table, Locking myself out only to find out that I am still in my pyjamas with a hurricane on my doorstep."
Lucy:" I thought you liked the rough weather, the storms."
Benjamin: " yes I do."
There is a long silence ntil Lucy breaks it with I'll grab the wine. Benjamin continues.
Benjamin:" Your missing the point I was locked out in the cold."
Lucy: " Ahh your looking for some sympathy."
Benjamin:" No well no er yes."
Lucy:" how much."
Benjamin:" a lot."
Benjamin sighs then continues going back to the start of the conversation.
Benjamin: " No I left my phone on the table with the keys for the front door it was good though I get one next time."
Benjamin ws walking out shouting he was referring to getting the picture of a perfect lightening he shouts from a distance in the next room where are the fresh towels.

Benjamin had got dry and changed his clothes he approaches Lucy Benjamin kisses her on her cheak, Lucy is surprised and smiles benjmain asks her this time around how was her day. When Lucy gives him an answer but for sure she did not give him all the details and did not say to much. They continued the conversation Lucy was twisting everything Benjamin said and now she was asking him how his day went when it was obvious that he had been locked out side for most of the day, in a storm only to let Lucy know that her bike had been nicked. Also forgetting to tell her about his keys tey were not on the table as he thought when Benjamin put it all to her it was quite a lot to take in. Lucy on the other hand theought it was funny and she ws trying not to smile Benjamin could see that she was about to burst into laughter, benjmaij wanted to know what was so funny he could not see the funny side of what had happened.

Lucy:" one of those daysi guess."

As lucy bursts out laughing.

Lucy:" Not so good then."

Benjamin:" Well what do you think."

Benjamin pours himesldf and Lucy a glass of wine.

As he hands her the glass he sits down besides her.

Benjamin does not speak for an whole hour Lucy is the same and is just as silence. The silence was welcome from both partys but Lucy was just about to speak but the conversation did not start as benjmain tells her to be quiet and gives her a promising shoosh. Benjmain was in grossed with what they were watching lucy trys again and again she was deinied, Lucy catches on. As Benjmain tells her again to be quiet, there is silence again.

Lucy sips from the wine glass trying to think why Benjamin had tried to silence her. May be he had a hard day. This was true in a sense but Lucy believed that what had happened that evening was to exciting and wished Benjamin the same. Once in Benjamins presents she offered him a drink again Benjamin was not listening and just agrees not knowing what he had said or agreed too. As lucy opened another bottle of wine Benjamin declined only to agree and join her getting drunk. After the evening of silence and booze Lucy was feeling down and could see what Benjamin could see what Benjamin was feeling, they were the same way. Benjamin was fast asleep and lucy was awake and sitting up right, after she had awoke she nudges Benjamin softly to awake him. They both had over slept and they were both late for work. Lucy leans over him slipping back down in to her beding, Benjamin now half awake speaks telling himself and then Lucy that they were going to be late for work. Benjamin continues how late, Lucy does not answer. While Benjamin groans with the pain of his hangover, he continues to speak telling lucy who was not in the room at that time, that it was not that bad and it was not that much. He suddenly leaps upright oh damn wide awake were late were his words.
Benjamin: " were late, what is the time dam why did you not wake me I'm late."
Benjamin jumps out of the bed Lucy was just about to answer his question, as she lays there saying the same the same words as Benjamin. As Benjamin rushes around looking for fresh clothes.

Only to realize that lucy had not moved and was still hinding under the duvet speaking softly before she screems The words that came from her mouth was that it was Saturday. Benjmain stops suddenly it was like he was moving in motion of what was coming out of Lucy mouth. He repats the words back to lucy. It is Saturday. He drops his trosers and shirt on to the floor like a teenager and gets back in to bed. Lucy tells him to shut up she wants to go back to sleep.
Later on a small conversation starts.
Benjamin:" You could of told me."
Lucy:" Was the alarm on no you know the rule you made it."
Benjamin says nothing else and gives Lucy the cold shpudler for the rest of the morning. However within a few minutes of Lucy making her self lunch and coffee forgetting about Benjamin and leaving him to make his own. An argument accurs. First a long talk to Lucy about her mannors then Benjmain tells her that punchualy she was all wrong and after she had spilt her coffee down her self bejamin continued to tell her as she is in the bathroom cleaning herself up he tells her that she is inconsistent Benjmain tells her straight about what it is like living under the same roof as her and being her partner having a relasionship with her. These words that were spoken were not compliments and lucy was beginning to get upset. Benjamin tells her that nobody and he qutoes nobody gets away with it what makes her so special. Lucy is puzzled why was Benjamin telling her this. She does not understand what she had heard.

Lucy was not particularly impreesd with benjamins lastest talk and was waiting patentaly to verbally attack him back. She was good at that, once he slips up whe then would intervene it would be her go. She bits like an animal and once she gets on she would no get off. Benjmain knew this already as he calmed himself in the kitchen getting ready for Lucy to bottle herself up. infact Benjamin was timing her. It usually took her around three minutes and then another minute to gather her posture . As she enters the kitchen looking for something in the cuboards to hide the fact for what she was really doing there. It was obvious to Benjamin. Benjamin counts the remainding seconds from forty down to zero. At that very point in time with Benjamin's timing. She starts to talk Benjamin is clever enough to bite back as he is bitten, the arguments starts. Again lucy was close enough to him to throw a few things at him like tins of soup the tv remote control which she brought in just incase. Lucky for Benjamin she was not aiming at him she just wanted to ake it clear that she was in the room. After she had run out of those things the odd saucer would fly past nothing that Benjamin could not replace. Before Lucy is able to continue not because she had not have anything else to throw at him. Benjmain starts over again as the argument continued.

Lucy:" what is all thos in aid of."

Benjamin:" sleep is sleep, you ahrdly touch me and when you do it does not seem right it is like I am being touched by a complelely different person."

Lucy is in shock and she does not answer him and Benjmains argument is beginning to level she starts it again.

Lucy: " well."

Benjamin:" well what."

Lucy: " Well you never touch me ."
Benjamin: " Yes I do."
Lucy: " Your numb all over it is your own fault I have given you everything."
Benjmain butts in.
Benjamin:" You can forget the immaterial things they do not count.
Lucy: " Yes they do."
Benjamin:" No Lucy they do not."
Lucy:" Ok no they do not."
Lucy walks out of the kitchen Benjamin was following her as she spoke. Lucy walks past there bookself, knocking off one of the books on to the floor. Benjamin picks it up not looking at the book and puts it down back on the shelf. They continue to talk in the living room. Benjamin is in shock as she continues until she come to the photographs of himself and her. Lucy hesistates and Benjamin ass her politly not to do it as Lucy pauses for a moment. Lucy tells him to grow up and that she was not going to smash them leading them further in to another argument via a quick conversation on weather she was or was not thinking about breaking the ormement. Lucy realizes what she was doing, this time using Lucy Benjamin tells her to grow up. this gives Lucy away back into the argument Lucy was blowing things out of proportion everything Lucy was talking about things that Benjamin had not even heard of. Things that were not even part of their ebrupt conversation and it ended with what about your mum.
Benjamin pauses for asecond then catches on.
Benjamin:" Arrh you nearly got me there. my mium we have not seeeen her for years."
Lucy: " exactly."
Benjamin; " exacatly, what."

Lucy continues exacatly and she walks out. Benjamin thinks that he had won. As he pick up his cup of coffee now half cold due to the argument. Only to spitthe mouth full out as in shock as Lucy walks in weilding a golf club. Benjamin tells her to stop Lucy does not listen as she begins to pick out curtain things in Benjamin's living room to smash benjamin cannot believe it and continued to her that it was because was losing the argument lucy had always deined that her actions were perceived by Benjamin. As she moved another object in to range Benjamin was having trouble controlling her amd it looked like she had lost her mind. Benjamin was looking right in to her eyes as she shouted radio system all Benjamin could do was shout that was my stereo as he looked at it in pieces. She was telling Benjamin if there were any other problems that he woud like to talk about. Benjamin said nothing. He just looked at her extremely surprised until she tells him to apologise. Lucy sits on the floor amounst the debrie Benjamin is keeping his distance as lucy starts again simply because Benjamin was to stuborn to apologise as he held his breath she continued this time it was the tv but lucky Benjamin was in front of it and Lucy was left to think about what item in the home was next.

For the rest of the day Lucy and Benjamin stayed out of each other way. It was going to be along appoligy from the both of them. if it does not turn back in to another argument. Lucy trys first to break the ice, Benjamin was not ready for the conversation or even apology from his side. He could not find the words. Lucy could see clerly that his approach was to early he said nothing he had stopped breathing, his eyes had changed as well as the expression on his face. Benjamin was not particulary interested and it was the words he had to chose them carefully as he did not want to start another argument. he probably did ot scare at that time in their relationship. Benjamin walks in Luy walks out was this her new game. This had happened a few times time s and Benjamin ahd noticed as much as Lucy had as it was obvious that she was running from something, was Benjamin still getting it in the neck. Benjamin calls Lucy in.

Benjamin: " Lucy."

Lucy:" Stay away from me jerk off."

Benjamin: " Lucy just Lucy."

Lucy had not settled down it jad been a few hours it was going to turn into days it was no longer their relastionship it ws there lifes. Lucy was not going to change. Benjamin could see that.

Benjamin:" Lucy come back."

Lucy ignores Benjmain again this was the fifth time that Benjmain had tried appoligised Lucy was playing a dangous game with Benjamin he was thinking that she was going to walk out.

Lucy walked in to the living room in the middle of the night Benjamin had tried to tidy up her mess from the previous morning. Insuprise Lucy walks in, throws down on to the floor a duvet and three pillows Benjamin was getting the couch. She tells Benjamin that he is sleeping alone, until she feels that she is feeling better until she can feel like she can not stand him in her bedroom. There is a towel in the bathroom down stairs she continued that he can wash alone. Benjamin knows this time that Lucy is really hurt. He knows that she is owed an apology even though the argument was not that bad Benjamin contiued to himself I guess that it really did hurt. It would only be a matter of time when he would get the chance to speak to her again. Benjamin with regrets is now thinking that he had aover reacted somehow Lucy was not going to buy it. Benjamin had ben put in an arkward position and Benmain knew he would have to reach out to find an answer to go with the apology, again.

It was not the greatest of opening lines that Benjamin had heard. Even so they were both on level grounds and Benjamin excepted her apology. Again the weekend had arrived they had time to think a few things to discuss. What they wanted, as Benjmain spoke. He was joking that the golf was a\ bit distracting Lucy cry's slowly as she smiles and Benjmain continued that he made her so angry and tells Benjamin that he does not know the power of his words. She continued that they can really hurt sometimes, then she replaces the sentence that she was saying to him his words can really hurt. Benjamin agrees.

As for the next few days things were looking better considerable better. Work was good and both of them were getting to work on time. Benjamin had changed a little and had stopped being fussy. Lucy on the other side had also changed her cooking had got better she had stped dreaming of poisoning her husband with her stupid idea of what actul food was, and cooked a desent meal someof the time. Benjmain to top it all off had started making normal jokes about each other. The relationship was no longer one sided and Lucy's beauty was beginning to show. Both of them getting compliment s from work mates. It was weird how there behaviour at work seemed to effect the way they werfe feeling at home almost certain the other away around.

One year later

Lucy had worked hard that year getting up on time doing the worst kind of jobs in the office. Benjamin was getting on well, everybody it was not unusual except things were back on the rocks this time uit was over drinkd and party's that Lucy had thrown just to keep up in society, it was the job only Lucy was getting something out of what was her plan to the promotion that she despratly wanted. She was slowly moving up the ladder. Benjamin was left to watch. He ws left behind. They would argue a little here and there especially in the morning on there way to work and when Lucy would do over time it was not like they needed the money. Lucy was not thinking about the money she would make it looked like from Benjamin's point of view that she wanted that promotion.
Things in the office were looking good for Lucy she had made all the right moves and Benjamin was being made to look like a fool. He knew it would only be a matter of time before Lucy would make them both fall off the ladder, and right then it looked like it was Benjamin that was going to fall first. Lucy was at home quietly watching the tv. Benjamin walks in drunk the argument starts this time with him Benjamin stubbles across the living room. And blamed it on Lucy, Lucy did not move or do anything and Benjamin was really shouting at her. Lucy would not stand for it and verbally attacked Benjmain back her sentence ending in your drunk, and then get off her as benjamin trys to grab her hand she pushes him away. Lucy's complaint started that she was no where near him Benjamin argument was she knew what was going to happen. She sits back casually and continues to watch the programme on the tv. Lucy continued putting on a professional voice he was telling himself to calm down.

Then she tells him that she was in a really good mood and if he was looking for an argument he was looking in the wrong place. She was not thinking of him and he should go else were. After Lucy had said her piece. This opens the door for another argument which was the first argument which was how Benjamin cumsly feel over on arrival in to the living room. Lucy was no where near him.

Lucy: " Benjamin you are drunk go to bed."

Benjamin repeats exactly what she had just said except in a slur. Lucy smiles trying to hide the fact that she was in total amusement and about to burst out laughing. She was imbarest and a little confused of where and what angle that Benjamin was approaching her from. Benjamin looks like he is about to fall over as he stubbles practicaly falling on top of her and Lucy shouting again get off. As he moves of her now falling backwards only to be steadied by Lucy who catches him. Only to receive a punch in the face form Benjamin. Everything stops as Benjamin stands watching waiting for the reaction as Lucy hold her face in disgust. There is a long silence and Lucy can not believe it she runs out puching past Benjamin leaving the door open. Benjamin is left alone in the living room still drunk and not knwing what he had done. Benjamin totally drunk passes out on the sofa, Lucy had hidden her self up in her bathroom she was still hurt and in shock.

Benjamin does not meet her in her room and does not see her in the morning as she did not wake him for work. Benjamin over sleeps.

As Benjamin awakes still a half a sleep is left talking to himself as for not knowing the time. And not knowing why he had been left alone on that particular morning. He calls for Lucy but there was no answer. Benjamin thinks she is up stairs and calls again but again there is no answer. As Benjamin rolls over after giving up on Lucy, he rolls of the sofa on to the floor grumbling again half asleep and calling for Lucy but there is no answer.

Finally Benjamin awakes realizing that Lucy had gone to work and Benjamin had forgotten about the assault which he committed the previous night. Benjamin is sobring up when the phone rings Benjamin leaves it ringing until it stops he was thinking that if it was important they would ring back. Besides he thinks who would call him at this time of the day. Benjamin already knows that he would be late for work, and it was too late to fgo to work he was also busy trying to figure out who had phoned him it was really unusual that he would receive calls at that time of the day as he would be at work. The thought of that phone call became Benjamin's torment of the day as he walks down stairs he cannot stop thinking of who it could have been. He is transfixed on the phone in the hall way. Holding the phone he checks the calls nothing unusual there were no messages and there was no number. Either way Lucy would be on her way home by now benjmain is thinking about greeting her to ask her if it was her that called. He was at a loss and thought it might have been her as the recepiants only called once. Leaving no message as benjamin is thinking another problem occurs Lucy did not cme home. She had not turned up, Benjamin was worried. Benjamin realizes that something was wrong. He traces back through the day thinking of what he might of done if anything he thought. It ws not like Lucy to be late Especially as her hours did not include the evening. As he looks at his phone as he was expecting her to at least call him.

Benjamin looks at his phone again he was waiting and just thinking even more slowly remembering the evening before. Benjamin realizes that he ahd done something to upset her. He knows that he ahd done something regrettable extremely stupid. He begins to question everything he had done. Continuing telling himself that it must have been him. Benjamin as the tears swelled up in his eyes and with his heart beating faster he calls out again in some kind of emotional pain the words again it was me. Benjamin cannot believe it and finally a whole day of waiting and worring realizes what had happened the previous night before. Benjamin after recollecting his steps continued to talk to himself knowing that Lucy was seriously upset. And looked like she had walked out. Or she was a little late getting home. Benjamin wants to talk to her as he picks up the phone he hears the door oipen it was Lucy and she had returned however it was not for to long. As Benjamin jumps off the sofa as Lucy walks in to the living room happy to see her. She walks past him fast not saying a word to him as if he was not there, she is talking at the same time with a half angry temperament. She was still upset as if what had done had just happened it was like a twenty four hour relapse a twenty four hour reconstruction of what happpend the other night. A twenty four hour reincarnation or a twenty four hour slow coffee break. As Benjamin is trying to apologise Lucy is busting to telling him that she was going to stay with some friends, she ment her mother. while Benjamin is still busy apologising Lucys mouth comes to a stand still. Benjamin was trying to care as he asks her if she would let him look at her syes it was clearly bruised. Benjamin got the message. Lucy and Benjamin's conversation moves going from the living room to upstairs then back to the living room then out in to the

hall way right up to the front door. As the front door is blocked by Benjamin knowing what he had done simply by looking at Lucy's face asks her once more not to leave the surgestion is ignord and lucy. Lucy is nice and calm and Benjamin is is questioning her behaviour telling himself that she had said what she had said and going to her mothers until she cools down. His behavoir now was that he was drunk Lucy was not buying it and Benjmain had slowly lost his temper. Lucy pushes him out of the way as she as being block the right of way.Lucy forgets something upstairs and has to turn around with Benjmain pushing her around as he is still blocking her way. Lucy was not having any of it as Benjmain is trying to sweeten her up with words. Benjmain continues to say that he was sorry. As lucy pushes past him once more more he lets her go past. Lucy walks around the house until she gets everything she needs. As Lucy walks out this time not harboured by Benjamin and Benjamin resists being pushy. As Benjamin steps aside from the doorway Lucy walks out. She tells him that he has a week.

That week had past and Benjamin had removed most of his belongings, he had put it all in to storage. Lucy did not turn up to pick up the keys, Benjamin was left waiting out side. After a long thought Benjmain was tried his hardest to hold on to them only making the mistake of putting them in rto an envelope and putting them through her letter box which was now hers. Benjamin walked away slowly wishing that he could see her again. It was not to be. Benjamin needs an excuse to get some time off the first thing her does is make sure that Lucy does not tell anybody that they had split. Until he gets back to the office, he had made a phone call fro his office to lucy's desk. As a one off making sure that Lucy knew that there relasionship had finished. He calls her again just to make sure that she got the message she did she did not pick up the phone. He believd that she would keep her word. Benjamin still trusted her and belived that she would keep her word. Benjmain and lucy agreed that he would call in sick, just to give each other some space. Nothing else was said and they had a mutral agreement.
A week had past and Benjamin knew that he wa going to get upset. Lucy had reuion there relasionship and it was also going to cost him his job. Benjamin who ws in the car park just arriving to work, on his bike. As Lucy had the car and had taken it back. As much as Benjamin tried he could not walk in. Benjamin was in a real mess. Emotionally he was a reck and his physical appearance was of a toilet, just his head. Benjamin was out side Lucy could see him from her desk window she says nothing benjamin looked up at her. She sees him but being Lucy she ignores him. Benjmain was losing his nerve and he was busy telling himself that he could do it he could walk in but as he said those words to himself the opposite was about to happen benjmain chooses to

walk out and goes home which was at this monet the back of a suoer market. Benjmain not thinking did not realize that he was tight for money and he did not like spending it when he had it he would not even spend three pounds o a burger and he would really try his hardest not to spend anything. Benjmain would not find himself a hotel even though he could afford one. He was happy just satying ina bed and break fast. However when Benjmain finds out that he has no money not a penny finding out that Lucy had cancelled all of Benjamins credit cards. Benjamin was seeing red he could not believe it. as he approached the receptionist at the bed and breakfast that he approached. The receptionist hands Benjamin's bank card's back to him.
Reception: " No."
Benjamin:" what are you sure, please try again."
Reception:" No."
Benjamin:" No what are you sure."
Reception:" No sorry according to your card you have no money in your accounts."
Benjami has to barter he had already been there a week the argument from the reception was that he could not just tell him yes as every tom dick and harry would expect the same, he tells Benjmain that he wouldm have to wait until he speaks to his boss. He asks Benja in to wait as he calls his boss on the phone that ws sitting alone in the corner of the office. After the brief conversation Benjmain is welcomed back in from out side the reception has some good news for him, Benjamin has one week and that was as much as the reception could do Benjamin is happy and sad and is in two worlds as he is thinking about Lucy knowing that Lucy had cleaned him out. Benjamin awakes thanking he reception. As he he given his door key's he smiles and thanks the reception. A few minutes later Benjamin

returns asking the reception for some beer. The man looks at Benjamin and then orders him some beer telling Benjamin that would bring it up to his room. Benjamin smiles as he thinks that luck is on his side on that occasion.

Benjmain quietly sits on the balcony sipping the beer the the reception kindly gave him it was a good view Benjamin thought as the skys were clear, no stars, no moon. Just the darkness with the brightness of the streets lights. What more could a man want Benjamin says to him self. As he swigs from the beer bottle making a salute as he swigs from the bottle again as he takes another mouth ful he says out loud again here is all to you. Benjamin did not realize that he was such a light weight. By the time that he had finished the second bottle he was quite drunk he could feel the full effect of what he had consumed. He was drunk by the second mouth full of the third bottle. Benjamin was content he had taken his mind of Lucy. And what he thought was a good relationship. Only to find out that he was sending himself further into dispear. Thinking and reminding himself that what was keeping him happy. Was it the source of the relasionships distrustion. Never the less Benjmain kept on drinking. Within his own mind and confusion he decides to step outside on to the hotel roof, there were chairs neatly placed it was somekind of social area there was a good view of the town he was thinking that he could stay there but then in a second thought he decided that he would be better off in his room. He changes his mind again and stays put as he looks for a smoke he finds his cigereetes and puts one in ro his mouth from his packet and lights it up. the cool midnight sky dark and half old he could feel the cold. Benjamin closes his eyes.

Benjamin wakes early in the morning eight am he is still stuck in work mode knowing that he would have to turn up to hand in his resination he was resigning he had quite his job. He could not work next to Lucy and he made it quite clear to his old boss. Benjmains boss was a little concerned and disappointed as he thought that benjamin was a strong person a winner. When benjamin gave him his envelope with a letter in side explaining everything he sat down in a little shock. Benjamin was asked a question. He was actually needed and it was made clear, but Benjamin had no choice he could see things going wrong it was all written down in a letter in the envelope however he did not mation Lucy. And his boss finally gave in the small meeting had come to the end and Benjmain was finally allowed to clear his desk. At that time was a good time as there was only one other person in the office at that time he had a chance to say good bye to is desk and his office, he opens his shoulder bag, putting what remained of his personal belongoing in to it. as he steps outside he opens the bag and pulls a beer out of it and opens it and drinks it straight down it was his way of saying good bye.

Benjamin did not think about asking about Lucy who at this time had taken a promotion. Benjmain did not hear about this until it was too late. She was no longer working for his old boss. And when Benjamin approached them for his job back he found out that he was denied. Benjamin was well upset and blamed Lucy for everything one for making him homeless and two the job his career.
All the talk for the companys boss please dod not leave and you are an assit, you're the best we can give you little bit exta. Plus the perks, it was all total rubbish. Benjamin whos eye he was looking into. It was not a friendly pair. Benjamin walks back to the bed and breakfast, As he walks in there is nobody at the reception and when he puts his key in to the bedroom door it does not move. Benjamin is in shock and worrie he thinks that the man down stairs has changed the locks, although this was only for a minute as Benjamin trys once more it opens. He smiles with relief, as he opens the door and steps inside closing the door behind him. There was a message on the table that could clearly be seen, it read that the doors of the bed and breakfast would be closed at ten until further notice. Benjamin drops his head.

Again when Benjamin approched his door he find s tat his door is locked again only to think that the same had happened again he waits for a moment thinking that he was being thrown ot and the man down stairs had changed the losks he trys his keys once more and again the door opens. Benjamin walks in throwing himself on to the bed in relief. Thinking vthat it was fine forgetting that soon he would be thrown out for not having any money to pay his arrears. It was eacatly four hours or there abouts when Benjamin has a vistor it was the reception, it started with a knock on the door, Benjamin knew straight away he knew that it was going to be bad news. He had no choice but to open the door. Either way he could not avoid the man he would catch upto him eventually, why not today. There was a spy hole in the door and Benjamin closely atches him at his door with a little swagger and a hard short knock at Benjamin s door as Benjamin gets to his feet he is being called. Benjamin goes to let him in it ws totally out of character and benjmain knows that he should open the door it was exactly fifteen minutes until Benjamin realized what he was doing. As he come s around he opens the door. As te land lord shouts his name he opened the door using a spare key. A conversation starts Benjamin is told tat he had to leave by the morning, Benjamin knew why so there ws no arguments although Benjamin begged.

Benjamin: " look please I can pay you I just need a bit of time."

Benjamin is interrupted.

Reception:" I am sorry I annot wait any longer it has been a week my boss is breathing down my neck the books have to be right."

Benjamin has no money and very few friends as he finds out everybody in his address book was either on holiday, at work, or with there familys busy. Benjamin was on the street, and he was on his own. It wass totally the wrong time he nights were getting colder and benjmain knew that it was going to get colder before he shouts leaving his suitcase aside, in ally way changes his clothes once more he strips naked down to his toes as he choses his most comfortable clothes and the garments that would keep him the warmest. The clothes to suit the weather. Once he had finished dressing he hides his suitcase in some nearby bushes at the back of somebodys garden. Covering up so he would not forget the spot and so he could come back later.
Once he was done dressed nice and warm with a coat, jumper, jeans, and not trousers though he had a pair and shoes for more protection from the rain as trainers would get wet and would not dry. Benjamin onced fully dressd stays put hoping that he would not be found or disturb anything he wanted time to think but no sooner than he had settled it was time to move on again the dogs in the little neighbour hood could smell him and the early evening barking, the echoes of the dogs barking forced him to move to another place this would happen a lot and Benjamin was going to have to agree that even though ally seemed a safer place to be it was not going to happen.

Benjamins first night went reasonabley well until he started to get hungry not knowing how to beg. Which was a problem and in the morning he told him self as he woke and gave himself a plan, he would watch other prople like himself he would follow them and watch them until he picked up the art of begging there was a style and a technique. Some of them would sit and other stand and most of them would play an instrument of some sort, the worst would steel and then just leg it avoiding the local authoritys when necessary. I took the style of begging to the back of the super market there was food and lots of going to the farms most of it was aday or two old to sell on the selfs. It was interesting the amount of food which was actually available, when looking in a back of a lorry it was quite incredible. Benjamin would arrive early to get the best food available anything that you could not cook and mostly packaged would do. Benjami believed that it was a gift he thought it was him not realizing how bad that actually sounded.

Benjmain has lost all sense of the time and was using the sun to keep the time. He could of done this the normal way simply by asking people as they past him on the high street most people ignored him that did not suprise him, as he asked a young gentleman the time the answer he got was buy a watch. Another man told him that there was a clock over the other side of the street then neatly looked at his watch then walked off saying ive have a meeting in five. Some of the time he was given the wrong time the last insult he got was from some bloke who insisted that benjmain should buy a watch. On one occasion it got messy and Benjamin for once in his life had to stand up for himself the man was a total stranger. Benjamin was sitting down and asked the man the time as he walked past. The man words were rude this upset Benjamin and Benjamin retaliated. After a few words and a small scuffle and on top of this Benjamin some how manged to slip his wrist watch off him. In the small fight Benjamin was impressed with him self as he ran off leaving the man behind him.

For the next several moths of being a tramp ws not easy. One of the things he did dislike was having to go through the bin the other one was finding food. Atahe most exciting bit was that you never know who you are going to meet and also time that ahe found a wallet on that one occasion. As he looked through the man personal piece of paper, I found the owners address, money not much and driving licence. As the owner was just around the corner I decided I would pop round and surprise them with my new found and return what I had found. As I neared the address it ws not in the most of nice places and I had one eye on my back as the other one lead me to his door. As I reached the address with out being robbed my self I double checked the address to make sure that I ws in the right place. I was in the right place and to my surprise when I knocked on his door he answered as he opend the door looking at me only to shut the door in my face and yelling to his house mate that there was a tramp at his door. The voice shouted out twicw sorry we have no money and again if you dodnot go away we willlcall the right aurthorirys. Benjamin stopped taking a step backards then took a step closer to the door ringing his door bell this time and refusing to use the door knocker. He received the same answer this time louder we do not do tramps please go away. finally after a few good minutes fifteen in fact he came to his door. Benjamin finaly managed to get him the massage that he had found his wallet and had came to return it to him. he finally agreed as Benjamin questioned him Benjamin asked him if he had a wallet he said yes then Benjamin asked him what was in it he, told me to wait at the door . He walked off then came back saying that he could not find his wallet

Benjamin asks him again what was the contents of the wallet, the man answers him Benjamin asked him to move ckoser as he checked the pictures to see if they matched the profile on the man cards. It was true it was him Benjamin gave the man his belongings with a couple of pounds which had fallen out on to the floor. The man thanked Benjamin for honestly he said thank you again and closes his door. At least Benjamin made a good deed of what could have been theft inside Benjamin felt good and he thought of the mans face the look on it made Benjamin feel even better. Mind you in saying that he really could of done with a cup of tea and was supried afterwards that he was not invited in as it was cold and Benjamin could have been warmed up. that was a thought even though the man thanked that was the thought that Benjamin ahd wished that the man had invited him in. It was plain to see that Benjamin did not have a clue about people as he half smiled to himself entertaining the thought he kept it all in his mind. He could of kept it. mind you with the way things were what was a couple of pounds it was a nice round number. He considered walking off with it. Benjamin was now thinking as he continues nice car to selp in would be something he is talking to himself instead of the allyways and the street. A little bit of honey as Benjamin sniffs the air. As he passes the bistro.

It was getting late and benjmain was looking for a place gto settle for the night in his pocket he had half a cigarette attached to half a pie which he had found earlier previously before he returned the mans wallet. It was rapped tightly so the left over conjeled grazy could not leak out in to his jacket pocket infact it had condnced into a large ball of sluge. Benjmain ate this quickly as he did he grunted and half choaked as he came to the end of the meal. As he swallowed the last of the pie it was clear that he was going to throw up he never said it but the words were there and having no water to flush it down did not make the consuming to easy. As Benjamin closes his eyes to finish swallowing deeply keeping what food he had in him down as it all might come out he swallows again the last mouth full. Thinking to him self what was he doing to him self he thinks that there must be better ways. Why am I here was the thought. He continud as he ws telling himself I have no money he says he says this like he was on the stage it was his performance it was like he was practicing his lines. He speaks out this louder arms sretched outwards in the cold darkness of the street.
Benjamin:" I am here because I have no money."
Benjamin raises his voice louder.
Benjamin:" Then again I am here because I have lost my job, my girl I am here because, because I am here simply because I am am here. I am here and I do not want to be here, I do not want to be here."
After Benjamin had shouted those words out a loud so anybosy could hear them as short as it was yet sweet he was really trying his hardest not to blames himself for his position his sight perdicument. He laens back against the ally that he was standing in watching the darkness half way in a bush trying to keep warm.

Benjamin at that point knew that he did not like his life. At that moment he was confident that it was just a phase and he would get things together again. He was confident that he would find his way back in to his normal life. What he ws unsure about was now he was going to do it. it was now that he had started to think. And also sees another side to life. He does not blame himself or anybody else over the things that had happened or were going to happen as he sits upright thinking that it was late and thinks that he should go back to his office and chill for a few hours and maybe fall in to the luck that seemed to follow him around if he is lucky he might be able to get his old job back. That was the thought. Which ws a good thought a positive thought always good for the mind. Only it went a little wrong. As Benjamin makes his way nice and timed he looks for a reflection of himself he does not look to good the dirty old used jacket long and to worn to wear in any place let alone a interview. Un shaven and with a fully grown beard that would make an impression he told himself meaning the opposite. He sits down and waits as the clock is ticking. As his old boss avrived earlyish normally before anybody else.a couple of cars pull up in to the car park. It was like Benjamin was invisible even dressed extremely poorly nonody noticed him. As more cars arrived benjamin wa s timing himself looking up at the sky. Micheal has turned up Benjamin thought that was a good thing as he thought that he would back him up being a old pal. Little did Benjamin know that Micheal would help no body at all.

As the car park became full, Benjamin was noticing old faces never the less he wass not noticed nobody reconised him. benjmain see that it ws the right time to make an approach. To Benjamin's surprise the secutary let him in straight up starirs Benjamin already knew that he ws pushing it as for his appearance the secutary let him in simply because she was scared of his appearance, she did not know how to handle it and did not want the argument of dealing with it. As soon as Benjamin was in the right place he was pleading for his job back and getting odd looks from old work mates as they did not believe that it was him. He was thrown out of the premises the sectuary called the sercruity Benjamin was thrown off there premises. Benjamin so called work friends were giving Benjamin the brush off. On Benjamin's removal from his old office he gets a little bit of agro things like what he smelt of.
Benjamin: " yes. Yeah I have been on the streets for a week."
Benjamin was clearly lying. He continued.
Benjamin: " yeah I have been on the streets for a week you try eating out of a bin. You selfish bastards."
As Benjamin is dragged out by his arm and left in the car park it starts to rain and Benjamin takes a seat out side on a bench only to be moved on as the guard tells him that he has no business here, and would either have a permit or he can dwell some place else. Benjamin was escorted off the premises. But not before looking in afew bins which is what caught the guards attention in the first place. He finds some food he raps it up with some old news paper which was from the bin also before he is caught and throen off the premises. Benjmain gets a shove standing up then again as he walks off.

The guard made sure that benjamin was lead right off the premises as he followed him pushing him a little as he was prompt straight to the end of the drive of the building. And some verbal directions were given,
Guard:" Now get lost."
Benjaminstays close outside of the building hoping, watching and waiting to see if anybody would come after him he knows that he must have been reconised by someone in there. Nobody came outside the company must of made a few changes. It looked like Benjamin was not the only person who had lost there job inside of that company. There looked to Benjmain that there had been a large huge reshuffle, promotions as Benjamin is slowly figuring it out. As he turns away he is half way up a laaarge road which is slowly turning in to a hill in it self. Past some woodland and past some strange buildings as he gets up to the top he knew where he was he ate there everyday and as it was close by him he knew it was a chance to find some food he thought that they would be kind enough to give him some food free as there right in front of him was the fish and chip shop. There was no harm in trying. Benjamin had always said if you do not ask you do not get, a classy phrase Benjamin thought. Benjamin approaches the shop trying to look as presentable as possible. He corrects his shirt which is under his jumper and straightens his jeans correcting the hem he takes his coat off puts it on his arm like he was netering a hotel or even more so meeting somebody. As he checks what he looks like by looking at his reflection through another shop window he corrects himself again until he feels presentable then onec done he aproches the chip shop. He had no idea who was in there his large reflection said quit a lot and he knew that he looked a total mess he was going in

never the less. Benjmain looks once more at his reflection his actual state was hurting his mind.

For some strange reason the atmosphere in the shop had changed this was not through Benjmains presents which he did not think it was but noticed it. Benjamin thinks twice before turning around and trys to walk out within seconds only to bump into a total stranger, through catching her eyes of a young lady that was also aside with her husband walking in with him, Benjamin of course being polite as he cheekly looks astraight at her in to her eyes it ws like everything had changed, slowed down just for that moment. Then it happened the hard shove and the words

Husband:"Are you looking at mny women." then

Wife:" Hay your fine he gets like that."

Husband: " Oy are you eyeing up my wife."

She gives her husband a shove, then continues.

Wife: " Hay that's fine he gets like that."

Then the words form benjmain he had prepared them quickly.

Benjamin: " No I am not excuse me."

The husband was blocking the door way and Benjamin could not get past.

Wife:" knock it off darling the mans a tramp it's ok. Mr tramp he gets a little aggressive. Here. "

The lady opens her purse Benjamins eyes lite up. she hands Benjamin the contents of the purse no notes just coins.

Benjamin thanks the lady as they shuffle aside, a few more customers turn up and then to top the day time off the manager wanted a word with him as he notices them and wants a few words.

Manager:" Hay look mate you cannot do that in my shop now get out."

They all look surprised. The husband had something to say.

Husband: “ well we will ytake it outside won’t we darlings.”
The manager:” good, please do.”
The manager is pointing Benjamin understands him they all walk out Benjamin is left apologising. The manger goes back inside and attends to his customers. As Benjamin was just about to walk off the mans wife calls him back the wife who is now called the lady kn ows that there is a second hand clothes shop around the corner and quickly runs after Benjamin tugging on his jacket until Benjamin stops.
Benjamin:” What.”
she invites Benjamin to the shop leaving her husbands side. He is left choosing the lunch while benjmain is with his misses choosing some half used clothes next door.
Husband: “ She never bloody stops. Where is she.”
As the husband looks around as he is orderings his food.
Husdand:” Pie and chips and er please.”
The lady is consistant and asks Benjamin what his name is.
Benjamin answers her saying to her Benjamin, that’s nice she replied.
Lady: “ Look erm Benjamin.” There is a pause.
Benjamin: “ it is Benjamin.”
Lady:” Look ther eis a shop a clothes shop just around the corner if you would like some fresh clothes I would be wiling to pay for them.”
Benjamin stops I his path as he turns around and looks at the lady he touches his mustash in thought it ws not like he was going to disagree. Even so benjmainmind was not focused on her he was watching the back ground he could not make eye contact with her as for the embaresment of the whole situation but Benjamin

agrees and they both turn around and head back up to the shops it was only a short distance.
Benjamin already knows that you do not get something for nothing, so he asks her what she wanted in return. He knows that the lady is cosure and she was just doing a good deed she seemd nice enough and Benjamin thinks that she just wanted to help somebody. She told him exactly what Benjamin was thinking that she just enjoyed helping people she continued that she does it all the time when she can. She continued it was making her feel better it was a really good feeling. She continued that she was helping some one who was not in the same position as herself. Benjamin agrees. As he bumps straight in to her husband. After a small hand out of exactly ten pounds Benjamin kits himself out Jeans, a pair that he paid for after he had put them on jumper, shoes and coat. He had left himself with exacatly one pound fifty just enough to buy himself a small bag of chips. With the one pence he had left he gave it to charity, all spent. Benjamin after everything that he had experience was still acting like an ass. He had an attitude he had changed as he thanked the hevenly women again while her husband was getting her the food which they went to the shop for in the first place. Benjmain thanks her again and departs back down the road bhack on his journey. His clothes were now clean and comfortable and warm, not really realizing what the lady had done he was more stubborn then he thought than grateful. The lady knew this as for the expressin on his face. It had not changed. As for the wather it was going to change for the worst not good for Benjamin as he had no place to go. Mind you after a little bit of hunting he found a place in a small woods enough trees and a small lake to watch. As he nears te wood from the bottom of the road. He wished that he

had his phone, Benjamin was in his eelement he loved what was about to happen. He liked storms and being in a small woods made the whole experinance a little more exciting. As the wind picked up amd the trees started to wave. He decided to shelter himself amongst the trees and bushes Benjamin was nicly covered and waiting as the clouds in the sky had turned and the wind was racing through the tops of the trees and then agai through the trees as te wind blows past Benjamin it was a ghostly feeling having the wind blow on you directly. Benjamin was absorbed the whole storm in to himself it was something that he really enjoyed as the storm neared the end Benjamin walks back out of the small woods and back in to the sight of the traffic which was coming to a syand still. He was near the bottom of the road and the traffic had obviously stopped after the storm had trailed all the way back to the top of road back all the way to the chip shop.
As Benjamin continued he choses to stay out of sight and takes another route through another woods nearby. Only to find a small lake, trees with good cover by the lake. It seemed a good place to wait and rest as the rest of the storm surpassed and changed. Benjamin stops by a large tree close to the lake the water of the lake seemed different to what a normal lake would look like. The water was a tranquil blue in the bright light and not over cast in the sky. Benjamin sits and watches the environment his surroundings until he is totally calm again after the shock of the storm it seemed to effect Benjamin's mind in a way that he could not explain the adreline and other stuff. As he is under a tree instead of looking at the sky his mind is transfixed he is watching the shadows of the trees to guess the weather again. Before it rained again. Which it did, so Benjamin stayed put until the second storm arose then finished.

The trees that he was under did not shield him as much as they did in the first storm fully. He got a little wet but had enough protection to be able to stand and watch and he noticed a dry patch close to him which he took advenagtage of as he moved from the underneath of one tree to the next. He took his jacket off and placed on to the floor. The jacket on one side was drentched as well as his jumper he was left a dry shirt. As he sat down on it there was a huge gust of wind then a crashing sound that was the thunder. Benjamin is happy and smiling over the fact that he had just brought the clothes and he had used them already. He could see that it was getting dark. And knew that he should be moving on to find a place with a few more people. He walked out of the near by woods on to a stoney concret pathway that lead him back in to another wood as he wlaked he could feel his socks they were soaked and he could hear sqelch with every step. After a while they had become more and more uncomfortable, Benjamin was thinking about taking them off. Just to ring out his socks which were wet. He finally agrees with himself and takes one of his shoes off. The first the right and then the second the left. Straight after removing his socks again the right one first and the second one left. At that tme he thinks that he would be better off bare footed, he gives his socks a squeeze as he llinps and walks oddly back towards the town. After an hour the ground infront of him had dried and Benjamin is able to put his socks and shoes back on they were still wet. As well as his shoes making the whole thing pointless as he took them off so that they could dry. He decides to undress again and finish the journey bare footed.

On the outside Benjamin is cold and wet, and now hungry as he nears the town the rubbish bin s become more noticeable. He cheecks them for food having no luck at first. He was thinking that he might find something closer to town. When benjmain gerts a good distance of where he had planned to go he stops taking a beep breath puts his well wet shoes back on with a squelch. He continues to his destination which was one of several parks in the area. He chooses one near his old home as he has a plan to spy on Lucy.
By the time that Benjamin had got to her home it was late in the evenong, it was cold and he was tired. Benjamin was in a good mood thinking that it was great to be back he had through his recent experiences lost his mind. However it was not so good as she did not turn up infact she was not going to as she was out all evening and all night she was on a late and would not appear until the early morning. Benjamin waits hiding under his hood of his jacket, which was kindly paid for and chosen by the strange lady back by the charity shop which was by the chip shop. Benjamin needs the time and the street out side of her house which he was on were empty and Benjamin only that he cared was concerned. As he is just about to make a move to break in to her house a car pulls in to the drive Benjamin has to move quickly he dives in to the bushes near by swearing and swearing that he had been seen. It was Lucy but it was not her car. Benjamin moves quickly avoiding the car lights ducking down between the bushes and trees near buy. They both had missed him and Benjamin was inch out of getting caught. Benjamin shuffles around sqeezing himself arkwardly further in to the bushes out of sight and Benjamin could clarly see Lucy ansd her new partner. As they both get out of the car not thinking of giving a caring thought. Lucy shuts

her car door as for the man who was with her Benjamin did not reconise him. As the man slowly walks past Benjamin stoping and standing close by him Benjamin is thinking that he was going to get caught. Benjamin does not move a muscle and to top it off hold s his breath. Lucy's new friend undoes his trousers and relieves himself in to the bushes that Benjamin is hidden in. As Benjamin had seen everything he was still dry just before he loses his temper he has no way of letting what was on his mind out with out being seen or being heard. He stops gripping the tree stup with one hand with the other in his mouth. Leaving claw marks in the bark as he man departs. As the man walks away Benjamin has one hand over his mouth trying not to shout or make a sound. Avoiding further bother of the wanting to shout. As Lucy and her new boy friend head off back to the house, Benjamin is left to do the spying that he wanted to do in the first place. Benjamin is watching carefully he is getting jelious as Lucy and her friend move from room to room Benjamin is really feeling that he had lost. It looked like to Benjamin that nothing was going to happen Benjamin was counting on Lucy to close the curtains. That way he would know for sure that Lucy was hitched and he would not be able to approach her he would not think about distroyong her relasionship. It had been about an hour and still the curtains of her house were open it looked like Lucy had a new friend and a new partner. They were probably just having a drink. As the time passes Benjamin catches on. He stays close not to far just around the corner on the next street so Lucy would diefinatly miss him in the morning on her way to work. It looked like Lucy was having a good time taking everything in to account Benjamin saw that as normal she was on the rebound he was sure that it was not to late to amend his actions. Benjmain nknew that he was really hoping although a smile on his face reassured him that the thought had left him made him believe it even more. Benjamin leans back against the wall and the small bushes brushed against his back like a massarge as the wind softly blew leaving the branches tio tickle him, he sits down on to the concrete floor pulling his knees up to his chest, it was getting colder. In the end Benjamin as cold as he was decided to stay close by he had stayed the whole evening and the morning.it must have been the early hours of the mornning as Benjamin had walked off, passing the house again. Lucy was late for woek Benjmain could see that her curtains were still closed he could clearly see the car still parked up it had not been moved. As it was the first day of winter and the cars wind screen was clearly filled with frost Benjamin was close to writing a cheeky message in to the ice on her wind screen. He declined the though only to think that it would make things even worse. He knew that it was childish behaviour. He did not want to sacre her he just wanted her to wake up a bit. In the end he had changed his mind and just as he past her car unnoticed, disappointed and unhappy. As for luck as Benjamin wlaks off he kicks some thing across the floor clearly not noticing it before. It was a wallet benjmain looks at it for a long moment then picks it up. he loks upwards as if to thank god. He picks it up opening it up and finds himself a picture it was of the man that Lucy was sleeping with. Benjamin thinks that it was a good excuse to approach Lucy of couse Benjamin would return the wallet but not before he has a spending spree but only the cash he would return the rest of he contents later on. Benjamin walks off with a smile on his face and in a better mood. He had enough money to pay what he owed and enough to pay for his bed and breakfast he was feeling rich again for the week.

Benjamin sits in a nice hot bath in a nice bed and breakfast. He is going through the rest of the wallet Benjamin is talkin to him self. As he pulls out the mans gold card putting it down on the baths egde as he opulsl the next card out. Benjamin was an honest person up until this point he could see why people steal. It was quite a rush he thought. He had to be careful not to do it gain as he tells himself that it could of happened to anybody and it looked like that he had found a bit of luck, he ws clever enough to think that anybody would of done the same in his position. Even though he knew that it would play on his mind. As for self factifaction he was getting loads of it in doses. He also knew there was now way of finding out theb card s actualm pin number he ws not that stupid and try he would return the cards back to there right full owner and speand as much of the cash as possible. Benjamin as going to have to wait and make his newly found friends which was a load of twenty pounds notes spent. As for approaching Lucy he would return the rest of the contents with the wallet he would make it as he found it he found the wallet and was returning it to her for him. he had already taken the money out he ws believing that he was the good guy in all of this, Benjmain believed that he ws making the right dession. Benjamin ducks his head under the water of the bath leaving the cards in his hands takening them under with him. as he does the same again only to spash the water on to his afce as he does the whole thing again. Benjamin is up out of the bath and drying, afterwards he heads off down stairs to find himself a beer. As there was no bar and having to go out side to find a local store he was goin tomhave a well waited good time.

Benjamin waited for the night time he preferred it he out of sight and simply was imbareest by the disapearence of Lucy. As he makes his way to the nearest shops he walks in stands around for amoment and then cheekly pul;ls the wad of cash that he had found out which he had brought with him and thinking about the money he had been left in the bed and break fast on the bedroom table. He had more than enough, the beer he said to himself as he picked it up, as he walks around eyeing up what he was going to buy next as he is half way through a chocolate bar which he ate keeping the rapper as he would need to scan it before he buts his cigareetes. As she hands the rapper to the gentleman behind the counte. Benjamin smileing all the way. He says to himself as he puts the rest of te things he brought down on the counter which included the large bag of chrisps not complaining as Benjamin already knew that he would basically eat anything. He would always say that he would try anything once. That was his kind of saying a moto. Once Benjamin had arrived at the till, the shop is prietty much empty only the cashier watching he was really tempeted to do a runner nobody woud know he had no address he was thinking that he could do it easy. Just for the sake of causing a bit of trouble simply because of his position. He keeps his cool asking he attendant for some cigerttes then pays the man giving him some cash. Benjamin hands the man the notes holding on to like he was wanting to take them back. After about fifteen seconds Benjamin lets go saying nothing he walks out with his goods in a bag once he is back walking on the street he puts his hood up he heads offback to the bed and breakfast.

A weeks passes and Benjamin is out on the street again after having a massive boast over finding the wallet and manages to pay back the small dept and the bed and breakfast the owner wishes him luck as benjamin leaves. The manager is happy that benjamin had kept his word and welcomed him back. Benjmai ditches the credit cards o his way out. Benjmain was thinking that it was a dirty world as he stood in the darkness by some parked cars for cover it was a nasty dirty world benjmain was thinking. He did not know he ws changing, as he was looking at everything from a home-less guy point of view. He never used to think in the waythat he was thinking at this time. He never used to think that way. I guess you would have to experience it for your self. It was like he could see things now form a totally different aspect. The other side of things benjmain was going through enough as well as understanding his plobems he was thinking about everybody esles. He never used to rthink that way, and the things that benjamin was going through. It could be lunch, or just a bad dession making or even making bad mistakes although benjamin would not complain he would just plod along looking for other answers and in doing so finding excuses to stop thinking about what was exacatly wrong. He would not push the problem aside and think nothing of them. It was the future and you can only taste the past for so long, so far before it stands up to you to call upon you and then your conscious starts to play the big game.

He could always go back and ceal with his problems like he was now although Benjamin would just say when it is done it is done. There was no way of changing the past but it would change his problems in the future changing the things of the past in his past. Benjamin sits down leaning backwards against a wall this was becoming his usual position. Not to far from Lucys house he wanted to stay close worried that he would or could lose his mind in the process. He puts his hand in to his pocket, he has exacatly one pound and fifty five pence. He was craving for a smoke as he fights the fact that he would have to go off and find some butts on and off the floor.

The sky was darkened and Benjamin agrees with the conversation he was having with him self, asking himself if the sky was getting darker he was sure the last winter was lighter and not so dark. Benjamin smiles at the thought. As he looks up at the sky which was doing the same to him it was looking down. As Benjamin looks harder this time at the moon and again it looks close Benjamin thinks that it looks closer to the earth than it was a year ago. As a child the moon always looked as if was far in space a reasonable distance, a few hours later he looked again this time it had moved across the sky it had moved considerably distanace in the same direction, Benjamin looked confused thinking that what he was discussing was thick. He stops smiling and confesses that he had not noticed it before, as for taking pictures of extreme weather he had never thought of the stars or even the moon. He wondered whyb he had not noticed the movements ofn that planet before.

Benjamin was in need of a shower he was really beginning to smell as he stands in a shop waiting to purcess a packet of cigarettes he found himself waiting by some of the shops other customers, a girl and her friends they implied that Benjmain was smelly and joked that benjamin needed a shower other thean that he wascalled a tramp the shop assistant apologised after he had served them telling Benjamin that they were just kids even though they both knew that itt did not justify it. they left the shop waving and laughing. Benjamin said nothing he just wanted his cigarettes, this was not the first time that this had happened. And it was something that he was getting used to. It was on the street. Just to make himself feel bgetter benjmain walks out of the shoptelling himself that there are no showers on the street just the rain. Benjamin said to himself that he would be damned if he was going to wash in a public toilet aagain. This happened a few days later after he ahd made the comment. As Benjamin walked in to te town cemter middle of the mornning waiting silently by the toilets and wash rooms, the wc. He is waiting poliety for the cleaners to leave and the toilet warden to give the ok, the all clear. Benjamin gets in first taking off his clothes rather quickly stripping down to his pants as he throws his clothes in to a pile on the floor. As he quickly washes in all the sinks there are four of them, no plug sockets making it in possible for the sinks to hold the water. As the water runs in to Benjmains hands he was splashing the water over his face and body until he felt clean.

As Benjamin washed quickly scooping the water up into his hands and splashin g the water everywhere except his face which some how you would think that he could not miss. The water was everywhere especially on the floor. As he speaks to himself praying that nobody would enter the toilet that nobody else would come in side. As he moved one sink to the next then finaly finding the soap, helplessly started to wasjh over again from the beginning. On the second attempt benjmian had afew visitors they looked hard and on wards as Benjamin continued as he thought they thought it was funny, Benjamin did not. As they left some remarks were made but nothing substanual just a few comments. Which would be normal. The first person words were been thrown have you benjamin conti ued to wash, the second comment was from a man who was a little bit shy of Benjmain and just drops a couple of coins in front of him and walks out, Benjamin shouts to hm with thanks, as he picks the coins off his clothes which were still on the floor. Benjamin realizes that the man wanted some thanks Benjamin says nothing the man leaves the wc, and Benjamin finishes his wash. He picks up his clothes and goes to put himself in the toilet cubical to dress out of the way. Once he has finished in the cubical he leaves the wc in a hurry using what is left of the toilet paper to dry his face as he puts what is left of the paper back down the toilet and in a near by waist paper bin.

Outside of te wash rooms and toilet things had begun to move there were people and the shops were just about to open. Benjamin was so impressed with himself he decides to take a look around. It must have been a few years since he had been anywhere near a clothes shop. Or even brought a garment from a shop in the high street, it was always Lucy who did the shopping. It was always Lucy who chose his clothes. He would just wear them it kept her happy with no complaints.
Benjamin was now window shopping, knwing that he was totally skint. The bright lights of all the shops seemd to light up the whole place. There huge advertisements towered up wards with te names of there companys gleaming and sucking in the customers. Benjmain was fascinated he was like a caveman a loner to this new relasionship. He ws looking at a manaquin it was fully dressed jumper, trousers, hat, shoes and coat.he was thinking that it did not look that bad as he spoke to himself as bejamin continued to gaze at the fake model in the shop window he was thinking that ws the style that he would wear he thought that it would suit him. he slowly changed his mind when he took a closer look at it he was standing outside a womans shop. Disappointed as he was he moved off to the next shop this time getting the gender right still impressed.

Benjamin stopped for a moment looking down at his clothes according to what he had seen in the shop window after finding the mens section he finds that he was quuite unfashionable looking down on the clothes that the lady had chose for him. As he looks down at his shoes and takes one of them off and compares them to what the male manaquin was wearing. Only to find out that they were wearing out not just in the sole but out of fashion too. This explained to Benjamin why his

walking felt so uncomfortable. But what could he do he was a tramp. Benjamin walks off feeling more imbarrest through knwing his problem. This explained to Benjamin why he was feeling so uncomfortable and why his feet were cold.
Benjamin needs a knew pair of shoes as he remembers that the lady brought him the pair that he was wearing aand the coat too, as he smiles as he thinks about how she approached him and rembering how he aproched her for some money for a bag of chips. Maybe she would be able to ablige again. Benjamin was not that far from the place were they met and now he was thinking that they could relieing on luck to bring them back together. Thinking that his theory could work and it was not imposible but now after a long thought now possible he makes the plans to find her again. If benjamins calcalations are correct he would be able to meet her on that exact day at the exact time of couse her husband would be there and they would be ordering themselves fidh and chips. This was good Benjamin thought it was like being a dectective. Figuring out all the moevments and the times. Benjamin laughs he knows he is on to a winner. Benjamin is pleased that he had found the answer to his problem it was justs a matter of time and benjamin knows if he would meet her again it would not be by coincidence.

The very next mornning Benjamin awakes around the corner from Lucy's house as he wakes up in the road with wet feet and feeling extremely rough. The wind is blowing and Benjamin could hear it whistleing in his ears. Benjamin tells himself as he tests himself again decideding that it was coming in from the east, Benjamin notices a old crisp packet blowing in that direction as it blows past him further in to the gutter. As a couple of cars drive by this had no surnifcants to where or what or anything that Benjamin was thinking as he planed his day. Benjamin is now hungry he was looking forwards to the day not only would he have the chance to find a pair of shoes for free and a possible meal a well deserved lunch. As he waits for Lucy to appear making sure that he cannot be seen she departs for work with her new boy friend by her side. Benjamin has to think hard he was easily tempted to break in and there was definatly no body at home. Benjamin also knows that if he had been seen it would be obvious that when she had found out that the blame would be on him.

Benjamin sticks to his plan and makes his way up to his old office then up to the chip shop he ws a hundread percent sure that the lady with her husband would appear. All benjamin had to lose was a pair of shoes as he tells him self this brings a smile to his face and he says softly under his breath and some chips. He laughs and dances around a bit like a child drawing attention to himself but by no intention. As he acts the cars that drive by are beeping and giving Benjamin a laugh. As Benjamin bows with thanks. As he nears the top of the road he is a lot quieter there is nobody around and the chip shop is empty Benjmain thinks that he is early he needed to know the time and was looking saround for somebody no body significant just somebody who had a watch on. He was surprised he had got there a hour early and was happy again. According to the opening times of the chip shop opening times which couod not be missed on the door of the shop. He waits just out side occasionally looking at the times on the door they were definatly opening Benjamin decides to take a look at the clothes shop with the second hands goods in. he ws hoping that they would have the shoes that he was waiting for. Infact they had loads there were three pairs in the window and as far as Benjamin could see some more futher in to the shop on the shelfs. After having a really hard long look Benjamin goes in after a minute the shop assistant approaches him he leaves the shop leaving the shop assistant surprised. Benjamin had walked in and out without saying a word the door bell rang as he left to wait outside it was now just a waiting game as he waits outside. While all these strange things are happening to Benjamin Lucy had been having a good time Lucy was standing down stairs by her living rom window her knew boy friend was sitting in Benjamin's chair. Lucy is beginning to miss Benjamin.

Her new boy friend had not caught on although they were both tied into the same job Lucy really did not want to tell him that she was using him for a foot up the ladder this worked both ways Lucy knew this and they were both aware of each other. Lucy could see clearly see that her relationship was not going anywhere in her eyes it was a career move in his eyes she was his bit of rough a piece of skirt his bit on the side. Lucy walks away from the window her new bloke was Micheal a different Micheal to Benjamin's work mate Micheal who turned Benjamin away the day that Benjamin needed him. Lucy knew that she ws playing a game. As Benjamin gets his new shoes and left over food he walks past the house Lucy is at the window she does not notice him and Benjamin is in full view as she closes the windows curtains Micheal asks her if she would like another drink, Lucy declines Micheals offer micheal asks her if he is drinking alone, lucy agrees pulling the curtains across seeing Benjamin but mistaking for the tramp she continues its that tramp he is back again. Benjamin could see her in full view Benjamin knows that he had been seen and is now worried that Lucy had seen him. He sits down in his normal place a road away and is left talking to himself.

Meantime Lucy was using what she had seen as a topic of conversation. A new converstaionhad started all about being homeless and tramps and even more stuff and Lucy was telling Micheal that they should go outside and invite the tramp in. Micheal surgests that Lucy was out of her mind. Lucy was saying that it was winter Micheal disregards that as an excuse. Benjamin is sitting down in his usual place hoping that Lucy would not find him and thinking hard about the situation it might be a good opener in winning his old girl friend back. Micheal is out he lead the conversation telling Lucy that the person is a tramp they are the lowest, the scum, the dirt. They were made in tramps they were made in to tramps for a reason. Lucy has a different opinion and wants Micheal to help that man Lucy does not yet know that the tramp is Benjamin. As Lucy knows the same as Benjamin that he had been seen. Lucy was still going on to Micheal about what she had seen and a conversation starts about the homeless. The other end of the subject.
Lucy: " There it was not that bad."
Micheal: " yeah I thnk that they are."
Lucy: " come on MicheaL you know it would be fun. When was the last time you had something for free I would like to give him a hot bath."
Micheal: " A hot bath, that guy is a tramp scum I will not go anywhere near him in am not making myself a part of that."
Lucy:" what about if it ws somebody you knew."
Micheal:" that's would be even better a larger bottle of beer for me."
Lucy smiles putting on her shoes.
Micheal: " o my you cannot be serious I do not believe it."

Lucy: “ I am going out side to find him he has been hanging around her for days .”

Micheal knew that Lucy argument was why did you not tell me. Lucy reply was he did not want to scare him with Benjmain and all the other stuff. Lucy walks off outside micheal stands by the door looking straight at her following her. Lucy is excited Michealk is not amused, whilst half drunk. micheal has no choice but to follow her.

Lucy: “ we can lure him in like a cat. Here kitty, kitty.”

Benjamin was close staying out of site. Lucy continued. Benjamin was close and he can hear her speaking he now to is excited as her. Lucy gets closer Benjamin loses hIs bottle and is up on his feet fast hiding after being close to the floor he puts his hood up throwing the chip paper down empty and swallowing the cold chips that he had found earlier in a bin, as he walks off but walking in her direction. Lucy misses him as he walks past her. Lucy misses him by miles as he walks past her getting a good look at her. Only to bump in to micheal whom Benjamin also gets a good look at. Micheal was to drunk to question the him as he passes by, it was good too that Benjamin and Micheal had never met. Benjamin apologises and contin ues to walk off. Once Benjamin is at a safe distance he stops thinking about if he had got away with it. His clothes might have been a give away. Benjamin had diapeared and Lucy and Micheel think and agree that they must of scsred the tramp that they were looking for off. Benjamin knows that he has to be careful. Micheal says nothing to Lucy about bumping in to the man. When he tells her the next mornning Lucy does not believe him and thinks nothing of it as she thinks the situation was over and it was just a bit of fun.

Lucy: " So what you saw the man ok what did he look like."
Micheal: " He looked normal I did not get a really good look at him, he had his hood up."
Lucy: " Ahh come on."
Micheal: " Seriously I saw nothing as much as you although in saying that there was something about him b but I could not tell that I would notice him if I was to see him again."
Lucy: " He smelt of fish and chips."
Micheal: " I was just about to say that how did you know. Do you know him."
Lucy: " No I bloody do not I am a little classier than that a tramp. A tramp that smells of fish and chips just forget it and forget him."
Micheal: " Poor chap I really feel for him I really do."
Lucy: " Do you think that we should tell somebody,"
Micheal: " what tell the authoritys why he has done nothing wrong. No just leave it. Lst the man live."
Micheal asks Lucy if she feels safe Lucy replys she is always safe micheal continues that if Lucy is having problrems they could make a call. Micheal continues as long as you are safe. Lucy agrees.
Lucy: " I am going up to bed that's enough excitement for me."
Micheal: " I am going to finish watching the programme ill come up when it hjas finished."
Lucy walks out looking concerned it was like Lucy was drawn to the stranger. Lucy had not finished thinking about him and says nothing to Micheal. A couple of days past the conversation arose again accidently.

Benjamin ahd walked away unnoticed but only just he was thinking that micheal he birds bits of stuff could remember his face. Lucy could pick it up and then no more spying on Lucy. Benjamin knew that he would have to chill for a while as for the incident he would stay close but keep his distance. Lucy in the meantime was getting on with things by the end of the month she had received the promotion that she had been aiting for. it looked like her hard work was working for her as well as her looks. Lucy was not as stupid as you would think most of the other women in her office were reasonable quiet which did not make things easy for her she liked talking and they did not talk at that time it did not make things any easier. Even though Lucy liked to have a laugh it ws still the bloke s in the company that had a laughed with her and of course complimented her. Benjamin was being foolish he had followed her to work. It was totally out of his character and to make things worst it was in another town. Benjamin did not know the area and he thinks that Lucy would spot him. he ws trying to go unnoticed he could see her car clearly and she ws still dating Micheal. Benjamin knew his name and that was enough he had heard it the other night when he walked past him out side Lucy's place. Benjamin was close and still unnoticed it was like he was invisible he seemed to mage to merge in not just on the street but in the woods and around corners.

Benjamin thinks that he is doing the right things as he questions his own behaviour he leves Lucy work place and head back home to his own town by the time he gets back Lucy was just leaving her office and heading home.
Benjamin now knows not to get to close he is sitting down hidden by the park acrs by the road the wather was not getting any warmer and bejmain could not fell any colder Benjamin was going to need a warmer place to be he looks at his hands and they are beginning to swell with the coldness of the air. By the nightime they were actually swollen and they looked panfull, they were fine just cold. His feet had gone numb and he could walk no further in the weather. Benjamin was thinking hard how to over come his position and predicament. As the night nears Benjamin is keeping himself busy as he counts the cars reading number plates and reciting the plates to himself. As he trys to remember them keeping his brain functioning. As the cold reslly sets in Benjamin is really trying his hardest to stay awake. In the end Benjain falls asleep. In the mornning Benjamin is awoken by some child proding him with his toy. The child was really aggressive as te light proding turns in to a kicking as the child tells Benjmain to wake up Benjamin is half awake. Puching the boy away. Benjamin finally awakes grabbing the kid and yelling where is your mother. Benjamin gently ushes the boy away with a gentle push. Telling the boy to stop and go away Benjamin is looking for his mother who is close but taking no notice as she is busy ion her phone not caring to take any notice.
Benjamin:" hay, go."
The child continues as he thinks it is a game. The child does not stop until his mother pulls him off benjamin and away softly apologiseing in a common acent.

Mother: " Oh I am so sorry."
Giving Benjamin some loose change from her purse Benjmain excepts the kind ladys offer. Ten just looks at her she gives him some more as she does he thanks her getting up onto his feet. He thanks her again only to get a kick in the shinfor his trouble he smiles at the child and walks off. The lady finally crosses the road Benjamin is out of danger. Again Benjamin walks off, Benjamin was cold the coldest that he ahd been for a while. On the streets for the first time being concerned he knows that he was going to have to cut a deal. He was thinking slowly building a plan. As he looks at his options benjmain puts one hand in o his pocket looking for his wallet as he looks through the rough papers he find the answer of keeping himself warm. In side the coldest part of his jacket he had found the bus ticket on it had the date it was in date, as he calculates the days counting back wards. It would be the perfect place to relax and it would be warm and sleep. Benjamin thanks the last man who wore the jacket. What had happened to Benjamin was pure luck. It was a good conversation piece Benjamin was thinking how did he manage to achive the predicament looking at his situation. as Benjamin waraams up still thinking how lucky he had been he was looking at the ticket it clearly had the right date on it, in big letters. Benjamin stayed on the bus all evening he spoke to no body and answered polity when approached in conversation only speaking when necessary avoiding the spoeple that looked rough. Occasionally getting off the bus to go for the toilet and catching the next bus knowing that one would arrive eventually, and he also got off the bus to have a smoke when he needed one or two, after he had asked for one of one of the passagers. While Benjamin washalf way up the country on bus Lucy is busy next to a warm fire

with a bottle of wine making jokes and making jokes about the tramp.
Lucy:" It was really funny."
Micheal:" Yeah yeah could you imagine if it was Benjamin poor chap, my god."
Lucy cannot stop laughing.
Lucy:" Oh Benjamin that is a name from my past."
Benjmain is getting off the bus looking around for a sign to tell him where he is. Eventually he stepa in front of the bus and on a big electronic screen he finds the name of the village that he was in. he was some where in the county side. Benjamin was happy again he did not care he was happy that he was just able to get on the bus. He gets back on the bus to get warm again. Mean time Lucy had enough of laughing and really feels for Benjamin. As micheal makes up more jokes until he says to much going over the top Lucy got angry. She shouts at Micheal and tells him that it was enough that the jokes were enough. Lucy said that a joke is a joke and the last joke was out of order I will not repeat what micheal had said. Not realizing that Lucy was upset by the joke Lucy tells him sto stop again what started out as a small drink turned into a fully blown argument.

As for Benjamin he had fallen asleep on the bus. And was being brought back in to the town. Lucy and micheal wer busy arguing they were shouting extremely loud at each other. Up until th epiont that micheal was asked to leave. Lucy was playing it cool Lucy knew what she was doing. Lucy had got what she wanted out of Micheal to make her next move. It was obvious to Micheal that she had been awaiting for him to slip up. The conversation about Benjamin was the perfect excuse and fitted in with the argument. All Lucy had to do was to throw Micheal out. Micheal should of seen this coming and after doing some quick thinking is back at Lucy another argument occurs whilst Lucy is still speaking Micheal had changed the subject and was talking and shouting about something totally different. A knew subject which had nothing to do with the first subject. This time Micheal is on top of it. he is talking as Lucy is packing not hers but his clothes.

Micheal :" You used me Lucy."

Lucy:" how."

Micheal:" You still love him." He was refereeing to Benjamin.

Micheal: " Please Lucy do not play games with me."

Lucy:" Love who. Before you say I have friends in high places, so do I."

Micheal:" Do not make me laugh, the most important person you is the bustman and that tramp yeah the one that hangs around outside your home."

Lucy:" Just go please end of conversation."

Micheal knew that she was serious.

Micheal:" Are you serious, you are serious."

Benjamin ignores what he had heard hoping that nobody was hurt. But hoping that there was an accident that would be Micheal. Benjamin walks a little further until he is outside of Lucy's place the cold air hits his face leaving him feeling the chill. He got cold quickly and it looked like it was going to be another cold night on the street. Benjamin sits down in the normal place he was glued to the ground. It looked like he had nade it his own personal place. Apart from the cars which he was using to protect himself from being seen, The wind that looked like it was going to get worst. It was not working and Benjamin could not get the thought of how badly timed his removal from Lucy's and his own relationship was. With no money and very cold Benjamin sits, he is talking to himself as he looks up at the stars and the light that was keeping him warm with the large trees and bushes surrounding him. the echoes of the traffic and cars nearby distance was louder than usual as Benjamin had lost sight of time thinking that it was late in the evening but infact it was late in the early evening he realizes that he could of fallen asleep angry for missing it. His imagination was playing games with him. Benjamin blamed the cold air and was telling himself that it could not be the evening yet but it was. Once Benjman had figured out the right time. Joking to himself for a moment speaking out to himself again telling himself that it must be the early hours of the morning and he must of over slept on the bus in benjamin s mind it all made sense and he was happy to be corrected what he thought was madness. As he makes himself even more frustrated and uncomfortable he stuffles along the concrete downwards correcting himself up against a wall that he ws slowly slipping down on to the concrete floor below. As he adjusts himself to suit the concrete and not himself with his jacket which was torn warm but still wearable he turns placing it down on the floor knees apon it and watches the house through a small gap in the wall. As he leans he stares tornmented looking at the lights that are beaming downwards on to the floor of Lucyd drive way. He ws thunking how he distryed a really good relasionship and how much that really hurt Lucy was the only god that he had loved. Benjma=amin shys away there was no way of knowing how emotional Benjamin actually was. He was realizing that hanging outside Lucy's home was wrong although there was nbo creime in it unless Lucy would find out and complain. Benjamin was going to move he decided to go back to the bed and breakfast to try and cut a deal with the boss. He could not remember his actual name. but it would give his a chance a place to get reaklly warm and a place to think about his actions. As the weather was set for the evening and Benjamin made a good call as it had started to rain.

After Benjmain walks off heading straight for the bed and breakfast he notices in a ally way he had never noticed it before it was dark like most places that are hidden and wet but sheltered and enclosed a place where Benjamin could stay it was close to Lucy's place and it was out of the way there were trees there and it looked safe. Benjamin ignored the offer that he made to himself and conti nued his journey back in to town walking like he was in a hurry but infact he was in motion and concentrated on where he was going. As heb was counting the steps while counting the numbers of cars which he was passing and taking more notice of there number plates which he would recite to himself. Just for fun and something to do he believed in keeping the mind busy. When Benjamin gats to the bed and breakfast he stays close under the cover of two large walls so that he could not be seen. But in a place where he could see the man behind the counter, Benjamin is trying to keep a serious look on his face. and was thinking fast thinking in which way he was going to approach the man. He stands there while Benjamin practices the lines he few moments later he had finished it did not really matter about opracticing the line s as what ever Benjamin had prepared would come out totally different simply because he had lost his nerves, and it would take a few minutes for Benjamin to understand himself what he ahd said. It was all down to charm, he was hoping that his comfidents would help him as he made an attempt, as Benjamin waits he is gathering his thoughts. He is watching the door hoping that it had been left open that would be job one done he could just walk in. tow would to be making the deal and the third would be to be haned the keys for the bed room. He ws Lucky he was in the first job was done. Benjamin was happy he did not have to ask to be let in that ment that they were open for business. He could make an unarranged approach. Benjamin walks in.

Benjamin:" Boy it is cold out there."
There was no answer from the receptionist. The man did not notice and it looked like the boss was away. Benjmain shys away he thinks that he is going to lose he takes a step backwards nerviously. Speaking again.
Benjamin:" Boy it is really cold out there, out side."
The receptionist does not answer again and Benjamin was just about to walk out and then out of the cold silence the receptionsist speaks Benjamin jumps in surprise. Leaving the entrance door to shut by it self.

Benjamin:" Look I am not going to give you a sob story I need a bed for a couple of days, I will have no money until the end of the week would you be kind enough to wait."
Recptionsist:" As it happens we do have a room but it is not so comfortable and if you say what you said yes my boss told me about you we have been waiting for you infact except we cannot offer you breakfast."
Benjmain was surprised and agrees to the receptionist terms. The recepionisist gives Benjmain some keys as Benjamin is taken to his room he was thinking that was easy and he must of left an impression, the receptioniasist opens the bedroom door letting Benjamin in, leaving the keys by the small table by the bed he walks off saying nothing. Benjamin thanks the man as he watches him he raises his hand I thanks and disappears around a corner back down stairs. Benjmain is cosy and in bed with a cuo of coffee he needed to have a good long think about his situation he was going to star thinking about it in the morning. As for writing some bullet points to see if he could reverse ssome bad luck. He could not believe it that he was a tramp and he was thinking could a women really do that could Lucy really be that powerful it was looking like it from where Benjamin was sitting and the view was not particularly good.

Benjamin first thing in the morning was to get a shower for a hour. Enjoying every minute of it, once he was out he got dry, after talking and a long song he takes his dirty clothes down stairs to be washed asking the receptionisit if it was ok. The recptionsist did not speak for a moment hen tuirns around and says to Benjamin.
Receptionisist:" Not only does he want a bed and a hot shower he now wants me to wash and dry his clothes."
I do expect that you would like them dryed.
Benjmain can not say anything and trys not to meet the receptionists eyes. Benjamin speaks.
Benjamin:" the last time I was here."
Receoptionist:" Here there here I will have them back to you in the morning in the meantime you can borrow some clothes from our lost property if there is anything that will fit."
Benjamin was looking as he frowned and slightly worried that the man that has been left to care for him was crazy. He turns around and goes back to his room. Within a few hours of waiting for some fresh clothes Benjamin is on his bed he is undressed striped down in his boxer shorts. There is a knock on his door the receptionist had returned Benjamin's clothes he had brought him up some knew clothes also which Benjamin declines but thanked also for his hospitality. Benjamin thanks him again and the receptionist leaves him the clothes and walks away.

Benjamin is impressed with what iss going on and is trying to understand. It looked like from Benjamin s side of things that somebody was paying his bills he did not want to think about it to much as he knew nobody gets something for nothing Benjamin chose to play along. Benjamin was thinking a negative thoughts he was thinking that either that guy was seriously easy going or somebody is making deals with out him knowing about them. as Benjamin continues to think about how he can get out of his predictiment. He begins to weigh up the pros and cons and odds was it Lucy that name was glued to his mind. Next time he sees the receptionist Benjamin would ask him hinting about who was footing his bills the receptionist was as good as the resistants he was keeping his nose clean. Benjamin raises a question which turned in to a fully blown out conversation Benjamin could not get out of it. The little man could not of been questioned any harder, although the little man had no answers. In the end both Benjamin and the man gave in at the same time both staying calm not one raised voice either end they both depart Benjamin walking off in a half a bad mood and the man did the same not knowing if he had one the battle of the converstion. The man was in a huff as much as Benjamin was in a mood. Benjamin says to himself that the only way to get knowledge information out of a person like that would to shooting them in the foot. Benjamin walks out and te receptionist sits in his chair saying nothing. After a minute or two Benjamin returns the receptionist already knows what Benjamin wanted and hands him a cigarette then offers him the whole packet. His words were take them all. Benjamin abilged.

The next morning with all the luck that Benjamin was having he was going through all his problems. Which was no home he asked the question why he questioned this over, he needed to tidy himself up and he knew this man before he wandered off he had to think about how he ws going to approach Lucy it ws going to be a job. All he needed was an address so he could receive mail. The bed and breakfast would be perfect. All he needed was a siut he could find a second hand one, problem solved charity shops in town, problem solved. The only problem was not a problem as Benjamin still found himself with some money, however he was cleaver enough to approach them with none. As they were a charity and if he explained his situation he was sure that he could get one for free. As all these thought flowed through Benjamin s head, he believses that he had made some progress. He knew that he coud easily turn his life around. The hardest part was missing Lucy. He still had feeling for her and she was also the cause but in his consciousness it felt like something completely different, was Lucy and Benjamin really fighting there real feelings.

As Benjamin is getting back on his feet only notv knowing who was footing his bills and through constant thought drives himself further out of his mind this insaness drives himall th way back down he had only just got back up. it ws a large kick in the face. he tries the whole things again it was harder than he thought. Benjamin is at te bed and breakfast, he is job hunting the receptionist had a spare computer, lucky for Benjamin. As he looked and searched there was nothing he comes to a stand still out of luck he was fed up with going around in circles. He was lonely and in love. Benjamin finally cracks is on a ladge he is drunk and he needs a cigarette he has one in his hand but does not notice it at first as he yells he needs a smoke. As he swigs from the bottle of whisky he can feel the air bklowing in his face through his unshaven beard. He was not thinking correctly. As he stands balancing stupidly on the roof top with a shoorled voice trying to speak a few of the bed and breakfast guests walk by saying nothing benjamin did not know that he ha an audience. Benjmain words become more vibrant he is now busy reciting poetry people down on te street are now talking and now speaking about him. this was one thing that benjmain could not get out of his mind he still lokoks back on the event today. And everybody says the same thing he ws very lucky if he had not got that phone call from his boss he would peobaly be dead. As benjmain takes another puff of the cigarette the receptionist down stairs is oin his way upstairs. He knocks on Benjamins door benjamian is else where obviously he was upstairs on the roof dancing with a bottle of whisky. Benjamin hugs the bottle like it ws a baby singing drunkern words nobody could understand him.

Receptionist:" whoa Benjmain telephone call."

Benjamin: " tell them to call back later."

The receptionist does as Benjmain had asked although the person on the other end of the phone insist that they need to speak to Benjamin he continues that he is busy and asks him again to ask them to call him another time. He says it again this time a shorter way. He was busy.

The receptionist tells the person on ther end of the phone that Benjamin was drunk and was about to throw himself off the building roof just as the receptionist was about to put down the phone Benjamin decides to take the call he does not step away from the edge he takes the phone call as he takes a step backwards.

Benjamin:” Hello.”
New boss:” We love your CV bow would you like to come and work for me.”
Benjamin:” And who are we.”
New boss: “ We not me, Benjamin.”
Benjamin:” Tell me the truth.”
New boss:” there is an opening at our company we received your cv and you have been short listed and if you can make the interview I am sure that you will welcomed.”
Benjamin hangs up, not realizing what he ahd done he steps away form the edge of the ledge.

The receptionist was behind him as benjamin explains he was ready to take a run and leapthe receptionist knows that Benjmain had lost his cool he gets close enough to benjmain to hold on to him and slowly softly pulls on benjmains arm pulling away from the ldge and towards him. benjmain gives a loud cry get off the man still had a hold of him. the very next morning benjmain knows that he hads to give the receptionist an appolgy it was going to be hard benjmain was not the apoligectic type. Lucy could of told anybody that. Benjamin tells him that he was drunk and it was just abit of fun the receptionist is thinking twice about Benjamin. He conti ued the conversation with now I have to watch you. Again the receptionist grills Benjamin on this topic the conversation leads back to wht Benjamin wanted to throw himself off the top of his building, the receptionist said that his actions this evening could ruion his business he conti ued how shevfish Benjamin was being. He would have health and safety all over him. just because he could not hold his liquor, it would probably make the evening news. Benjamin does not realize how bad the events of the evening were. Or the kind of mess he would leave himself in in the near future. Or the mess that he was thought to be in. Just to make things worse he realizes through his actions he may have lost the only way back in to Lucy's heart, the job offer. As Benjamin polity asks the receptionist for his phone as he hand s him the desk phone he asks him who is he going to call he was also asked to keep it quick and continued that they were not a charity and he was running a business. Benjamin starts a new converstion asking the receptionist if the phone had a call back button. The receptionist asks him whythe receptionist asks him for the phone as he is looking at it

then presses a few buttons and hands it back to Benjamin. He looks at the phone staring with confused eyes as he looks for the number that was left from the caller last night. Benjmain wants the job interview that he was offered the previous night. Benjmain was diapionted with his behaviour he tells himself this as he has nobody to tell him. he was acting stupidly what made him feel even worse he was under the influence of the bottle. benjamin goes off for a long walk he ended up right out side Lucy's house not inteniously as he sits down in her drive way this time around the back of her house again he questions himself. He was trying to think about the places his feet could take him unconsciously Benjmain was thinking that he could just walk and his legs would take over the journey and he would not even have to think just walk. Even though it had to be right outside the women that he had loved. As he turns to walk away and is just missed by the car pulling into her drive. He now knows that Lucy again had yet another boy friend Benjamin knew as he did not reconise the car or the man that stepped outside of it. Benjamin manages not to be seen, as he loses total control of him self as for what he saw.
Benjamin:" Who is it this time no wait it is your boss." As the word come out Benjamin is a little slow in controlling himself and realizes what he had just shouted. Leaving Lucy at her window again. Only to think that she hearing things as she welcomes her new boyfriend in right in front of Benjamin. As he covers his mouth for the wanting to screem loudly. He leaps in to the nearby bushes so he would not be heard or seen. He jumps and stamps hard on to the muddy ground despretly. Lucy had invited the man in side, Lucy was at her window not forgetting wht she had heard. As he closes the door within a few moments she closes the

curtains. But not before she takes a long hard look as if there was somebody there and there was Benjamin.

Rough poverty

It had not occurred to me as I woke up exacatly where I was. It was night time and all I could see was a rather large water fountain, why I could see this I cannot tell you. When I looked down I found myself in clothes that I thought were not mine. I ws fully dressed, it took a moment for it to sink in. The only thought as I squeezed my eyes apart then together and at last open, looking down at my dress again. What had I become, the coat that I was wearing was not rhe coat that I had put on it was not mine, I could not remember, back in the day I would not wear clothes like this it was not my kind of style, it was large and w hen I say large it ws three sizes to big for me to fit in to it. Along with an over sized wooly hat, trousers which had no belt but replaced with a peice of string to hold them up. and a pair of old fashioned work mens boots with no laces. I was a tramp. I closed my eyes again putting my hands in to the worn out coat only to find an worn out wallet. It was empty, where was I as I looked around down and then up a long a path, black, I could not see a thing only feeling the cold ground and the coldness of my feet in the cold boots on which I stood in and on. Besides myself was a bench I must I thought but How, how did I get here. I did not remember myself I was in a different place, a different place to where I would normally live. I was in the wrong clothes with no money and I was dressed like a tramp. I was looking around the only object I could see was a used whisky bottle, by the bench by my feet, it was half empty.

As for the surprise of waking up in a park, dressed like a tramp I was tryimng to figure out who I was. I had no recollection of being in the park in fact I had never been in a car park not onec or even twice not even with a dog, or even just to play. As I looked around dazed and confused pacing frantically as I woke up. I was thinking I was not one of those rich kinds these things do not happen to me, I was not from a poor background. I was from a middle class family with brothers and sisiters. I looked around again with frustration with nothing to greet me but the darkness of a large field with nicly cut grass and the smell of whisky on my breath I had never tried whisky what ever was on my breath was obvious cause for concern.

As I looked upwards still thinking where was I, I just wanted to go home. The thought of home was a real thought it must have been real as I remember I there there s a pause, I had forgotten my address. I decided as I did not no where I was that I would stay put until the morning at least I thought I would have an idea of where I was of where I am.

I had no longer had a memory of my self for some strange reason. That part of me did not function it did not want to ecept those thoughts of what I was trying to remember. It felt like my mind had been replaced what was in side of my head was not my brain. I was trying to remember to think the thoughts and memories were not mine, they were fasle. I was telling myself that these memories were not mine I was busy telling myself by myself that theses memories were not mine and if that ws the case then who's were they and where were my memories the real memories. The memories that I had been receiving were really poor and old as I thought of them it was not like I was one to think, in fact there was a time that I would have to stop thinking and let god take over. So I had to question it I had to oprn my big mouth. That was just me weighing up the pro's and con's. if this was me and I had one question the only other question was how did I get here and how did I become a tramp. Those thoughts and these questions I questioned as I sat on a bench they kept on reoccurring over and over again. This is great I said not only am I driving myself crazy with the thought of findng a thought I have now forgotten my who I am Benjamin looked down at himself once more it was true I was a tramp.

The only other question that I would ask myself at that point in the park was how did I become a tramp it ws a good question at the time as I curled up on the park bench. Waiting for the mornning to arrive. Not onwing the time I closed my eyes and waited for the darkness to dispurse and the nothingness to arrive. I had only known of what I had seen on tv about what I would expect from people for being a tramp would be. I had all of that to come. No more smart clothes, eating food which had proberly been on the floor before it had been half eaten and kleft in a bin. A crappy bin not one of the good ones. If there is such athing as a good bin, the scrouging, stopping people total strangers in the street for money, the sleeping in the door ways of shops. I hated the person that had done this to me. I really hated the person did this to me, there was no good things about being in this situation. even the good things about my situation were bad.

The time seemed to of slowed down and the air in the air around me seemed to of stopped moving. The coldness of the air had seemed to of kicked in. and the hunger had started. I had no place to go and I had no friends in the area. It did not surprise me that I was in this situation on my own. I must of done something on my own to some body as my mind did not fit my predicament. As I finally started to think there was no way that I would be getting any sleep it was just to cold. Infact in saying that the only thing that was keeping me from the cold was looking for somewhere to sleep. Some where a little more comfortable. It was colder facing the north so I turned around facing the south and the wind was off my back. Even though I had moved my position a few times maybe actually six in all.

in all before finally setting down in what was a bin infact a wheely bin around the back in some allyway.

That acton did not make any difference I was still cold and I ws still tired. As occasionally the odd rat would appear and would crawl and make this horrible scratching sound waking me up every few hours as they came out for a feeding. They were as scared as I was and once they had finished they would disappear and there would be silents again. When they ahd finished thre turn of scrounging off the waist they surround both the bin and myself leading me to believe that I was in some kind of danger. I only had myself to blame.

Everything that I had or had happened within those few hours gave me a sense of direction. I could see how people were so greedy ok. I was in a n bad position no home, no friends, no job, no money they could not of given me more. Of course theses were my words now. And if you would ask me the question forty eight hours ago I would of probably of thought the same. I could see whee I was coming from. Now that I was in that position it was a real eye opener. As Benjamin shuts the bin top and pulls over him some doggy cardboard for warmth. Only to feel a squelch on his face Benjmain knew straight away as he leaps upwards in disgust grabbing what was on his face and throwng after removing it from him as he throws it out back on to the street a dead rat. As he lowers the bin lid shouting the words that echoed of each side of the ally way walls it had to be me.

After the removal of the rat which was inafct a mouse when Benjmain finally took a good look at it he says to himself that he needs help in a joking manor but a serous comment. And had no idea where to start or even look. In the morning the streets were extremely busy a good time and place to hangle himself some money no taxes just disappointment of being gturned down. It seemed like I had been there before it was like I was watching myself. Why was the thought, is this what I am looking for as I was looking for some place to sit. Still not believing tha facts of my new found situation. As I sat down seated for the first time within a coupke of days. I was trying to figure it all out, why I was approaching people for money free money.
The theoy was that I had none I begged the more I got. I moved to a new spot this happened quickly the more I moved around the more people I would get to see the more money I would be handed. I ws beginning to think that there was a system to this. There was no point in asking children for penny's I was targeting certain people children had no money it would be by sheer luck if a school kid gave up there lunch money for me there was a ninety minute oquation that said no. the boys were the same. Most people were on there way to work and would just ignore me as they did not have the time to stop, I suppose that tey could of got up earlier. Mind you they wer already peobably late. Again a no. I had been beging most of the day and I was ofen told to move. It was a wake up call as one tramp that refused to move used a stolen vebdors licence as an excuse shouting back at the aurthoritys holding it up yelling he had the right to be there. The people that nicked him had other thoughts. So you had to be carful.

All I could hear was a mans voice his words as I sat there was why do you not wisen up.

In the end I guess I was to lose the first round of trying to understand my new and promising position and with no money and obviously not knowing my true address if there was one. I could see the rest coming and when it came it came hard and fast I had spoken over a convertstaion two men were having, it was late too and they were taking everything including my coat they were drunk. and to top everything off they linched my sleeping bag. Which I found later the next mornning, they were both left in a nearby fountain. As I pulled away at the sleeping bag pulling out of the fountain as I pulled the sleeping bag out of the water, I could not see but there was not much left of it, the coat was also distroyed there was not to much left of that either. I had nowhere to dry what was left of my belongings, little did they seem as it was a big thing at that time. I spent the whole day gurading them. and got them dry by simply leaving them on the floor outside of the same shop the incident occurred. I was in poverty and I did not like the sound of it. the sheer thought echoed through me it was really sinking in and I was sunken in where I was trying to figure it all out was even harder as soon as you get to the top of your first problem your set with another then another it is continuous. Everything had been timed I was insinc with everything else with what is going on. It would be easy getting in but extremely hard getting out. I was actually at the differcult part getting out. I went from the getting in to the differcult simply because I was not in so the only thought at the time was to get out.

It was getting late and Benjamin was hungry although the thought of food quickly left him as he thought of the dead rat. That he had slept on first. I could still the presents on my face which slowly which slowly put me of the idea that I would want to eat anything. For the next coupkle of days Benjamin felt the same way. With no money and no place to sleep still Benjamin busy looking for new place to dwell not to far but close enough to the town high street. There was always some bosy there so Benjamin was not alone. He would get the occasional beep from cars as they drove by. And occasionally get some dodgy half eaten food chucked at me. and the occasional drink which always looked liked urine, Benjamin never attempted to open the bottles he was to scared. He aalso had te opportunity to scrouge the odd piece of chicken and cold chips out of the bins from outside of the chicken hut. Disgusting I know but that's the way it was for now. Beggers cannot be choosers and with that thought it entered and left Benjamin quickly. Benjamin was losing his mind and the thoughts that were left were none he was looking at his reflection over a puddle. He noticed that he ahd grown hairy he needed a wash and a shave but they were the last thing on his mind.
As the cold air was coming in fast probably from the sea Benjamin was no weather man and he was only guessing. However he can remember it was always the same. It went from some thing like there will be cold winds to snowing to lots of rain blusry of course to a little dryer and shower it all made sense honestly it did.

With the smile on his face with the impressions of the weather man. benjmain is feeling a little better. Still lost and not knowing the time or place where he was. Benjamin was waiting for the early evening as he contin ued to look for food. He did not know but he ws looking through bins for food infront of everybody. Within a few days his beard had grown not saying that it was the food as you would expect the opposite to happen. He was looking dirtier and feeling dirty he needed a wash. As he turns away from his reflection he growels uncontrolabley at an old lady who is walking past him. Benjamin realizes what he had just done he realized that he was at his lowest point ever, he follows he a bit getting in front of her to grab her attention and then apologises, The old lady screems beleiving that she is being mugged. And it did not stop there some young workers from a nearby shop leaped to help the old lady from Benjamin who was busy shouting his apology there was a little scuffle and nothing more until the words were put across to Benjamin your right tramp as Benjamin is pushed then pushed again and then proded they were telling him that he could be in trouble if he was to do that at that time that was nothing as Benjamin had done nothing, he continues to applogise as he is slapped on his long tramp like jacket. Again Benjamin is proded and then tells the man after grabbing his finger that this could be grevoius body harm. Benjamin lets go. In the end the boys leave Benjamin who is in quite a bit of shock. A the lady who over reacted was taken in to the shop foir a cup of tea Benjamin is left to deal with the thought she decided to have her hair done whilst she was there Benjamin could clerly see that it was daylight robbery. As Benjamin watches the old lady remove her purse and takes out the money benjamin is wishing that he ahd stolen her purse.

As benjamin weighs up the pros and cons of what he is actually doing in the place the only thought was that he was in hell. Apart from that the facty that there were people around him even though he did not feel dead or have any other problems he could not heqar either god or anybody else. And so gthere fore considers himself alive although ofr dhould I have said even though all I had infront of me was what was behind me was poverty. As I finaly got the lady out of ny head, I continued to do the window shopping as I set out to do. It was not so great dressed in clothes that were not yours, and to have to watch a man stuff his face with food that has not been in a bin. And just to top it off having children laugh at you because they know no better. Why was I drawing so much attention, question was I in trouble answer probably.
It was slowly becoming obvious I was not used to my new surroundings I was not farmilar with the area that I was in. The people in this town seemed, I suppose you could call it tight although in saying that most people were.
I had found anpther door way to shelter under a place which I cjoose wisely and sat down in it it was early evening the sun ws going in from the coldness of the winter was slowlyb creeping in. there was plenty of people around still you know the ones that brave it the question was would they be polite enough to stop and drop a couple of pennys in his hat.

Music

It must have been as month and I was picking up knew tricks on the street and according to the people that I had been watching there was lots more there was crazy stuff such as petti steeling petti crime the most obvious one. I was just standing there on the street surrounded by people watching. I was with another home less guy I did not know him personally infact I had only just met him briefly I would not of classed him as a friend more an aqaintance. It was the way that he did what he did which took me by surprise. It was the way it had style the way he lifted the old mans wallet. I ahd to try it so I waited as he did he had my back. As I was standing close to two maybe four people all waiting targets as I blew in to my hand's I started to watch and I started to follow people around. Especially old people, they were the easiest. Except the mans wallet that I lifted was a young man he was as small as a teenager I did that because I was getting desperate and I could not feel how sorry I was as he walked out of te shop telling his grand daddy that he had lost his pocket money. It was straight out of the blue the next vitem had no idea who I was as he moved down the que I was tight right behind him. as I moved my hand closer to his back pocket it was obvois that he was loaded as for the size of the shape of the wallet that was in his back pocket. As he slipped his wallet out of his pocket I was waiting nervously for him to return it gently I ws going to do that for him. Except when it is returned it would be empty. As I made te second move bumping in to him removing the item for him and proded him gently just enough to give him the same feeling as going in ti his pocket. Taking my hand away leaving him with a nudge. Phase three stepping backwards and giving him a tap on his shoulder just to ask him a question would you have a spare smoke. Just to take the feeling of being robbed away. he would always have the thought that it ws me but as I was to far away from him he would drop the thought as it was impossible for me to reach him form the distance that I ws after I had met him. Before he turns around I hand the goods to my aquintance who is leaving the shop. Job done. Of couse the man says yes, as he removes his cigarettes from his pockets. From the opposite side of his jacket he hands me a smoke as he tells me to hurry up rolling as I do I thanked him and walked off.

Apart from a twenty pound note a couple of credit card a driving licence there was nothing else. Most of it was pieces of paper, bills, I could not make anything else of it. I threw the papers away with the credit cards and the wallet I sold for a fiver keeping the mans address I was making this stranger my target as I had his address I might be around to visit him and see what else dwells in his property. With all te imforamtion that Benjamin had gathered from his first robbery. The twenty pound's was split two ways leaving Benjamin the grand sum of ten pounds enough for a couple of packets of smokes he was thinking if was all that stress and worry really worth it.
Although with the stangers address he might pop over and introduce himself. I was busy doing my usual rounds people that I would see now everyday wer beginning to notice me.this kind of upset Benjamin as he thought that it would cause him more problems. It soon would as now every other day I would meet with the sucruity guard who would watch me as he moved me on from place to place espacialy the places that I was trying to sleep in. then there was te cleaner and then after that there was the bin men, the dusts men. They would also say a welcoming weird hello. I was becoming quite a celeb amongst the poorest of folk. Their was a lady that would open her shop up every couple of days, when I was there she would say hello she was not sure weather she should of approached me at first until the day that she had greeted me through a phone call not to me but to the local police as I looked at her she shunted away that's when I knew I just knew as she was not there to greet me she looked at Benjamin with a dirty stare. This time she was watching me walking towards her she was obvoiusly sacred of something as he panicked rushing back I side her shop.

and turning over the door sign closed it said in big letters. I thought her behaviour was disgusting and I felt it I felt for the first time like a second class ciziten. The notice on her door said closed.

As I looked at her through her shop window she was not being the how nice to see you the message that I ws recioeving was get lost you're a weirdo and I guess that was her message she obviously was not the kind person you would think maybe I blew her cover she was scating like she was scared enough. Her shop was closed so it was go away. I did not know her true intentions but shortly afterwards her neighbours a shop a little further down the street had caught on. It seems that news travels quickly. I was on the receiving end and I wanted to get my own back when you go looking for trouble you normally find it. I thought about doing her place over. When ever I could I would watch her till at the end of the day I would watch her count her cash. Knowing one day sson I was going to rob her. I was still outside sleeping rough in was outside every morning. I was quite surprised that she had not noticed me and if she had she had not spoken of it. I was quite surprised that she did not ask me to move. I was well in my rights to stay there, if she was to complain it would have been the park bench for me probably the coldest place I could think of. As I calcalted the robbery taking it all in, timing every movement she made with the shopping centers clock right outside. I guess time was on my side. I had not forgotten her for the next few days the job wa son my mind. I chose to stay away move some where else to settle down but just for a while. Keeping the arrange ments of the shop in mind keeping the thought to myself. Why was I feeling this way question because I was lost and needed to be found even more I was trying to be myself, Benjamin.

I had a choice in the place that I was going to sleep the first one was to go back to the park, if I ahd the bottle as I heard through the towns people it is not tat safe. mind you in what I was dressed in would scare you as it scares me. It would scare anybody, or I could just stop at the high street and use a door after thInking about it hard Benjamin finds another option he has the strange mans address the one he lifted out of the wallet. He could try him. It was something to do it was going to be a long night. Benjamin needs an excuse and is thinking finding one quickly he decides to say that he found his wallet whilst looking for food in the bin near the shop were he robbed him. Obviously leaving the the robbed bit out and would say that he thought he would return it to him. It would be a smart way in to his home. Question was I really a theif as well a tramp? Benjamin ah no answers to his mind he is just cold he starts his journey. As Benjamin decides to go along with the idea approaching the strange mans house after robbiong him in the shop he clearly found his sddress and is going to use the mans wallet. As he strolls in to the richest bougher in the area he isb looking hard from street to street. He could not find te address that was written on the inside of the wallet, until he found a taxi driver in his taxi as Benjamin looks on wards it looked like he was in luck. As Benjamin is watching by total coincidence it was the man that Benjamin was looking for it was te man that Benjamin had stolen off. Benjami is indelight and is jumping around doing some kind of funny dance. The taxi driver drives off leaving Benjamin to follow the weird man home. Benjamin had begun to scare himself he had never storked a person in his life and was not sure if he could call it that. He was behind the man just keeping his distance just enough to see him his dark shadow. With one eyes over his shoulder he walked casually to a remote place in the trees nearby benjmain was sacred for tehe first time probably the night or even that fact of what he was doing. As the man takes a gilspe over his shoulder clearly seeing Benjamin now believing that he was being followed and he ws not wrong Benjamin had slipped up. Benjamin watches the man he stops pulling out what Benjamin thinks is a phone in fact it was a tazor Benjamin gets close as he explains his self as Benjamin was just about to hand him his wallet back. When Benjamin awoke it was to the sound of music, he begins to fake it a little bit more. As I had been taken in Benjamin had a big smile on his face.

On the street

When I had left the mans home after being filled in question why was I in that mans bed and so I was back to being on the street. Unfortuanatly I did not get the chance to have a good look around. Although knwing my real intentions he invited me back. I ws out on th street yet again as we said our good byes I was thinking that the man was extremely polite and nice and thick. Although he had good manors he had offered me a chance to approach him again. It was the afternoon as we said our good byes, as I walked down his road out of his sight I had lifted his wallet again I was telling myself it ws right and I had no choice and I wondered if and when he would notice, when I looked back in to the office again twenty pounds probably for the taxi. I guess he would just have to walk you win some and you lose some wast he thought. Question was what about if you could win and keep winning. I was back on the streets knowing that at least if things got really bad and being in that position already and I had not realized that I was there already there and I had not realize that. As I climbed back into the wheely bin and closed the lid I fell asleep only to be woken by the noise of te early mornning bust bin men after being greeted with a good morning I climb out of the bin said my good mornings with a little prayer knowing that the cleaners would appear next with the rush of more and more people. As the early morning rush slowly came to its end again realizing that I had slept on another dead rat which was stuck to my face as I quickly jumped out of another large wheely bin whipping him off my face ss I rubbed the mess that ws on my righthads dwn my knees and on the nearby wall.

Benjamin needed to watch the high street more as he wanted to watch other people like himself the homeless and others he was watching some guy with a dog. And he was weighing up the pro's and con's. asking him self things like where does the man get his mo ey to pay for the dogs food and other things he already knew that he could get his clothes form the second hand charity shop. He talked full faced and well I was just about to find food heaven. As I followed him slowly he walked with his dog it was his guard when we got around te back of the shop I thought great a car park then as I stood aside the dog started to bark I was busy looking at the time it was half past seven the man camled his dog rubbing his hands together within a few minutes a large lorry pulle up in tio th car park. As we both looked hard at the truck as we looked at the karge doors opening. Infront of me were five large trollys they were all pushed out and within less than five minutre the man s jacket was filled not with just food it was filled with dog food I asked the man what about himself he says it is for his dog, I felt at that point he was really kind and I thought that I should match him. Question is everything a game to Benjamin. The man calls to Benjamin telling him he has got about three minutes Benjamin is already on board filling his coat with anything that he could fit in it he was not even looking what he was grabbing. As he leaps off the truck he is heading the mans way who has a smile on his face as they both enter an ally way split the proceedings and go off on there separate ways, Benjamin never saw the man again.

Even so benjmain had enough food to be an[ble to dstuff his face for the next few days I ahd chocolate fingers and I was feeding the seagulls with peanut buttr sandwiches for a week until it was over.

As I finished the last meal at the ten oclock on the second day I needed a place to stash my food if it happened again. I was temped to eat all of it all at once. But I was full and I am not a greedy person, I managed to stash some of the food in a near by bin I counted what was left by date so I would collect it one day before it all goes out of date and kept it as close to the date of the next delivery. The new food would arrive there was bread and peanuts and there was some meat which I had forgotten about. It went moldy when he felt it squidge in his pocket he jumped thin king tht it was that rat again taking out of his pocket only to throw it as afr as he could landing on a coffee table of some coffee drinker only to cause another accident Benjamin laughed almost straight away and not being able to control the thought continued to laugh the most of the day. The meat would have gone off by the time Benjamin had got back. Benjamin ahd got more than he had thought as he looks down at what he has left this included carltons of drinks, baby juice lots of chrips some chocolate bars sausage rolls and a few other bits. Benjamin must of eaten everything else. Benjamin says to himself that he had to agree that he was a little disappointed he thought there was more so once a week at ten oclock he was there out side te back of the shop waiting for the truck occasionally some other home less guys would turn up aaaand they would devise things amongst themslef on how they would do the job. It looked like nobody noticed nobody said a word. Benjamin agreed that he should smarten up now that he had found away to feed himself. He had very few penny's he was planning to buy some new clothes from the charity shop Benjamin was always welcomed. It was going to play a big part in Benjamins life in the future. Winter was coming to the end I was still trying to figure out how I became a tramp of course I could asked a doctor if there was one. I heard that they had left and gone abroad, however they do not grow on tree s or just appear to people in act they are hidden, however it was little more than complicated than that I'll take myself through it once more. Benjamin ws getting some advice the man in front of him was telling Benjamin that he would have to be poorly before any doctor would see him and after hus sickness be referred. It could take weeks and by that the he would feel better so there was not much point. The strange man continued and said that people who used doctors are either really old, really sick, or ingeneral feel sick. However I was none of these I had just lost my mind a sickness that you could hide if you are clever enough. Tu shay. Benjamin was looking for a doctor who could tell him the same as he had just heard. As he says that he ws none of the above. There was no way in as the deseases that I have is called tramp. I had found myself ona park bench and I do not know how I got there I have no memorie of how I got there. Is there a cure for this Benjamin asks Benjamin was questioning hims self.

It was clear to him however he puts it across to him it was not clear what he had said. I had always thought of being outside I never thought of it like a tramp to be a desease. It must feel and be addictive.as Benjamin slowly comes to terms with his situations he is slowly excepting who he is. At that point he comes to the terms that he is talking to nobody. He is excepting the fact that who he is now. Benjamin still beleaves that he has no memorie, Benjamin still agrees that he was a rich person and trys to return himself back to his class. Realizing that there was going to be some trouble as he is yet to have an address and with out an address he cannot have any money and with out the money he cannot have the bank account. With out theses simple steps Benjamin could not get his life back. Benjamin was out on the street.

As Benjamin comes to terms with who he is and what he had become he was questioning himself as he went along the smile slowly disappeared for the first time he actualy looked worried and tells himself that what he had become was not him. As Benjamin spends a lot of that day drawing up conclusions each time giving up as he runs in circles. He goes to his food stash only to find he has less than he had thought, he was not to up set. By the time it was dark he had lost track of time he does not know the time of day or what day it actually was. He thinks he has missd the weekly hand out, of the out dated goods that he wanted to receive. This worries Benjamin even more. Benjamin with all the thopughts of the day as frustrated as he was and tired at the same time goes wondering off to find the time and the day it is. As he does reminding himself that he needs to know theh time if his calculations are correct. As Benjamin stuffs himself with the out dated food until he is gorged full of bread and juice. He tells himself he needed more eating food for Benjamin had become a luxury and a buzz. At this time it ws better thn a pint of larger. As Benjamin gulps his last mouthful. Throwing the remander of the sausage roll in to the nearby bin. He cheers to himself as for getting the shot in first time as he runs around circling the bin pretending that it was the final basket in a basket ball game which never was. He continues until he was out of breath. He continues shouting loudly Benjamin scores, he races around the bin. Then he stops correcting himself and come sback to realatity and normality.

As Benjamin comes to terms of what he thinks is an elusion and he believes that he is diluded by his position he spits out the last mothfull on to the floor. Benjamin is walking around in is usual patch again he realizes that he has become drawn to this place he notices familiar faces except it does not break the ice. On a couple occasions he manages to make conversations. He thinks that it is being friendly just friendly people on the way in to town he catches the bus. He is on it only to find that he w standing next to a blind person the man next to him must have been hard of hearing as he went to get off the bus and cross the road unaided. Benjamin could see what was going to happen. The man does not wait for lights and crosses the first part of the road not thinking obviously he attempts to cross the second part of the road not knowing of the traffic ahead. Benjamin is cool with the man as he hands him his arm, and with a fasle godly like voice says to the man take my arm. The man steps in to the road, Benjamin is ready to gently touch him to guide him in the right direction. Benjamin was thanked by the man they both went on there way. This gesture of help began to reacure it seemed. Again another example was an old lady she was caught up I the local market making a mess with packing her shopping and another time. Benjamin was doing good and the prole around him were slowly noticing that Benjamin was little more than a tramp. People began to approach him simply because he knew things that he did not think that he would know, he was realizing it himself.

Benjamin was going to be helped in the future he did not know. And when he was finally approached whilst standing by te waterfountain People were beginning to notice that he was educated and now he had filled his mind with even more knowledge people did not want to see him in the position that he was in. In the first instants he was listening, that's is what he did best. He was just about to walk away form the help. Which was good in a sense but shows that he was just as arrogant and stubborn and needed a little shove to wake him up. Benjamin realizes this. Benjamin was to alte to except the towns offer the opportunity had gone. Benjamin was telling himself that it did not matter as if it could happen once then it would bound to happen again it was when it was just a matter of time. With this thought Benjamin resured himself that he would be found. But were and when was now the topic of the day. He was not trying to hide the fact that he was beings welcomed. Benjamin rolls a smoke, thinking and feeling a little more welcome. As his own presents has given him a place back in to society. Benjamin swakes up in a door way as he looks around at first right upwards at the celing then the cold concrete walls as stretches out as he wakes up looking outward only to bump in to an old lady she was blocking the light withn her trolly when Benjamin looked again he could see her shopping the trolly was full of food. Early morning breakfast was all Benjamin could think about. It was delivered free by an old age pensioner. Benjamin smiles not repeating what he had just thought. The old lady looks at like he was real scum and is disgruntiled with hers and his position.

Benjamin gives the lady a huge loud good morning. As he leaps up and gives the aldy a hug knowing not to touch the trolley and wait. He knew that she would offering him something. As the old lady is still surprised as she wriggles her hand down into her trolly and pulls out aa can of crab meat and hands it to Benjamin. To this day Benjamin believes that the old lady was god, even more so as they met every morning since that day, she was just a granny. Her realsionship with Benjamin was basic she was a granny and it looked like she enjoye his company and she was helping him. Benjamin always thought that it should be other way around. He brought this up in a conversation. over tea. There relasionship had gone form a conversation in a door way to having tea and cake. As for company that ws good they would sit in th coffee house for a hour each day. They would speak about old fashioned things and things that you would not think about. Her last words of the day and she had to be the one with the last words were some thing a long the lines of the future. To this day I still do not understand what she ment. She also said you never get any younger. She continued I know that for a fact. Even though Benjamin had found a friend he ws still reluctant to share hs true feelings about himself he was thinkng tahthe could be a little bit more open. When the converstion came to him he did lie I suppose you could call it that. As slip of the tongue you kn ow your just talking and you say something you did not want to say and the truth comes out. A few other things come out on th way a journey of speech had begun certain things are mentioned and added to the conversation that you are having.

The old lady that loved having Benjamin in her presents the lady would talk all day and Benjamin could hadly get aword in edge ways. He never got the chance to express his feelings if there was such a thing a feeling. It seemed to be a bad conversation as the granny talked away Benjamin wanted to speak as it came for the lady to leave she continue until Benjamin realized he belived that she was cracking up as she sopek on this occasion she would not stop repeating herself and then the conversation was lost she ws saying the same things everyday lit was like she was drumming her words in to Benjamin because one she wanted him to listen and two she just awanted to be herad. One morning at the coffee table she had got up and said her piece and then walked off. It was less than a few minutes leaving her coffee behind her.

After wishing Benjamin a good day Benjamin was surprised that he did not notice her she had been at the table everyday of the week. And he had listened to her for a good hour each time he did not say a word. Benjamin could not a word in edge ways again. This left Benjamin believing that it ws her age old age. As the lady contiued her conversation it seemed like she liked talking about the future. Benjamin believes that she was trying to tell him his future. Benjamin kept up with the conversation just. As the old lady continued saying Benjmain only understood parts of the conversation some of the things that were said were extremely powerful and hidden in side of her words was the knowledge. It was in her.

It was all in the mind phyically Benjamin had his own. Though he had not had the chance to express himself yet as he knew better than to boast about things that probably are not true. He had a few ideas of theology and politics which he kept to himself. He was thinking about what the lady was thinking about.

As te lady asks Benjamin to help her with her words Benjamin looks puzzled the lady just as Benjamin's about to speak finishes her speech that conclude the leeon today. She fiddles about with her bag looking for her purse obviously Benjamin was going to get paid infact it was qiute the opposite as she pulls five pounds exactly out in to the sight of everybody and puts it side on the small white saucer as a tip. Benjamin just looks at her I suppose you could call it disamusemnet. As she turns to Benjamin he was deep in throught he was thinking. That was a hard one, do it was the thought Benjamin looks around there were to many people around and Benjamin just looks at the money wishinbg that it had been a little more as every penny counts. The final thought was no. the five quid stayed put. Benjamin was still there with the look of craziness on his face. he had the chance to take the money the lady would not know the lady probably would not have noticed. The old lady finaly gets her answers as she asks Benjamin to hold her as a guide. Benjamin takes her arm. As they both walk out on to the street. Again Benjamin is thinking about askng her for some money he wa sthunkng she got to give him some thing for his time. Benjamin was polite but to shy to ask her. The old granny could feel this she did not miss a thing. Benjamin thought. As they both neared the bus stop the hard concrete ground was getting to hard for the ladys shoes the lady says nothing as they walked te lady continued that it was her agE mixed with pride and stubbornness. Benjamin thinks as they make it to the bus stop. They wait a few minutes and the bus turns up on time Benjamin waits and watches she get on to the bus before he walks away.

Benjamin is still unhappy and is disamused by the old ladys actions back in th café he leaves the bus stop grumpy a new turn in Benjamins mind this type of grunting on this seemed to happen when he loses quite often as you can imagine. Benjamins day was not over yet. He still had the night to consider he was getting good at approaching old ladys as they would come out of the bingo hall and some out of the clubs always avoiding the men avoiding fights as he could see himself brawling wth some drunks. So he stuck to talking to the ladys he would give an occasional compliment to brake the ice and then he would use his charm not really wanting a relasionship just the offer of some street food like a bag of chips or a some thing meaty. Most of the time Benjamin would get an answer most of the women were drunk and most of them abilged, mind you when it came to insults they were prity good to most of them would just step around him, with the words he dirty or something worse who put these scumabgs on our streets at night. Tramp. Benjamin was clearly amused by the insults and chatter that he was causing. Even though what he had just heard was nice but was an insult compared to what other things had been said about people like him. Even people like him in the same situation said they had seen a lot worse and hared even more. Through what had been said. Benjamin knows not to hang around for to long in the place that he was in the evening, the bingo halls and te clubs he had to time his arrival and his departure. As it can be a little rough and a little noisy.

As the night slowly went by benjmain ahas a hat with exactly five pounds in it apart from being puked on by some drunk girl and been apologised to by her friends he was given an extra few quid for the incoveneince. Benjmain ws in a position he ws not fine. But carried on with the seven pound he was happy that he had met them. This meant food and cigarettes Benjamin liked the feel of the money. When you do not have any just the feel of a pound coin would excite Benjamin the word s was a frill. Benjamin was sjust handing some money to the assistant it is a fiver he continued to leave the man inquestion until the man finally gets fed up with Benjamin joke he was playing around pretenting to give the man money thenwhen his hand is out he would quickly snatch it away he persisted in doing thois this the assistant was not amused. The assistant finaly gets fed up with Benjmains act. As benjaminis now verbally anoining the man by constantly repeating its ok it os just a fiver. The man has a reply to this it was like give me my money get out of my shop and if you do ot I will personally kick your head in. he said this as he waved an extremely large knife. Of course Benjamin paid the man. and afterward shouted at him and runnimg out side in to the street only to bump in to a crowd of drunken men and girls. He insists to them that they should not go in to the shop. His question was why. Why should we not go in there. do not speak to him sophie he is a tramp. No wait why she continued I want to know why wait do not worry she is drunk.

Benjamin ask the girl a question are you a puker the girl was clerly over the limit what is your name is sophie. The girl looks up and polity asks Benjamin to move out of the way as she asks him his name only to be sick Benjamin did actually move just in time. Only to turn around and throw up again this time on her friend. She was not having a good time. Eventually she is draged off with cheers and singing sophie is a puker. Benjamin continues to watch as he takes another bit out of the kabab that had left him with it to hold as she was being sick she had forgotten it. Either way Benjamin had reslved himself. They were off there faces and heading toward a taxi Benjamin is still watching as they all bundle in. The cab driver was not amused and I think everybody could of herd his complaint. Benjamin now with out the company as for that. Benjamin looks down and for the thanks of god is looking at a purse the young lady dropped it, it was now to late to return it and Benjamin knew that she woud be too drunk to come back and look for it. Benjamin jumps with the excitment of picking it up. Erm was a good thought as he rumbles through what was mostly business cards and of course taxi money. And to top it off an address. Benjamin was more than happy with his find, making sure that he does not go back to the kabab house. Only for the thought that she would be looking for it and was probably waiting around there although this was only theory. Knowing that he would return it within the next few days but not before he has a spend I guess love was nt o his side but money was.

He closes his eyes once more giving thanks as he leaves the towns high street. Not really knwing where he was going to dwell. In the middle of the night he decides just to walk and see where his feet take him. it was quite a lonely thing to do.

As Benjamin walks he is talking to himself, the night time weather is good and the sky is clear he looks up at the stsrs but only sees the moon, a quarter cresent. Benjamin looks on the ground for some cigarettes butts. After trying his jacket four times he has his lighter in his hand, Benjamin had walked right out of town he knew this and he knew that all he was going to see for the next couple of days was concrete motor ways and the ocsaional country path. Benjamin was having second thought should he stay or should he just walk. And as he was already walking he might as well continue. As for the route he would just follow the motor way and there was very little traffic at this point and the road looked like it was lit all the way. Benjamin tells him self that he was going to give it a go he prefered the challenge. He continued as he started off twenty three miles to go, by tomorrow afternoon I will be on a beech if there is one. Benjamin with no money and no belonging starts his journey. Talking to himself as he walks leaving the small town behind him. they would probably forget him within a week. Until he appears again. Benjamin was happy, the expression on his face would tell his story the smile was a give away. he was now even more comfident as he walked he would think of the town he had just left behind him hoping that he would find a better place in the next one.

Benjamin was walking he had the whole country side to play on as for the traffic nobody ever stopped. Having no traffic around him concerned Benjamin. Benjamin thinks and within a hour is feeling quite thick as it was late evening and most people were in bed fast asleep. There was the occasional truck that soared past him. but nothing unusual. It was just as he thought it would be. Even if a driver of a lorry would stop it would take a lot of convincing that the driver was safe most of them were foreign and you could be agreeing to anything if you did not understand there language.
Benjamin is aproched more than once and he still denies his right of way he was happy walking for now. Benjamin wass now in motion he ahd picked up a rhyhem he only stopped to do a leak go to the toilet although he foud this frustrated as he would cool down quickly and he wanted to be warm. So he stars over again. This closely avoiding the high way police Benjamin says hello and they say hello back Benjamin smiles for some reason Benjamin thought there actions funny. That was the end of it, although it looked like Benjamin was the wrong position he actually felt much more safer walking on the motor way than walking on the street. While walking to his new destination. Benjamin would see the odd road kill, however in act it seemd to be everywhere on tis strip of road. Benjamin felt intiled to say a preyer to everything and anything tht was lying dead on te motor way side. he was getting some funny looks but he continued never the less. As he prayed he got a few beeps from on going traffic and s few people shouted giving there opinion they were mostly teenagers with the breea-ze from the traffic had a bit to it with the wind blowing it would hit your face with a sting, it muct be coming to the mornning as Benjamin notices that there is more traffic.

Benjamin was right the road was getting busy and more people were arriving bleeping there horns as they past it was a little bit enoying at first. As he walked it was having a effect on his mood. Although he was happy that somebody was giving him some attention he was not treally on his own. It was feeling good and Benjamin was feeling popular. As Benjamin nears the fifteenth mile that was as far as he could walk at that time. He was going to try and hitch a lift the next eighteenth miles he had no idea of how far he had actualy walked and how far he was trying to achive. He had made a guess on the distance of the journey by mistake it was now obviously longer than he thought. As he was going to hitch part of it he thought it would be easy infact it was one of the hardest things he would have to do on this journey. He had required a piece of carboard and a marker pen on thecard bord he wrote his destination he continues to walk showing the boeard out facing the motor way it read lift needed. The marker pen and cardboard was thrown at him by a passer by earlier in the day. Benjamin thought of it as a guesture how nice he thought. The timing was good the idea was now, Benjamin clearly remembers the driver he was a young man probably in his late teens. Believing that I thought that he was doing me a hindrance, or making a joke and helping me at the same time he threw the marker with the card board straight at me. in to the lay by. I collided with them. As soonas the motor way ws lear I was left to chase a piece of card board down the fast lane. Benjamin was kneeling down on the conctreted lay by he takes the marker out of his jacket pocket and write s oj te card board in extremely large letters.

The bank job

It had taken Benjamin a few weeks to settle down, Benjamin was over thinking about the things as he was on his own nt knowing why things were going wrong. he had the chanace to make some friends buta agai his mind let him down. As for his circumstances they ahd let him down. After basically getting upset he stopped greeting two other tramps that were in the area.

Benjamin was sitting on his own believing that everything was ok it was not but invact it ws the opposite he was slowly beginning to miss his own town the lady and the granny and a few others but however Benjamin was a fighter and did not want to give up. he agreed he needed a change and that is why he came to this town. He did not want to give in it was half a chance. As another man approaches, Benjamin has to make a decision, he decides to stay.

The houses and streets looked similar to the town that he is missing they seemed theb same but were different they seemd really old and went to lod places that you would not even think you could live in asuch a place there were massive mansions that were large enough to hold a large family of cubs the memoreie crys to think to think about the gardeners they could easy be re introduced.
Everywhere Benjamin looked he seemed drawn to the town was there some thing there for him a person waiting or maybe some gold lost and then found a gift perhaps may be a thought.

It seemed qiute posh and upper class the roads were clean and the bins removed even the bin lorrys were nice and clean.

The people seemed smarter as well forcing Benjamin in to looking more out of place he missed there to fit in. the people spoke differently Benjamin was quite amused. Once in a while Benjamin would get the odd look. Benjamin was still keeping his head down, and only spoke when he was spoken to if that. The street bins were empty most of the day this was a problem for Benjamin. As waist was his best friend he would say. If only there was some. He closed his eyes wishing that somebody would just throw something away. Benjamin wanted to sit down it was not like him just to give in, even haslf a cup od tea would do it ws something. Benjamin needed to change his dress to fit in. He could be a little smarter he thought. As benjamin is acting like himself and not anybody else he was watching the local bank for amusement he was dreaming of money alhough now that with the thought was he being watched himself. A strange man appeoches Benjmain he is wearinga bobble hat that acts like a ski mask the man tells Benjamin that the drop off will be after the heist and the drop would be on gte fifth floor. Also on top of that they will do and he repeats himself again will do the jewlers as well
The man hugs Benjamin ahd takes his hand leaving a huge wad of Notes in it. The man walks off, Benjamin does not get the chance to explain and knows that he has been mistken for somebody else.

Benjamin shouts a robbery but those words were not enough. He wanted to swear but he could not find the words and when he was finally there his words were hamburger came out he had shouted as loud as he could.

Benjamin sits down not knowing what to say, think, or even do. He was in shock. As the man straightens his dress leans over to Benjamin pretending to speak Benjamin would not of knowb what to saty back it was by pure luck that he was where he was when the man turned up then the man walks off Benjamin is in disbelief. He had the idea that the man was some kind of ganster, a crimsal. The man in the hat seeme to think that he knows Benjamin. Benjamin takes his hat off and puts it to his heart and thanks god. As Benjamin now has thencash the first thing he does is to go in to town and smarten up. the second thing he does is gto get abed and breakfast. As he is down stairs near the kitchen he orders himself a cup of tea this seems all to fimiluar he also orders himself a full English breakfast and after a lare piece of strawberry cake. He sits at the window watching while eating the passer bys, as he was quick to eat his food and he was stuffing so fast he got anaudience. He slurpe his half dark chocolate cup of coffee. Before realzing that he had left a large amount of cream attached to his face he wipes it off smiling at the passer bys. Asking himself that they did not notice. As he reaches for the napkin wipes his mouth again as he calls the waitress over to oreder the same food again. He leaves the café and tips the staff excatlt one whole ten pence. For te next week or so Benjamin is content with visting the café. And he would order something different each time he was there he was their he was trying to eat himself through there menu. He was doing it fast, he was.

Benjamin thought that he was being watched while stuffing his face and after evry meal tipping the waiter exactly ten pence. He drinks his tea as usual with a slurp wipes his mouth and pays the bill as he leaves.

As he shuts the door behind him some of the local people are gathering outside cusing and cursing it was a lady night in a night club. As this happens it sends Benjamin's thought all the way back. He just stands there for a second then wakes up and continues as he passes a couple of lady's who are talking he asks them making them jump. He asks them a question it was where is the local park. The two lady move away the lady on the left who was not particularly pretty I suspose you could call her ugly one as she smiles and takes a fancy to Benjamin showing him her teeth it looked like there had been a war in her mouth. Benjamin tells her straight that he was no debtist and she introduces her shelf as Sophie the name rings a bell but Benjamin cannot recall where he had heard that name before. Although she is polity spoken Benjamin had a chance to speak to her but in all the commotion Sophie is dragged away. she shouts the direction of the park to him it was a left left left down that way. Benjamin was well amused as for the girl he could not stop laughing. Simply as she had some of her teeth missing and when she smiled it was funny Benjamin thought. Benjamin smiles as he disappears in to the crowded street. Benjmain laughs again this time saying nothing. He is left alone and happy with the compliment. Benjamin goes off to find the park. Recalling the directions of what the girl had said.

It was the same the reacuring attitude and actions is that life Benjamin thought to his self you would do something and you would go back and do it again. Even more so with people who have really real bad problems do not know when to stop. Like now I guess you must be really quite clever. If evrytghing you did was recauring like a sports game receiving the ball perfectly then for it to happen again I guess it could work in patterns only for it to happen again. I guess that is were my problems occur, you beat it amnd again another problem occurs another one arises like a chain reaction or similar. Like the pass in the football game. Life I am right. I know I am Benjamin is talking to himself again as he thinks he has to pick up the card board package it was his treat a half eaten Sunday roast in a sandwich to Benjamin it was a delight he closes his eyes putting it into his coat pocket for later on. Benjamin is acting sane as for his predictament as he realizes that his movements had been the same he thinks that it is a warning as his life seems to be areacuring mess he does not know if it is a good thing or a bad thing. At that moment he questions his self again how would he change his life. Plus action make a decision. Stick to that decisssion wait for the right time posibely pray. Benjamin is looking back at every decision that he had made since he hasd came in to this new town. He was weighing up all of the answers and all of the decisions that he had to make. He was looking at everything that he had said in recent conversations. He would change the area which he belived were wrong to the ones that were right.

Benjamin sits down on the park bench casually as he was watching a few people in the nearby distance they had a dog and they were playing with it. there were some other people nearer by in the park tey wer also playing with a dog there were large trees twice the normal size and they had there branches over hanging so you could shelter there if needed. And small bushes that some small children were playing by as well as the dogs. Benjamin could see he was visualizing it there was a large preastoric creature learking in the larger places and the ocsaional space being Benjamin was thinking if the planet earth had been visited. A lost tennis ball bouces in front of him he grabs it his actions are fast, and nobody comes looking for it. so Benjamin returns it himself simply by throwing it back in the direction that it hahd come. A few moments later a girl with her dog appear it was her dogs ball apologises the little girl looks at Benjamin he knew what was coming next. The little girl bursts in to tears. Screaming hat that man had taken her ball. Benjamin looks around there are no people around there ws nobody there to inquire about what has happened he trys to calm her down only to make things worse benjamin walks off quickly to another part of the park. Away from the crying girl some place peaceful.

As Benjamin gets over the crying girl feeling really grotty for losing her ball he sits quietly minding his own business almost instnainiousky he is disturbed again this time it is a football until the owners come to find it as Benjamin is approached by its owner Benjamin, he looks up as the owner looks down again he is apperoched by a little person the boy stands there like he is waitibng for a treat Benjamin says nothing auntil the boy speaks except the boy says nothing leaving Benj amin to believe that the ball was his but the boy wanted more he wante a conversation one he wishes that he did not start as the boy wanted to know everything form the colour of the sky to if there was a haven and what was it's purpose. And to top it off who would be the next prime minister. I did not want to say it but I did proberly you. In the end Benjamin started asking questions also where did the boy come from if he was an alien, which of couse comfused the boy. Benjamin was just about to give him a prod just to test his own sanity as he did notv think that the boy was real. As he continued the conversation with the boy As the boy continued Benjamin was thinking that he is a little bit intelligent he was just about to open his verbal dictionary when his mum turn up. as she thanked Benjamin telling her son how many times have I told you do not speak to strangers. As he is pulled away the lady thanks him again. The boy was upset and almost instantly bursts in to tears. Benjamin thinks it was him infact it was because the little boy ahd forgotten his football.

It made Benjamin smile to hear the young boy being told off only for her to come back to him asking for his football. Benjamin fetches the boys ball it ws behind him not to far. When he returens the ball the boy is wquick to ask hime another questionthis time as he is being pulled away form Benjamin and is shouting hisstaricllly how far is the moon form the earth. His mum apologises again. Dragging him away with another telling off.
The boy left benjamin with a large smile on his face to the point that he had to laugh as he finishes laughing he says the words the moon, the boy did not think it was that funny however it was.
Benjamin looks down his eyes on the floor he finds a smoke a cigareete and then chceks hi own packet to see what he had left. By luck he has a fresh one. He puts the used cigarette in to his packet as he does he removes the fresh smoke lights s it up. benjamin thinks about his actions this thought was reacuring he then changes his mind blaming it his actions with the fact that he was smoking and he could not lie that it was addictive he questions his actions and then questioned the question that you do, conclusions, will power. These words obviously ment something the question stops as benjmain pulls a smoke the one he found in front of him out of his jacket pocket. Blowing the thick smoke out of his mouth in to the air at this point I was feeling like an interlecual thinking that if there was not one and again if I was one. Could I be the first one how much brain power do I need how and what ws brain capacity I had never heard of this term before. Can I recreate myself with out blowing a fuse in my mind or with going out of my mind or with out thinking that I was actually mad. When I said those last words going

out of my mind I realized that I had. That for an interlect or an intellectualy thinking in liked the sound of that it suited me down to my t-shirt. Mind you if I was called that I might get a little up set.

As the darkness seemed to take control my life, it was time for me to find some food, there were around five maybe six bins near me I had first and glorious pickings.

As Benjamin found that the bins had changed no open tops just srewed in lids harder to reach the food and you never actually get to see what you are getting or what you are picking up. it was not unlikely that you would not come across poo. Although the first bin of four I rolled up the sleeve of my jacket the bin looked wet although I had not experienced any rain may be I missed it even though before I did the deed I looked at the ground it was dry. It looked like now that some c=body probably a drunk ahd left his bottle in side spilling over the contents. I removed the top. What I pulled out was the most disgusting thing I had ever received wet bread with a fizzy drink. This had happened to me on a few occasions this happened to be one of them. The bread was soaked but still in it's rapper. Just as I pulled at it pulling it out of the bin it's rapper fell off it as I rolled it back up and put it in toi my jacket pocket in the inside. I had left it in there so it could dry out. Bin number two a packet of chrisps of course it was half eaten and probably spat upon. Bin number three, Nothing, and bin number four again a half eaten sandwich. Scrambled egg and it tasted like cheese. Bin number five was empty apart from a half used bottle of water if it was water but I had never trusted that one. Bin number six, lots of used smokes and flat half drunken bottle of beer. The last bin was the best bin it had inside of it more chrisps, half a sausage roll half a scotch egg more chrisps and some baby food. Who ever I was I was quite impressed.

Benjamin was nice and happy but not knowing that the man that gave him the stash of cash is wanting his money back when Benjamin hears this benjamin found out what the man found out knowing anyway Benjamin did not really want to return the money. Or should I say what was left of it. It was clear to Benjamin he had a debt one the man. Benjamin had spent at least half of the money and was back on the street. When the man finally caught up with Benjamin everything thing he ahd spent was being accounted for. Benjamin was in some serious debt. It looked like from Benjamin s view that he had lost. Fist the his watch then his clothes and bank cards plus his address they did not believe that he was on the street though they did not care, finally the wallet. Benjamin was found in the local park on a bench stark naked by sophie and her other friends. He was not beat up just cold and hungry they had rapped him up in some blankets. They kept there distance as Benjamin deals with the shock. He was a emotional wreck and clearly not ncontrol. As Benjamin was busy still telling them to keep there distance as he shouts loud well it was more like a holor it was quite loud as it removed the birds from the trees. The crys from Benjamin were mostly half jumbled words, In the morning when he awoke most people had heard. He was the talk of the town people were talking about how Benjamin had frighten of some burglers and had got caught up in it. Benjamin kept his mouth firmily closed.

Benjamin is sitting down stairs in Sophies place it ws or should I say weird when Benjamin calls upon Sophie does not answer straight away. Benjamin thought that she was half deaf or deaf. But infact Sophie had a secret. Sophie was not her name and she ws hiding that from everybody not just Benjamin. Benjamin was thinking the same. But excepted the fact that she wanted to be called Sophie so be it. Benjamin looks atb her strangly as she brings him some clean clothes.
Sophie:" What."
Benjamin:" Oh nothing."
There is a pause both of them silent.
Sophie: " What."
She answers again and then again.
Sophie: " What."
Benjamin:" I would just like to say thank you for retrieving me."
Sophie:" Oh."
She continued.
Sophie:" That's fine all in a days work."
Benjamin:" Your name it is not really Sophie is it."
Sophie: " Er sir yes it is."
Sophie walks out in a huff. Benjamin shouts out to her.
Benjamin:" Thanks."
There s a long pause.
Benjamin:" Sophie." He says quietly.
Benjamin is talking to him self after Sophie leaves the room, he is feeling guity as for questioning her so soon. Benjamin is getting redressed as he is just finishing tidying himself up. Benjamin is called for some food. As he eats the food that was left for him he is being sure not to over stay his welcome. As benjamin had finished and just about to walk out of the door the girl sophie catches him just in time to give him her gift. She calls him back in benjamin has no way of avoiding her

she pushes the gift in to benjamin s hands it was rapped decently.
Benjamin:" what is it."
Sophie:" Open it and see."
Benjamin puts the small parcel in to his pocket and tells her that he would open it later. Sophie agrees as he disregard the girls feelings and walks out on greeting a person almost straight away. This action seemed to up set Sophie quiet a bit and for a whole day does nothing but shout until her two friends turn up. Only to up set her even more when she has to explain. The two girls begin to tease Sophie in to a conversation to help her.
Sophie:" Act, why bloody me, I always get it wrong."
Friends: "It was not really Sophies fault it was just bad timing. Even though he knows you know just have the affair."
Sophie: " He might come back. I could not even tell him my real name. I am a real sucker for punishment. Am I not."
They both huddle around her clutching her and then silence.
Benjamin is quite centered all for one and all of that if he could take Sophie back with him he would of done so he could take it and not give anything back. Sophie on the other hand was lying about who she was. And she was worried that Benjamin knew. This did not make things any different or easier on her behalf Benjamin had the right to think about who he is speaking to one minute being recused the next pamperd and the gift he was not the one to be sucked in it was obviously clear. As the evening went on Benjamin had returned back to Sophies place and Sophie was now up set a bout that as well.

Sophie continued to say things about Benjamin things like you know women things, it was all womens talk. Benjamin catches on the next time they meet, Sophie Trying it again. This time grabbing his attention as she gives him the cold shoulder. Her two sisters insisted that it was her problem she had created it so the both of them refused to interfere. Sophie would have to deal with on her own. The first thing she does that she had is offer Benjamin a wet shave no normal man would deine it. as she makes a total mess of his beard and then his mostash leaving the chair for some air only coming back to pull and push his face, then to finish him off she slaps him hard on the face leaving Benjamin dazed with an facial expression that showed the way she was feeling. Later that day at lunch time after she had taken Benjamin's order of free food Sophie on purpose drops cold food down Benjamin all over his new clothes that she had provided, Benjamin still had not caught on. As for being an interlec as smart as he was. Benjamin leaps backard thin king that it was hot he was just in shock. Sophie that was cold. Sophies reply to a badly waited meal was that she had picked up a jug of water which was on then table and pours it down Benjamin on to his lap. Benjamin this time around catches on.

Benjamin:" Sophie what. I have obvoiuly upset you what have done you have been bullying me all day, do not think tht I have not notced."

Sophie trys to speak but Benjamin refuses her the chance. Until she looks like she had something to say. Sophie co0ntinues but Benjamin butts in.

Benjamin:" Oh it is the gift."

Benjamin pulls it out of his jacket pocket and continues that it is wonderful. He tells noticing tht he had not even opened it realizing hoping that she does not notice.

As Benjamin hide sthe gift under the table and nervoiusly and quickly removes the rappings he continues.
Benjamin:" Ah a watch how wonderful and nice. I have always wanted one."
He straps it to his wrist.
Sophie:" Oh wait it is on up side down."
Benjamin:" Oh, "
Sophie:" wait, let me help you."

Sophie still upset stamps her feet in a childish fashion making her self look spoilt she runs out side, Benjamin looks onwards in disbelief. Benjamin was left inside at the table asking her two friends what had he done. The two lady and Benjamin start to laugh. Sophie was neither impressed or happy to be in Benjamin's presents for a while. Benjamin understands that he has upset Sophie. Telling her friends that he did not know exactly what he had done and he blames her instead of taking the responsibility. He says to her two friends softy that he has no cause to up set her and when sophie re-enters the dinning area she hears everything and that the fact that benjamin was planning to apologise. Sophie was close and could hear him, she smiles knowing that her friends knew she was faking it. Now it was Benjamin's Turn to get upset when he finds out about how much sophie.

Benjamin is in the café at his table and sophie is his for the whole day. Sophie was the hoist and benjamin was going to have some fun with Sophie he begins with making his order as the order was just about to appear as he had changed his mind Sophie takes the plate back. As she come out again he changes his mind again as these changing are happening he is adding more food to his order. Eventually Sophie begins to question his behaviour. As soonas he thinks that sophie had caught on he uos and leaves not before sophie has a word as he leaves while half way through there conversation, her words or half of them were you have changed.... Benjamin was off like a rocket. As he leaves the table he shouts to her ending the converstion which had just started. That he would never sit down in the café again. Benjamin does not know whst he ahd said yet. He walks out her two friends which are her sisters also burst out laughing. Sophie does not get the joke. Sophie throws he table cloth down and is up set yet again leaving her two sisters to gossip between themselves.

Benjamin needs some time from the hustle and bustle of the town as the country side waqsareasoble close he made his departure, telling nobody.
In Benjamin eyes the country side was a lonely place filled with frills and spills especially in the night time. As Benjamin calcaltes the amount of people there during the day and explaining to himself it is no different than the morning Benjamin begins his journey making sure that he has some food and he knows that if he waits long enough he would be bound to find some road kill. He could make a camp fire if the weather holds. As Benjamin makes his way out of the town he is thinking of Sophie and he is clarly trying to think about what she is lying about. He takes his mind back to the first time tht they had met. It was a romantic time and a romantic meeting. As Benjamin stroll down a conrty lane he feels in to his pocket for the gift that Sophie had given him. benjamin cannot find it and thunks that he may have dropped it somewhere along the road half panicking he stops looking down and finding it on his wrist he laughs grabbing his heart he says nothing and continues to walk. Only this time to wonder off on to a different route and in totally the wrong direction it was getting late and Benjamin was lost.

Benjamin was lost but still he did not seem so bothered infact he was thinking that he was clever. Instead of thinking about the destination he decided to just follow his feet. He was slowly approaching the area that he wanted to be in. It did not take him long to find the right directions, and paths. As he remembers certain things such as fields, bushes, bends in the road and of couse the road kill he finds his way back on to the normal route in which he started his journey. As he walks through an apple orchard he picks soe apple that had fallen from thee tree on to the floor. He did not pick them from the tree. This ws good he thoughtas he was always hungry and there was anabundence of fruit infront of him. the trees looked wet Benjamin thinks that they were probably over watered or simply like that as it had rained. Maybe they were like that just because that is the way they were. Benjamin thought that they were extremely easy to reach. He did not acre about what ws on the floor even more when he bits in to an apple sucking and crunching all the way until there was nothing left. As he continued to walk from field to felid as he walks he notices that the apple trees ahd changed from apples to pears and this made Benjamin even more hungry as he lent up wards grabbing afew and putting them in his jacket. Benjamin was delighted he had not had a pear in years. Even better Benjamin thought as they were ripe. By the time he had finished he was feeling better. After he had finished he had followed a pathin to another felid there were more pears inafct after Benjamin and to his surprise it was a plum orchard.

Benjamin shkes his head in disbelief as they were ripe too.

As benjamin laays down by a tree like Newton, filled with the farmers food and not having to pay a peeny. He smiles and congratulates himself in making agood decision over the thought of coming down into the country side. All was well for the moment. It was getting dark again and again wassout in the nightime. As he was filled by fruit and already laying down he would not have to find breakfast in the morning as it was now above him. he says this to himself he stays put as the weather changes he raps his coat around himself in oder to keep warm. Benjmain closes his eyes it was easy for him sleeping outside. Benjamin agrees that it was harder and it looks that way as Benjamin had a mind that wonders.

The worst thing about sleeping outside is the morning it always brings out the life on this occasion it was slugs. Benjamin did not like them they were slimmy for one and for two they always came out in twos or threes and they always seemed when they moved that they would be moving towards you. And on top of that they always invade your space. And they look like they had been put there on purpose.

Benjamin decides to think about something else something not son hellish, slimmy, and poor. While Benjamin was sitting down not really thinking about anything but taking notice of his surroundings looking uoards notices a large oak tree. It was standing about tem meters way Benjamin was thinking if it was there before he noticed it. In fact it was. It was around thirty foot in hight the width well Benjamin could not tell you. Benjamin had to touch it just to make sure that it was reall and he had not imagined that it ws just put there and his mind was not playing games on him. it looked a little more comforting that an apple tree so he moved and took cover underneath it.

Benjamin follows his mind and moves closer to the large tree threes a small stump next to it at the bottom of tree. Benjamin was happy to abilge. He had not woken up the farmers yet. Benjamin sits down looking at the life in front of him trees, bushes , and in the sky birds. As he occasionally watches the sky it is changing from mid day to early evening then to darkness then in to the night.

Benjamin wanted to stay up not thinking about the time he was in no hurry to get to his destination he was hinking that he would see some wild life it was the country side. To Benjamin s surprise there was not much and he found that it was a bit of a dispiontment. As you would think that as it was the country side there would be creatures of all nature he thought for that moment maybe it was his presents. He finally comes to is own conclusion that he was in the wrong place in the country side to really see or hear anything.

As the morning took ages to arrive and the morning dew was settling, leaving the uncut grass path way harder to find and not so easy to walk on. With the muddy tracks filled with water in some places on the ground. After the tracks of the tractor had left them behind. Benjamin was cold and wiches that she had stayed put. He ws looking for some where a bit warmer. As he finally comes outside of the country side, he finds the village the one that he thought was there but ws not sure where it was. As he moved closer he was aproched by a man with a dog and greeted, the dog did not look a gresive. Benjamin gives it a stroke complimanting the man and the dogs beauty. The dog w soff it's lead and it looked like it ahd taken a likening to Benjamin as it had left it's owners side and had decided to walk with Benjamin. The dog owner whistles to his dog the dog stops then turns around he goes back to his owner. Benjamin was happy and dog owner just as. As a coverstaion arose with the owner they were discussing if Benjamin knew the land Benjamin continued that he ws just passing through Benjamin looks at the man the man looks at benjamin they both look at the dog who was now sniffing Benjamin as he pounces upand down he ws back on it's lead and the man tells benjmain to be carful then pauses telling Benjamin that these were his lands. Benjamin is taken by suoprise not knowing that he had just met the famer. As the farmer pulls the dog back using the lead asking Benjamin toput the stolen fruit down onto the floor. Benjamin had been caught the farmer was in his rights. Benjamin had no choice but to do as he was told. He puts the apple s down on to the floor one at a time and very slowly. The dog bows down and the farmer pulls him away form Benjamin. The farmer says to his dog good boy.

Benjamin kindly makes his way the farmer had not finished yet as benjamin walks off past him the farmer says to Benjamin whilst pulling his dog hard backeards it was clarly disrobed by Benjamin's presents. That he does not want to see benjamin on his land again. Benjamin walks off knowing that he had been told. He walks off back on to the main road. As Benjamin ahd found the village he goes off to have a look around. There ws not a lot to see in this village, infact it was so small he wondered if it was called a village. It was small a row of old cottages and the place was slient not a sound there was no birds nothing but the road back out of it. Benjamin was used to being on his own there was no problems that way as he looked over his shoulder he could see a cat at least that wa something as the topic of his conversation was that the village ws a quiet one. The cat was walking cooly as most cats do as it was minding its own business, Benjamin thinks it is watching him and it probably was. Benjamin continues to walk saying a few words about the cat as they both disappear in opposite directions. It was obvious that the village was a quiet one and the people that were in it were quiet people. Benjamin still exploring after an hour continues to walk through this seriously quiet place. It was like a ghost town, the only thing that was missing was the ball of hay that the wind should be pushing. The road was longer than he had thought and Benjamin was lost for a few minutes and then completely. As he did not want to have to go back on to the farmers land or go back into the village so he keeps on walking.

As he walks he can see his suroundings change even the air tasted and smelt different. His only concern was at that time the sound of the traffic. It was getting louder meaning that he was close to the motor way not kn owing where he was being lost I guess was part of the trill of being in the country side. It was exciting. And that was the exciting part. Only to have that taken away as he finds out hat he has found another village. The large bolted down road sign with the village name upon it not missing the welcoming piece of graffiti. Benjamin is quizzed thinking that what ever he had seen was just a warning saying do not enter this village or if it was just a joke. Benjamin was worried but disconcerned the last thing he wanted was to cause any trouble. As Benjamin is walking he falls hungry. As the thought past him by he walks straight in to some road kill a pheasant, dead lying right by the side of the road. Benjamin looks around him there was no traffic and nobody around he crosses the road and looks at the poor bird, he says a quick prayer aand then picks it up stuffing it in to his long over coat. He thanks god again for the gift. Benjamin had the idea that he could seel it to the local butchers if ther was one and as it was a village there probably was one. If there ws not one he would pluck it himself he knew how, no body loses. As Benjamin walks in to the town it was similar to walking through a western movie picture, people stopped what they were doing. And would run inside and you would hear doors closing. I was quickly greeted by the local posie a group of teenagers. He was the talk of the town within a instance. Benjamin keeping his cool he gets the odd look. Anybody if they were as badly dreesd as he was the long over coat was a bit of a give away. it was a little bit obvious that Benjamin was a tramp. The group of young men were happy to share the bench with Benjamin as he aproched them he was neither angry or upset with there comements.

There movements were synconised as Benjamin aproches them for a seat on the bench it was like the party of the red sea. They all stepped a side Benjamin felt his coolness. Benjamin sits down as he does he says to them all hello holding out his had waiting for the boys to shake his hand, they all refuse to greet him. It looked like they lacked the respect. Benjamin thinks that he had met some square kids. The group of teenager did not know what to say to Benjamin they did not understand what Benjamin was trying to say. He realizes that they were a little to normal as for the graffiti on the sign. Benjamin was in the clear just for now. The boys said nothing and did nothing they did not understand what Benjamin was trying to say. It was not the correct street talk. As Benjamin continued some of them agreed and shook hands buy touching there hand s not Benjamin's but there friends. He could see clearly that they were faking it. He was still focused when one of the boys aproched him holding his hand out he pretends to be off the street as benjamin thought Yeah he said as he touches benjamins hand nice yeah. The boy continued. He says the word respect to benjmain as he trys to hide his posh voice. After a few minutes of Benjmain introducing himself the boys leave the area going off one by one in twos. Benjmain yells after them.

What is up an doude you still want to hang out with da brother. There was no answer form benjmain who ws watching them all dispaear in different directions further in to the village. Benjamin rememberts the dead pheasant. Benjamin trys to smell it but ye smells nothing but thinks that the pose of teenagers had smelt it scarying hem off. They did not mention it. Benjamin was tring to recall if one of the boys were holding his nose.

Benjamin smiles and speaks to himself saying the word smelly he looks downat the floor just under the bench there is half a bottle of juice. He picks it up and says orange I shall have that after the bird. Benjamin settles down on the bench as he sits quietly for the rest of the evening eventually in to the night. He is busy watching the people as they walk by ands with the posh and the rich boys in there cars he decides to stay the whole evening with the weather being a little better and it was not so cold having the dead bird next to him it was keeping him warm.
In the morning it was usaual the early mornning would bring people and Benjamin was being greetd with a few hellos hoping now that the police would not trun up, a s he grabs a few pounds of some passer by. And smokes a few cigerattes from off the floor, just for the sake of it. in saying that their was nothing worst. It was apsolutly disgusting. Just the thought of now made

Benjamin feel faint. Benjamin thinks what he is doing he recalls needing a smoke it had to be a soggy one from the nearby park. The smell like poo was there but it was much worse than that. He was actually putting others peoples and substances, chemicals that he could not see in to his mouth. I hold the thought to that. I suppose you could call it a science experiment.

Benjamin says to himsle as he picks up another butt of the floor. As he does he is approached by a workman he ws dressed like a builder at first I thought he was going to offer me a job he had short hair with large wellingtons boots he seemed to be the same age as me. the builder finally ushers Benjamin off the flor and offers him a nice new unsmoked cigarette. Benjamin is happy with the assistants as he takes a smoke from the packet the man tells him to take two if he would like Benjamin says nothing as he pulls another one from the packet. Exchanging names they both stand side by side taking until the man finishes his snoke. Benjamin was trying not to insult the man and in the end he just shouts seven oclock, Benjamin geumbles alittle as the man trys to hide his laughter. As the man was clearly trying to pick him up. what the man said Benjamin would not mention it. It was not right by any means just funny. Benjamin had noticed his hands and his peirced ears being that guy must have been painfull Benjamin thinks. Benjamin was quiet and keeping the compliment to himself. Before busrting into laughter at the man behind his back as the man walks back to his van. He beeps Benjamin as he drives off. Benjamin agreed if he had a voice like that he would die. It was a really out of character thing to say Benjamin thought afterwards, he gumbles a bit before giving him a aplogy. Benjamin was fine until the burger van pulled up. with benjamin feeling so hungry he wants a burger but poor benjmain has no money thinking quickly as the smell reaches him him from cross the street. The smell of burger and sauce and the sound of grilling meat. He slowly walks off in the same direction crossing the road. Benjmain could of cryed. But hen something incrediable happened a customer who was addressing his lunch, was not particularly happy with his burger that he had

purcessed from the van, as he takes another bite speaking with his mouth full which is extremely bad mannored in Benjamin's eyes makes his complaint. It was something like this er what the hell is this this tastes undone I want my money back their converstion continues as he is letting his thoughts known not only this he was trying to pull the public around him to help him. As the man walks off unsuccessful with his complaint throws the burger in to a near by bin. Benjamin seeses the chance, he looks up at the sky and clouds thanking god, Benjamin knows that he is going to have to wait but on this occasion does not as the man had totally disappeared. Benjamin approaches the bin. The only obstacle was the van burger man. He was clearly upset with the mans comments and when Benjamin complimented him after grabbing, re un rapping the burger, he smiles now knowing that his food was fine though taking in to account that Benjamin was a tramp and would of eaten anything. The burger man does not move his van to his next destination and continues to speak even though there was nobody listening.
Burger van man: " I have my eye on you."
Benjamin looks upwards, he thought it was god at first then realizes benjamin slowly lifts the burger to his mouth, takes a bit still focused,as he takes it out of his mouth rapping back up and putting it into bis jacket to join the pheasant.

The burger man was clearly upset with what had happened and seeing benjmain eating the burger had upset him even more he continued.
Burger van man:" Look mate I know you obviously have no money but you cannot do what you just did in front of my customer's."
Benjamin looks at him funny, as he looks around to see that there was nobody there.
Benjamin:" now look it is only a burger it only would of gone to wasit."
The man gets angry and reply's to Benjamin.
Benjamin: " Would give me a free burger."
The burger man: " No I will not. You just had a fee burger and just to remind you it was out of the bin."
Benjamin looks at the man and the man looks at Benjamin. The burger van man continued that Benjamin ws just as bad as the man that threw it away. as the man grew calmer he asks Benjamin to throw the burger away, to put it back. Benjamin does so and is prasied for the effort knowing that he would come back for it later.
Benjamin: " If it makes you feel better."
He says this in a different he was pretending to be upset it was his up set voice. It was clear that he was lying. Within a round fifteen minutes the burger man van closes up and disappears. Benjamin does not waits to see who else was around. He stands by the bin thinking that his actions are a little bit obvious either way he sticks his hand I to the bin and pulls out the burger still in the rappings floded the way it was when he put it there. This time he puts s it in to his mouth straight away He eats this quickly like a starving man like he was at that time.

As he chews on the meat as he does he is trying not to bite it to hard or eat it to quickly as he has an audience as there are people passing by watching him. Benjmain is thinking what was going on he decides to to them as he eats the burger. As Benjamin shouts what the food comes right out of his mouth. Even so that little bit of bread was not getting away benjmain he kneels down picking it up off the ground in front of everybody and puts it back in to his mouth. Again benjmain was surprised ans satisfied. He goes back to the bin in search for some more. He is looking for a minute or two he is in luck as he shifts his hands through the rubbish, as he moves his hand s to the left and then the right. He feels something soggy it was an egg it must of fallen off the burger, it was still warm. Benjamin goes in to the bin again this time he is looking for cigarettes and as usual he finds some butts. He picks them up and puts them in his jacket with his road kill the pheasant, the burger, and now the butts. He wipes his hands down his long smelly jacket. He produces the rest of the meat as he does pushing the egg to his mouth swallowing it in one go. As Benjamin swallows the expression on his face changes. Rapidly from a smile to help as he goes bright red as the egg is stuck in his throat. Benjamin turns his head to the right of him the on looker keep on looking as Benjamin he turns left holding his throat as he choaks he puts his hands in to his pockets emptying every thing out on to the floor grabbing a small drinks carton sqeeses what was left in to his mouth, it was just enough to help what he had tried to eat further down.as he dislodged the food he takes a deep breath. He sits down on the parth on the curb looking at his bits.
As Benjamin is sitting down talking to himself he was obviously in shock as he speaks he says.

Benjamin:" Do not worry Benjamin it is ok, that was close I thought I was a goner."
After a few minutes Benjamin smiles and feels a lot better. In all the excitement he shouts out does any body want to bye this dead pheasant to his surprised an old gentleman said yes. Benjamin ignores the man as he thnks that he is hearing things too. Much to his surprise the mans comments were real. The man looked well dressed and spoke polity, he was well dressed and balnced on his walking stick. He wwore trousers and his shoes were polished. His shoes were brand new. The man prods Benjamin twice with his walking stick. As he wants to take a look at the bird. Benjamin thinks that the man was interested he opens his jaccket and shows the dead bird to the man. The man looks at it and then says that is know pheasant. Benjamin checks again as it had slipped around the back of his jacket, the man says it again that s no pheasant Benjamin asks him to wait as he is having a hard time retrieving it. once he finds its he grabs it the old man who looked smart but blind makes Benjamin a deal. They start talking as they both haggle. Just as Benjamin was going to start the cinversatio another older person arrives and stands right next to the old man, this man was younger bright looking and also he was smartly dressed. There was now two customers in front of Benjamin. And again when Benjamin was just about to start the bidding another two people turned up, there was now four people bidding for the bird. Benjamin was looking a little bit excited and bewildered. As he starts the bidding.
Benjamin:" ok going for ten pounds benjmain changes his tone almost straight away putting ona posher voice. He continues going for ten pounds, anybody for ten. Young man at the back."

Benjamin was going to lower the price again he goes. Benjamin:" going again nine pounds."
Benjamin is getting what he wanted there is a little bit of talking and the price of the bird goes up again. he lowers the price by ten pence. The old man woth the stick raises his stick.
Benjamin:" going."
Another old man at the back of the small crowd enters the bidding. The bidding goes on for anyother five minutes and it felt like hours Benjamin continues going to the old man with the stick, once, twice just as Benjamin thinks he has sold it another man bids, as he raised his stick the bidding starts all over again. Eventually at last Benjamin makes his sale. It was sold. Benjamin:"going going gone to the man with the glasss and walking stick it is yours. You sir its over all to the man with the stick for nine pounds exactly."
Benjamin was just taking one last look at the bird. He was just about to change his mind the old man prods him woth his stick fussily holding out the ten pounds Benjamin hesitates to take it, which was unusual for him. he snatches it quickly telling the man has nothing smaller as Benjamin reminds him that it was nine pounds and not ten. The man was happy and kindly says to Benjamin he can keep the change Benjamin thanks him. as he hold sthe bird as the man takes it Benjamin again is thinking again and the man has to pull the bird as Benjamin was not letting go. Eventually Benjamin finally lets go of the bird. Benjamin not sure weather he made a good decision on thn deal he thinks he should of got more. But in the end he was still thinking that he should of kept it for hmslef. Even though the ten pound s would go far enough for now. It would last two days exactly he would ssend it cigarettes and a sandwich. Eventually the smell of the crowd the

old people despearses and Benjamin is left alone again apart from the odd car that drove by. Benjamin sits on a bench looking at the ten pounds.

When Benjamin finally settles down, he is looking up in to the sky quite a long way up. He visualizes space to join in what he is looking at. He sees the sun trying to fgure out what the actual time was the little escalaid with the selling of the pheasant was fun and seemed to take all day. Benjamin was totally forgetting that he was swearing the watch that sophie ahd given him as a gift. In remembering that the image of her came straight back. The girl he was really missing her as much as he thought. And the thought of the thought of missing her made him smile it was three oclock in the afternoon. Benjamin takes his watch off his wrist he puts it in his jacket pocket as Benjamin takes the good off he is thinking of the girl while putting a brand new smoke in to his mouth. Benjamin lites up the smoke hailing deeply taking a huge drag in to his mouth. Eventually watching the sun set and the moon came out the darkness was to come next over the bench that he was sleeping on. Just by him was a shop he was not in total darkness completely the shop lights gave him enough light to see, just. At that time it was enough to lite a ciggerete. But not enough light to keep him awake. As the bench was now his home for now.
Benjamin could smell and he was reasonabley good at it by now. It was the smell of rubbish that was on his nose. The sweet smell of the chip shop, Benjamin smell the air it was clear to him that is what he could smell. As he continues to smell the air he can almost smell his next meal he gets up and follows it up the street looking excited in what he is going to find. It was just around the corner. This gave Benjamin the opportunity to be greedy.

Benjamin sat down the occasional bus would go past Benjamin thankijng that he found the chip shop he thinks that it would be esay picking simply for the fact that it was busy all the time. Going back to the buses they would go past him all the time he thought about just up and going and taking a ride out iof the village back into another village as the bus passes by if only he had a bus pass or a bus ticket or even some pennys in saying that to himself the bus that went psat was full so he had got that the wrong way around Benjamin felt stupid with the thought, but continued anyway besides he had just got here. He was in Eastry. There must have been something Benjamin did not believe that the chip shop could be so popular. However Benjamin gets the better of himself again when he finds out that it was. Again Benjamin questions himself and his mind. Benjamin was still in the same position infact he was caught in the system that he created he can not get out of it, There must have been something going on Benjamin did not believe in it. Benjamin sits down thinking occasionally saying odd things as people walk past only to change his verb but kept saying hello to people.

In the morning he was feeling better Benjamin thinks it was something thatbhe had eaten he also thinks the felt that way because he thinks that he has over stayed his welcomed in the small village. He thinks that h has no body left in the village to talk to he did not see the elderly in the village paying for there paper's Benjamin's hat was now empty.

Again luck is ion his side as he looks at his situation he finds his watch he speaks to himself saying I could go back I guess, I suppose Benjamin is happy with the thought and he had created a solution to his problem almost straight away.

Before Benjamin makes his way home he decides to check the chip shop bin, to his delight he finds himself breakfast he knows that he will not eat for the next couple of day and a half as he would be walking back home this time Benjamin eats and enjoys what he he eating. Benjamin was sued to eating out of the bins now it was normally cold something that we would all do Benjamin finishes the early norning meal putting the rapping paper back in to the bin. He sets off on his journey. Leaving the small village aside the weather was good too as it ws now spring and Benjamin leaves the way that he came in. in the same direction it was different it was like he was watching every step. As Benjamin makes it out of the country side he enters the motorway. Benjamin is least the tired he was on his adventure home. he was full of energy he was waiting for the adrenaline to kick in. as it does Benjamin was in his element. As it was the morning there was not that much traffic Benjamin does not know the araea that well and if he had walked any further going to his destination he would of ended on the coast Folkestone instead he chose to go no further. As the early morning traffic begins to appear Benjamin is pacing it his head is down and all the rest it was a real buzz for him.

After a few hours and looking at the motorway signs to make sure he was still moving in the right direction Benjamin thought that bearings and time were off balance thinking that he was in a pkace that he was not. And thinking that he should of reached that place by the time that ws on his watch. He had only walked four miles in around thirty minutes that is fast walking he checks the time on his watch it was his imagination and he corrects his mind by calculating the journey infact he was walking at a steady pace and he had walked he had

walked four miles in twenty five minutes, he smiles and is pleased with the being impressed with him self. For correcting his mind with time.
It looked like it was going to be a fine morning the sun was out and there was a soft wind blowing this made it ten times more interesting for Benjamin and ten times more easier for Benjamin to walk it also made it safer. The concreted road was nice and smooth Benjamin recalls the day when he was a child the concrete bitting at his feet only only to put him off walking for the rest of his teenage life he never got over it. As the smooth concrete released his demons with every step Benjamin was feeling fit for the same reason Benjamin would close his eyes whilst walking just for a few seconds he could feel himself falling but only for a couple of seconds then he would open his eyes what he believed he was doing was doing was blessing his journey and himself with a prayer. As he thought everything was the same neither the less any way Benjamin moved quicky as he reconizes some of the journey as he tells himslef that he had been there before now knowing and feeling more comfortable in knowing that he was walking in the right direction. He was trying not to think about where he was it was more wanting to be focused on the walking. He did not want to know where he was. He was trying not to think about it. but it was funny because after that thought five minutes later a car pulls up next to Benjamin he stops walking the car is moving slowly the man sticks his head through his window he shouts to benjmain asking him if he was thirsty.
Benjamin explains, as soon as he has finished, the man, the stranger kindly throws Benjamin the bottle of water it hits him on the chest it falls on to the floor and rolls off the lay by onto the side bank. Benjamin follows it finally picking it up. Benjamin thanks the man who

gave him a bottle of water as Benjamin drinks it he explains why he was on the by lane on the motor way. The man drives off shouting that is my good deed for the day. Suddenly there is a bleeping sound Benjamiii jumps looking around thinking at forst that he has a bleeping bottle, he is looking at it the rest of the traffic is picking up again, he knew that he was getting closer to home.as he looks at the bottle holding it up holding it up then he takes his jacket off thinking that it is in his jacket realizing that it was neither in the jacket or the bottle. He listens carefully as he gets closer to it was some where on the bank, somebody had lost or probably dis ownd there phone. It was now in Benjamin's good hands.

Benjamin picks up the phone not thinking twice about answering it I suppose you could call it bad timing as the person on the other end was trying to finish the converstion with Benjamin. He was clearly trying to listen above the nosy traffic just at the side of the noisy bank of grass. Benjamin was trying to hear but in the end the man on the other end of te phone gives up and hangs up. Benjamin thinks that he is thinking the same as the man on the phone he puts the phone in rt his jacket pocket in the inside of his coat. Believing that if the man really wants his phone back he would call it. as of for company for a minute or two Benjamin was happy benjmain cotuinues to walk. As he slips down the bank back on to concrete of the hard shoulder on to the motor way he continues his journey back he ws on his way home again knowing that te phone ws in his pocket giving him something to focus on and think about. Hoping that the man phoned him just for the sake of having somebody to talk to. The sun was out and Benjamin was walking ij the opposite direction of it. the sun was nice and the heat warmed Benjamin just enough Benjamin was thinking aonly a mad man would do what he was doing. There was not much that Benjamin could do atr this point in time. As Benjamin takes off his jacket and throws it over his shoulder he continues to walk he is walking at a steady pace there is no traffic and Benjamin is alone apart from the ocvcasional bird that would fly above him Benjamin believd that he was being watched by it it looked like a condor it was to big to be a crow.

Benjamin looks at the bird it seemed to be flying around his direction. Another sign form god Benjamin thought benjmain looked upwards and thanks god as he thinks that the bird is protecting him guilding him and watching over him. As Benjamin noticed that his pace was slow and he needed to have a rest, he stops at the sign post where he stoped when he begun his journey. The gaffeti was confusing his situation it seemd to be everywhere all he had to do was find the right piece then he would know that he was on te right path. Benjamin stops at the sign he takes a good look and sits down at te bottom of the sign. He was thinking if he should try and thumb a lift. There were no lorrys and the only problem withb that ws that he would meet the wrong company most people thought that it was ascary thought hbenjmain was thinking positively as he sated himself on another grass bank. He was watching the on coming traffoic form the other side of the motor way. It wa sgettung a little nosiy. As benjmain confronts the noise that he had gripled with for that hour benjmain is feeling a little bit un comfortable being that close to the on coming traffic. He decides to move as he finds that he is being bad mouthed by the passers bys he was shouted at. As this happens the sun hist him straight in to his eyes. He felt that he was blinded for a moment as he stands up and slips on the muddy wet bank. As Benjamin gets up he wipe his hands down his jacket. As he slips again in the end Benjamin gives up he was stuck. He removes the mobile phone for a better look fro his jacket. He was waiting for it to ring it was a little qiuckeer than Benjamin thought. Benjamin was not in a rush to get home.

After Benjamin had played aropumd with the phone then not having the knowledge to continue. Puts the phone back in to his jacket coat pocket. He slips back down the grass bank. On to the nearly dryed concrete road. He continued his journey it would take a good several hours just to make it half way. Benjamin still excited about what was a head of him. and the walk was slowly turning into an adventure. As Benjamin walks he is totally focused even when their was traffic ahead of him and round him. there was that soft breeze which seemed to come to Benjamin like a ghost, the breeze blew contiuiously on his face and through his hair he was being kept cool. And knowing that the evening would be cold it was lways colder on the motor way a lot more than Benjamin could imagine. And the cold streams of air that the cars leave behind them added to the pain adding to the frustration of the journey. Benjamin was thinking it would hbe nice if they had built the roads at least the walkers and people that enjoyed walking and cycles had a place to be it was a good thought it could happen if it ws put to the right people. Leaving the thought left Benjamin concentrating on the journey a head. He was in motion occasionally looking up wards to free his mind only to look down again this was not a bad thing as Benjamin decides which style he prefers.

After he has finished making jokes about the way he was walking and other things a extremely fast sports car drives past him. with a police cars to follow it. it was obvious to Benjamin what was going to occur as they both pull over in the near distance Benjamin not knowing what he is really doing pulls the phone out of his pocket and takes some pictures it was clearly set on camera motion as Benjamin snaps away getting getting some closes ups and all sorts, the police are making an arrest Benjamin is filming the incident and locving evry minute of it. until he is told to stop. Benjamin does not stop until he is told again. he polity stops and continues his journey he wanted the picture of the man standing spread eagle, arms on the roof and legs spread wide. As the man waits to be patted down. The police man warns Benjamin again. Benjamin does not know the law officer and he is now focused on Benjamin. As the officers spartner continues to arrest the man the police officer asks benjmian for the phone Benjamin has no choice but to hand the phone over Benjamin was disappointed that he ahd found and lost his new toy. As the officer flicks through the pictures on the phone the first question that the officer asks Benjamin was is it his phone. Benjamin had to really fight as he answers no and tells the officer that he had found it a few miles in te opposite direction, the officer looks at him. he asks Benjamin a second question and Benjamin does not answer it. in stead asks the officer if he was being arrested. The police man says no. He had not commited a crime. The police man looks at the phone when he finds a name he turns to hs partner they both step aside and have a conversation the man that was being arrested had just told him that he had lost his phone the officers question the man agin about his lost phone the man describes it fully to both of them the police turn to

Benjamin asking him where he got the phone from. Benjamin still not listening says in an exciting voice and being excited are they arresting them. the police catch on.

After Benjamin had played around a bit he finally gives the police the information that they needed to return the phone to the original owner which was the man who there were arresting. Benjamin agrees and is ok over handling the man's phone. They were both free to go they all disperse and Benjamin is left alone to continue his journey back to te town.
Benjamin thought what he had just experienced was quite funny. The man being arrested over what looked like false pretenses. He was sure the police did not see what they were doing as funny or see the funny side of it. the camera was the funniest Part Benjamin thought. Benjamin tells him self that the whole thing would be a laugh at the dinner table for many years to come.

Benjamin continued his lourney although the road s were not as he predicted there was a lot of traffic more than usual as he puts his hand in to his pocket for a cigarette packet ripping some of the paper off putting it in to bis mouth ofr a few seconds until they were wet and rolls them up in to small balls and puts them in to his ears, ear plugs Benjamin thought. It was extremely noisy as each car drove past the saliva from Benjamin's mouth was to keep the ear plugs in place. It was cold as well and the air tasted of sweat at first and the cold was soft. As for blocking the sound out realzing that he had some cigarettes pulls one from the packet as he was trying to think where he had got them, as he is looking down at the packet and turning away to hide form the wind lites it up and smokes. As Benjamin smokes his smoke he puts his lighter away. he takes a drag on the smoke inhaling and exhaling happy with the sensation and continuing to walk. Happy with the out come of the brush with the law. As the sky seems settled and the traffic was as bust as ever Benjamin feels the pain of the walk his feet were beginning to hurt. That was the warning to stop but in his position he gas no choice but to continue. As he gets in to a stride another part of him was telling him to keep on going. This had now become a test of faith. Benjamin is on his last legs eight miles to go. He would reach the small village. As Benjamin trys his hardest to reach his destination he is forced on to his knees and now is crawling the last part of his journey. He is telling himself and anybody that is listening that this is the furthest that he can go. Benjamin needs a rest and even though the skys were settled it was clear and bright the sun would be going down in an hour Benjamin crawls in to the bushes sayig to himself that he would atay there until the morning and wait until he can feel his legs and feet again. benjmain awakes he has over slept. It was late morning how he over slept he would think about that later. As he wakes he can hear the birds singing it was the tweeting that woke him up. he checks the time by his watch. Benjmaij is up fast and out of the bushes as he brushes himself down he looks straight down the road that he would be taking to get home. as he takes the twigs out of his hair and shakes his jacket off. He conti ues to look up this time at the coulds there was going to be a rain storm. Benjmaij knows that he has to find shelter some where he had also fallen hungry. Remembering not to saty to long as the farmer would be watching. After realizing this as he chose to change his plans. It ws not good as instead of four miles to go he had twenty four miles to go he obviously had miss calculated the journey Benjamin blames this on his self he was dreaming. Benjamin was at that time thinking of how if possible if he was clever enough to avoid the farmer. And as he had already been warned about hanging around on his land. The last time that he had settled there for a day he ran in to trouble that benjmai did not need. Either way it was on the way home so that was the end of that. Benjamin would try his luck. And if all was well and everything was rosy Benjamin would go on his way. Any way Benjamin continues as that was a thought and it was something to think about. Also when he gets there, as the storm satrs it starts very slow. However that was going to change as the light blue skys change to grey with the clouds, with thunder and darkness. The darkness and thunder came together with massive ligtening in the distance it had to be in the direction that Benjamin was walking in. Benjamin thinks he is stupid but he would attempt it any way. Only a crazed man would walk in to a storm.

He would think he should be walkng in the other direction. Away from it and not towards it. there was no traffic and Benjamin does not want to stop he is in his element as he wants to reach a safer place and destination.

Benjamin was counting his steps he had walked around ten thousand steps. Only leaving around five thousand to go if his calcalations are correct. However he is disconcerned with the weather. The fact that he is now walking through a storm luckly he is not struck by lightening. Yet it would be the very first time if it was so. As Benjamin gets closer to his destination the small woods he would be able to rest and watch the rest of the storm. He did not mention it earlier there was along ally way and country path a sheltered place just before the farmers orchard. As Benjamin gets excited only to get upset, as it looked like picking season had finished and there was no fruit on the trees or any on the floors. Benjamin looks up at the fruit trees there was nothing left. It looked totally different dis fimliuar with his surroundings. He continues to walk. Eventually after having a good search he finds one piece of fruit he was looking up and around the trees until he found it. It was bruised and wrinkled, he reaches up and picks it of the branches and then takes a bit out of it, Benjamin was happy again one for getting to the farm and two he had found the piece of fruit. Even so it was a small piece he gives his thanks that it was there. Benjamin knows where he is and as for the season to be out the farmer would not be around, Benjamin walks free again, his boots are covered in mud. The ground had not changed yet and Benjamin sits down against the large oak tree. He closes his eyes. He was thinking that it was good to be there as Benjamin was nearly home.

The first day at the orchard went well although there seemed to be more people around him. There were some chidern playing around him there perents were shouting for them they had a dog. When Benjamin is finaly rested he continued his journey after being intoirduced to the children who seemed to be confused Benjamin put it down to his dress. The chideren were contept on mentioning his coat Benjamin wants to know what was wrong with it he thinks it was fine. He beguns to question them but before he gets the chance there parents appear and an other question is brought up. the chikd in front of him hits him softly on his jacket and the smaller gorl kicks in the leg on hard enough to hurt him but enough to upset him. they both run off back to here mum yelling tramp. He hears the childerns remarks again if once was on enough there s a tramp over there and he really smells were childerns words. As they all disappears in to the woods behind them to find there parents. Benjamin looks around confused as they pass him him by as they were all on the path that would lead them all back to the village. The children had not had there fun yet and as they were all walking in the same direction they tease Benjamin again.

Mum:"Do not worry he just a tramp."

The boy behind him interrupts

The boy:"Excuse me I need to get by."

As the young family pass Benjamin is looking over his shoulder.

Farther:" come on." The man pulls oin his sons arm. " leave the tramp alone."

He says this loudly the boy is tugged again as he pushes his sister and he man calls for his dog.

As Benjamin greets them with a bow as they leave as he does a little dance as the little girl bursts in to tears. And is told again to move along by her dad. As the small party of people leave Benjamin s presents Benjamin was on his own again. He was going to stay put until the morning. Which gave him the chance to same sonme energy before the long journey back in the morning when he would start his journey again. if the weather holds out nobody likes walking in the dark. Even if the weather is good however there was more of the chance that Benjamin would be able to thumb a lift. This did not happen to Benjamin what did happen he managed to get to the edge of the start of the small town as he finds himalef cold and hungry. Benjamin is knackered and cold although he is hungry he is happy that his walk is nearly over. He is struggling as he walks through the town to get to the edge of it to continue the last part of the walk. He finds the head stone he is in the right place he kneels down and give thanks and praises for finding it. he puts one foot in front of the other he was now home. he closes his eyes opening them to double check. Benjamin tells himself that it felt incredible. He sits down and waits for the morning. He sits by the stone.

As Benjamin gets off to finish his journey he is back in town. He is heading toward sthe café he gets some seriously dirty looks and as he sits down to rest in his normal place, he waits for Sophie to appear. Sophie does not appear Benjamin knows his way in the dark and continues further in to town as he nears the café he stops and watches there is nobody around it is appsoultly totally quiet Benjamin questions himself is he in the right place te right town. As he nears the café it was a little short of a welcome back. Benjamin is disapointed mind you it wa slate amd if he had been there in the morning he would of got a welcome. He finally get s the courage to approach the café. He looks hard at the number balanced half on and half off on the café door. It says Sophes place above the door. He knocks on the door and waits a lady answers it after a minute.

Benjamin:" Hello I am Benjamin is Sophie in."

Lady:" There is no Sophie here."

The lady goes to shut the door as she walk back inside.

Benjamin:" where is she."

Lady:" Lucy."

Benjamin is quzzed

Benjamin:" No Sophie."

Lady:" Lucy."

Benjamin:" Sophie."

Lady: " Lucy."

Benjamin fails to understand they continue,

Benjamin:" This is Sophies place 44. "

Lady:" yeah."

Benjamin:" Then where is Sophie."

Lady:" You mean Lucy."

Benjamin:" If I had said Lucy I would have said Lucy but I did not I said Sophie I am looking for an answer the lady sophie where is she."
Lady:" There is no Sophie here."
Benjamin still struggles to understand.
Benjamin:" where is Sophie.?"
The lady looks down on Benjamin sorry full. Then tells Benjamin where he can find Lucy she tells Benjamin that she is away on business and she was extending her business and she would be opening it up tomorrow after some Tramp named Benjamin. Benjamin stands his ground pushing out his chest like he was going to get a grilling. Protecting the fact that it was him. The lady did not catch on.

Benjamin sits down at the tables just out side of the café. He calls the lady to him and asks her if he could have a coffee the lady replys that they are not open. Benjamin is still making his order not listening to what the lady had just said. The lady asks him if that was all. Knowing that she was closed. Benjamin does not reply and the lady walks off Benjamin is thinking where was Sophie and who is now Lucy. He thinks that she had just changed her name. He smiles at the thought not thinking about his old friends. So if sophie was not sophie and was lucy and then where is she this brings back the thought that if sophie was Lucy it could not be his old friend lucy. Well Benjamin thought she sounds nice enough. Benjamin is waiting for his cup of coffee the lady ws not coming back and as he lookled up he catches on she had just turned the opening sign from open to closed. Benjamin thinks that he does not know anybody in the town called Lucy. Benjamin is waiting for hs coffee realzing that the lady was serious and she would not abe appearing again until the morning.

For some strange reason Benjamin is told that the menu is on the house this morning he thinks of what he is going to oreder supiously. He was also delighted that it was all free. The lady whom was serving him was Emma.
Benjamin:" Emma a gift."
Benjamin thought he pulls the watch that Sophie gave him out of his jacket and places it onto the table. He looks at it once more his smiling face as if it was just given to him. He puts it to his ear once more just to hear it ticking it made Benjamin think of Sophie who was now Lucy so it seemed.

Benjamin had waited on his cahir by the table all day Sophie who he thinks is Lucy did not appear even more Benjamin had eaten most of the menu and when the lady came out to offer him more he got up quickly and said that hye needs some space more fresh air even though he ws already outside.
As Benjamin manages to hold everything down he had eaten that morning and looked to do the same in to the evening after disappearing for a while he returns as he straightens himself he walks casually back to his table then walks in looking for some more service he had not finished yet. He approaches the café bar only to realize that there was nobody there. He still asks for large glass of water.
He walks out side and waits, Benjamin is trying to be calm he passes around feeling uncomfortable thinking it may be some thing he ate, he walks back inside throught the large door in to a small area looking at the counter then out of nowhere the lady appears asking him if he had asked to be served he calms down and says yes and that he would like a glass of water. finally Benjamin says the chilli was hot, hot. Benjamin stops he is leaning both arms on the counter with his legs crossed. With his feet onsome kind of bar which says go no further on it. he can smell some thing it smelt like fish at first he looks down at his shoes they were clean he takes of his jacket and smells it it was clean he hangs on the old coat rack in the corner of the room. It was a long pole he looks at it Benjamin makes sure that thee is nobody around and then with a smile on his face smells the underneath of his arms he says to himself that ws not the smell he sniffs the air and could swear that there was a smell again he was drawn back to his jacket as he lifts his jacket up and puts it back on, but

only for a moment and takes t off as the smell comes back.

Again Benjamin looks at his jacket on him, then realizes it was his jacket he places his hand in to slowly into the right side of te jacket and nothing he trys the left again slowly and again nothing. He presses softly listening two he feels the squash he closes his eyes putting his cleanish hand in to the inside pocket removing the smelly gone of dead fish, erm he said as he bites in to it. He continues to eat the fish it was wet and cold. As he is interrupted by the a the waitress snatching the fish form Benjamin and throwng out side she tells him that they have more manors than that and if he wants to eat here he better wisen up. She points to the kitchen and tells him that the lady that he wants to speak to is in there. Sophie was back. Benjamin answer to that was could he have a glass of water and he had uped his manors within an intsants he actually said please.

Emma:" yeah sure."

The girl replys that the kitchen is that way as she points him in the right direction. With a look of confusion on his face Benjamin takes himself off to the kitchen. Considering the size of the café Benjamin knew that the café was a little bit to small there was enough room for the pan washers and Sophie was nowhere to be seen. Benjamin walks back out telling he girl that there was not to much room in there Benjamin had walked into the older kitchen and if he had looked like Emma had said he would have found her wisen up Emma said to Benjamin as she leads him all the way. Emma tells Benjamin that he had walked in ton the wash room and Sophie was upstairs Benjamin sits down again and take another mouthfull of water.

There was nothing wrong with the food although now Benjamin had eaten the whole menu. Benjamin was looking rather fat. He un does his short buttons leaning backwards in the small wooden school chair like a school kid with a big smile on his face. Benjamin did not know that there was more to come. He leans forward resting his elbows on the table. Emma comes back out with another menu.

Benjamin: " what is this."

Benjamin says filled up and looking like it too.

Emma: " It is our desert menu."

Benjamin: " No."

And with that it changes his voice and the expression on his face. he continues shortly afterwards.

Benjamin:" ok yes. Yes I would be delighted."

The girl looks at him and pushes the menu in to his hand's. his arms tied of lifting the knife and forks he now had to lift up a desert spoon it was just to hevey Benjamin is left with the menu and his eyes wide open. As he looks down the menu card. He shouts to Emma as he continues bto look at the old plastic covered menu card. The menu was a bit rough looking Emma answer to that was uh. He continued.

Benjamin is quizzed by his eyes being bigger than his belly as he picks the first desert. As he places his order starting form the bottom planning to work himself to the top. Now he was going to fit it all in to his mouth god only knows. Benjamin continues one boel of desert to the next. He w shaving a good time.

Things were qiute in the town Benjamin had begun to fit in to everyday life a few more each day would notice him apart from his taste in clothes he seemed he was seemed to think the same he ws going unnoticed and he could see this and feel it too. Benjamin was becoming more confident. And his face had a new shine to it. as wellas the smile on his face. that greeted people Benjamin was beginning to feel at home. and knowing that Sophie Lucy was his new name for her. She was around to help him. He was pretty much happy. Sophie Lucy who she was called now had just come back from her mothers, she was the lady that owned the business infact it was their family business. It had been handed down from generation to gerneration. Benjamin was present at her arrival this was an unarranged meeting. Giving her a big hug on greeting her whisly straight after pulling her through the door way she was shocked a good move by Benjamin even though it was not necessary. They were all in the coffee bar, Benjamin supposes a toast. Benjamin was acting like he was going to prepose. He was excited. He did not they were all happy to see her.as she walks around looking at thing, touching things, and making compliments. She hands her coat waiting for some body to take it Emma takes it hanging straight on Benjamin coat Benjamin notices and removes his coat not of any reason uther than that he had a smelly coat. Only to make things worse as he how was holding it and it really idid smell, Emma takes it from him all of this was happening from behind her back.

Emma throws his coat outsideit lands on the chair perfectly like she had put it there. the lady says to her

good shot, Sophie Lucy and Emma and Benjamin look at each other beleildered as if to say how did she do that that it was obviously a flook. The lady takes off her gloves and drops them with her bag and the girl does the same again. Emma places them on the table neatly.
Mother: " Not bad, good."
In her posh accent.

How mum the girl asks it was going to be a short conversation.
Oh fine the old bat she is thinking of moving.
Benjamin is dazzled by her new approach it was obvious to Benjamin that the journey and te visit to her mothers had completely changed her she looked different and spoke different she had deffinatly changed person. As sophie Lucy had changed the grils tell Benjamin the same and tell Benjamin while they both discussed it that it would wear of some it was her mum. It had something to do with te air in the country side it ws different to the air in the city. They both looked at each other and laughed. Supiously with there eyes half closed. Benjamin is sophie Lucys first appointment of call. Like a new kady is content with telling Benjamin that he really smells he was content in saying that it was not him and that it ws his coat she tells him other wise he was smelly and it was him. end of as she tells Emma to run a bbath for him. The bathroom was an qiute place to be until the water was turned on.
Sophie Lucy: " Stop."
Benjamin was trying to tell her that he did not want to wash. Sophie Lucy insisted. Turning the taps on knowing that she could turn them off until she tried and found that they were stuck. Everybody panicked and Emma was busy turning out the custoamers as she cried out. There was going to be a flood the great flood has arrived again. while Benjamin was being undressed and complaining about it and having to get the bath not knowing what had happened. Benjamin has a choice to strip down. He falls to the floor not moving trying to give a sicky the girl looks at Benjamin as he looks at the girl.
Sophie Lucy asks Benjamin for his clothes Benjamin refuses to undress. Sophie Lucy calls Emma and they

both pin him down and undress him. Benjamin was having the time of his life as he shouts what for this made no sense he continues shouting the words to wash. As Benjamin gets away of stashing a load of food in his jacket he finally agrees to gets in to the bath. Sophie Lucy not knowing that te taps are stuck and is left wondering where her customers had disappeared to. Benjamin hands the last of his garments to Emma she tells Benjamin that it was ok she would not peak. He answers I know you won't. Benjamin on his tip toes gets in to the bath. he did not think that he would enjoy it as much as he did. Within a few minutes he was back to bis normal self. The girl sits down with Benjamin and they start talking. She does not notice that the taps are still running the answer was left with Emma who was down tne other end of the street. Trying to ush her customers back in to the café, but Benjamin does. He leans forwards strtching out his arms for the hot tap first he cannot turn it he then trys the cold tap it does not move at this point the bath ais getting hotter Benjamin wants to get out the girl completely astonished does not know what to do. Benjamin had started to sizzle as he waits for the Emma to remove her self from the bathroom, aafter Benjamin gives a loud shout as the water was now hotter. She realkizes with an apology knowing now that Benjamin wanted her to leave the room so he could get out if the bath in the p[resents of the girl. As he shouts towel extremely loud. She looks at him not taken must noticed as she was more focused in Benjamin's body. As she was still trying to figure out what was the actual problem even though it was in front her. Benjamin was bursting to stand up and get out.of the bath tub. As the girl finaly catches on. She leaves the room. Not for only rushing back in trowing a Towel at Benjamin. As Benjamin jumps out of the bath not meaning to stand up. Benjamin is un happy with ten occurrence abut dioes not mind he polity tells the girl that he thought it was a bad idea from the start and it was. As from the bath over flowing the girl manages to stop it by stuffing Benjamin s pair off smelly socks up the tops only for a while as the water is redirected giving her enough time to find a plumber who seemed to arrive quickly he told Emma that he was in the area which was true he was.

Emma : " You were quick."

Plumber: " Yeah I was in the area."

Emma: " It is up staors in the bathroom."

Plumber:" lead the way."

Emma: " Go there your self."

The girl walks off leaving the plumber to figure it out himself. He stops drops his head then continues. Benjamin is just finishing redressing. When the plumber walks in.

Plumber: " Is this it."

Benjamin was on his way out of the bathroom.

Benjamin: " yes it is."

Plumber|: "Old taps."

the plumber said as he finally takes his hand off his head.

Plumber: "No problem I will be five minutes."

Benjamin looks at him as he tucks his shirt back in. Benjamin walsk out leaving the plumber to talk to himself.

As sophie lucy tends to Benjamin's wounds it semed like Benjamin had an audience he could clearly see through the café window and he was being praised the people gathered around cheering and shouting. And even taking potographs which ened up in the local paper. Tramp catches fire in bath it should of said tramp burns in old bath or even worse tramp traps himself in hot bath tub, Benjamin was not amused he was not upset as such. He just wished that they had got the head line correct. Benjamin insisted that he did not catch on fire and the burns were from the hot water. He merely got stuck in the bath, a hot bath. As he complained to Sophie Lucy she had to smile and just to calm him down she said that it could of happened to anybody. and it was her fault for not checking the taps. Things like that happen to people all the time. Benjamin's question to that was where, when I have not heard of anybody. Sophie Lucy interrupts him.

Sophie Lucy: " India."

They both look at each other.

Benjamin: " oh sure."

Sophie Lucy: " The kids there are so poor, In that country they do not even get to wash, so thnk your self lucky."

Sophie Lucy just stands there.

Sophie Lucy: " ok."

Emma butts in to save Sophie Lucy she knows that he was going to blame her. She takes SophieLucys arm dragging her away from Benjamin and the dispersing crowd.

As Benjamin has his small but painful wounds rapped up and creamed he returns to Sophie Lucy who is busy looking at her teeth and mouth for some strange reason as she turns to Benjamin and smiles Benjamin does not notice at first sophie lucy smiles at him again then frowns. Benjamin thinks that she is playing games as she smiles once more. Benjamin then realizes that he ahd not seen her super sized big white teeth. There s a long pause between the both of them as Benjamin tells her that she had teeth the size of a horse. He tells Benjamin that she not ever missed a day of brushing. Benjamin points at her as a compliment, she points back. As Benjamin walks towards her passing by her to correct the mirror Sophie Lucy walks out. Benjamin calls after her.

Sophie Lucy: “ what.”

Sophie Lucy meets Emma in the coridoor as they pass each other Emma whispers to Sophie Lucy he did not notice. As Sophie Lucy’s relationship with Benjamin was looking rocky. And it looked like Sophie Lucys assistant was Rebbeca was in it. Rebecca stands in the kitchen arms folded leaning backwards on the café bar top talking tp her self.

As she stands there in the kitchen she can hear somebody tapping tap, tap, then silence then over agauin tap, atp, then silence again. rebbeca looks around she cannot see anything so she ignores it then rebbeca looks up at the celing. Her eyes glued to the celing and then it happened the plummer did not do his job as before rebbeca had the chance to shout for help the celing collaspes right above her she was soaked and un hurt jusy in shock there was water everywhere. Sophie Lucy finds her and is apologiseing over and iver as she runs them both outside, Benjmakian was not around he would of known how to treat her. Rebbeca just wanted to lie down. Rebbeca got her request as she was handed some fresh clothes and a towel. As she trys to tell Sophie Lucy that she was fine, and that there was no physical damage done to her. The thought of Benjamin some how helped her through the trauma as she metioned his name as she was coming out of the shock. As Rebbeca is sent away Sophie Lucy is assessing the damage no celing and no bath she was a very lucky lady. As Sophie Lucy looks at the damsge on her café floor a bath tub and al ot of celing.

As all the commotion had settled the blame for the of the celing went to the plumber. Sophie Lucy was busy weighing up the pro's and con's of what could happen not looking at as it had happened she could only think of the worst. Going back to yesterday when Benjamin was in the bath she continues if it had happened then why did not the plumber notice my celing he did not say anything Sophie Lucy shouts Rebbeca you are lucky. Sophie Lucy looks up at the whole I her celing which was no longer there and then looks at the mess on the floor. As soon as benjmain got back he ws filled in he did not thiunk anything of it but that was Benjamin to a tee. He was neither angry or sad. He said it was a warning and it should be dekt with with then he said it was a doggy plumber and he should of known better I was just in the area indeed. Sophie Lucys answer to that that she was not that superstiuos. Benjamin agreed and said sorry. Sophie Lucy was now in a bad mood and tells him to knock it off. Benjamin catches on and makes up some other jokes like it could have been a sign. Sophie Lucys answers to that was from who. Benjamin look supwards pointing as they both say a sign from god. Sophie Lucy looks up and tells Benjamin that he has got her thinking about things now. They both smile and walk off in the other direction. Benjamin shouts a cup of tea I think is due. Sophie Lucy stays put looking at the rubble and carnage on then floor.

As Benjamin and Sophie Lucy decuss the celing and a few other things Benjamin insists and says with out that celing makes the place well he said a littke bit open plan. Sophie Lucy looks at him with half a smile he continues smiling

Was that two much input Benjamin says Sophie Lucy smiles again it was ok Sophie Lucy says it will be fixed within a week as for now we are closed. I have the finances and now I could not think of a better time to renovate so now it might of well be now. Benjamin says nothing. He is looking out side of the window as he is nodding his head. Hay Sophie Lucy prods him.

Sophie lucy: " Wake up."

Benjamin:" Erm what."

Sophie Lucy: " who have you got your eyes on."

Benjamin:" Nobody I was just thinking."

Sophie Lucy: " Oh yes go on."

Benjamin: " Being out side is so different now back in the day if I was to walk in to a town you would have been flogged right back out of it now adays everything and eeveryone is so relaed its like take it easy man every body seems so ….different. I do not expect you to understand me."

Sophie Lucy: " Oh no go on please."

Benjamin:" It's the people there different they have changed."

Sophie Lucy: " Its not you Benjamin people change it's true we move with the times."

Benjamin: " Is it true that I talk total rubbish."

Sophie Lucy: " well it could only happen here."

It was like the old days where you would steel something off the market man. Now a days you would ask and if you asked nicly enough there would be more chance of you getting what you wanted not like back in the days. I know it is not like you would just stick the goods on to your jacket, although it still happens today. Once your done you would leg it down the high street. Or nip in to the local pub for a quick pint, and a bit of wheeling and dealing. Spot on you cannot go wrong. Benjamin calls for the waitress, realinzing that he was not being served.

Rebecca was not back so sophie Lucy takes Benjamin's order.

Sophie Lucy: " No not yet ill make it what was the order usual piece of cake and a pot of tea. I will be one minute.

As sophie Lucy makes her way to the kitchen Benjamin is busy to dreaming as the skys turn inwards and the sun disappears and he could clearly see that the moon was out at the same time as the sun slowly moves itself in to it's new position as it goes down leaving the light of the moon to shine above him. Sophie Lucy walks beack in talking holding a sliver tray and a small tea pot.

When the sun moves finally behind the moon and it ws nightime again Sophie Lucy and Benjamin had a realy long talk. About everything, Benjamin laid half on and off the table he had his arms out with a smile on his face hidden by the cold empty tea pot. As sophie lucy stands up removing the tea pot she is looking at Benjamin and he does not notice. As he continues to stare, Benjamin sees her as he is also looking side ways he asks her what she wanted sophie Lucy was quizzed for that moment.
Sophie lucy: " You have changed something."
Benjamin looks up.
Sophie lucy:" You have had a shave."
Benjamin:" yeah this morning."
Sophie Lucy: " there is some thing else."
Benjamin was just about to tell her, sophie Lucy moves around the otherside of him. but before benjmain has a chance to tell her she butts in.
Sophie Lucy:" wait." There is a pause then she continues. "I have got it you have had a hair cut."
Benjamin:" Yeah." Benjamin was just about to tell her.
Sophie Lucy:" A new suit as well and a uh a tie."
Benjamin:" spot on." He smiles " you have noticed."
Sophie Lucy turns around she walks out and shouts at him telling him that she was impressed.

As for waiting around for twenty minutes or there abouts. Sophie Lucy returns she did notknow that Benjamin was going to question her about her real name. Sophie did not return as she decided to have the conversation from her kitchen. As she prepares the food for the day from her kitchen that she would be selling for that day. Benjamin decides to walk out and goes for a walk. Not realizing that Sophie Lucy had began to speak. He leaves the small café. It was qiute true that more people had started to except Benjamin as he passes the children that seemd always to be there out side the café as they played. They seemed to always be there. they were polite enough to say hello. And so on as he walked down the street. He was continuely greeted with hello's.
As he walked past the water fountain it reminded him of the first time he entered the town. It was not a good time for Benjamin, even so he does not stop to think about it but stoped just by it to listen to its tranquil behaviour. The sound of water I think that everybody would think was a qranquil one. He was thinking about Sophie Lucy in her kitchen he looks in his pocket for a coin and he was lucky to find one to see if he could double his luck by throwing the coin in to the fountain. He does not find one in his pockets after having a good look what he did find was a coin on the floor. He thinks that it would not be good thinking about somebody esles wish so in the end he did not get a chance to throw a coin in to the fountain and make his wish. He places the coin that he had found on the floor and places it on the edge of the fountains wall. He waits for a moment then picks te coin up and throws it in to the fountain not making a wish. He stands there for a moment.

The wish that Benjamin had made was not his, as he had found the coin it was probably owned by a child or maybe it was just dropped and forgotten even though a wish was a wish and with that thought Benjamn continues his new journey walking off woth sense of his destination. He is enjoying the excitement and the adventure that would be ahead of him. where he ws walking but he would take his surroundings in to his mind so he could find his way back. On this occasion he had lost the time. He looks in to bis pocket for his watch he finds that it was not there and remembers that he had given it to the young girl Emma. He double checks again there was nothing in his pockets jacket or trousers. He takes his long over coat off the one that was smelling of the old fish that he had found in a bin somewhere on his jouneys. Benjamin sighs at himself like he was fed up or in a bhaf a worried mood. The watch was a gift and he nows understands Sophie Lucy. He really regrets giving it away at least he would know it was in good hands except not his. He knows that it was irreplaceable as it was a gift from Sophie Lucy.

Not having the time Benjamin has to go all the way back to reading the sky. Not having the time disenlougens Benjamin for a few hours as time was still moving he was left to catch up. for part of that time Benjamin was sitting down at the road side. He was wishing that he had the watch. He takes his mind back it was easy except he could not find it as he gives up as he climbs back on to his feet he finds his way and is in an area that he recognized. As for the time he could not guess at it for the first time.

Benjamin was outside the mans house whom he followed that miserable evening. My god Benjamin said to him self as he aproches the gentle mans house the kman who Benjamin befriended whe he had got out of the taxi. Benjamin thanks himself and smiles easy pickings was what Benjamin was thunking in a nice way. Benjamin begins tao walk up his drive on to his path way and right up to the door he is a little hesitant as he puts his hand out to te door bell and cheekly preeses the button jumping backwards not knowing where to look. Not finishing off the move and ringing the door bell this happened twice, Benjamin gets no answer so he knocks instead there ws no answers on both occasions and Benjamin has to force himself away. As he turns to leave he gets an answer the hallway light which was off is turned on. Benjamin surprised he speaks believing that he is in luck yes, yes to himself. As he turns around and stands readying himself for a greeting. Benjmain is underneath the mans doorway. The door was a large one it had a large lion knocker one that made the door of the house look. important

Benjamin stands there waiting thinking that the man was coming to his door infact it was quite the opposite the light is turned off again and Benjamin is out of luck. Benjamin stands thinking that he would eventually notice him. the ligt gies opn again and is left on still after waiting there is no answer. Benjamin is still waiting on the door step as he waits to be noticed.

The man does not notice Benjamin for a long while as Benjamin is waiting it starts to rain just Benjamin's luck. Benjamin is thinking that it was a good thing as if he is lucky the man would look outside his window to see the weather and notice Benjamin instead, this was true as Benjamin thought of this miricle it happened. As Benjamin ahd decided to give in he walks away leaving the underneath of the large door way. He was in the rain as he was getting soaked on perpose as the man would soon have to take notice. He ahd made it look like he had been in the rain which he was and he makes himalef looked soaked right through. The man finally comes to his door. Benjamin was impressed with his arrival and was laughing to him self thinking like a telelpath. The man opens his door he remembers Benjamin and invites him in. he was in luck.
Old man: " Hello Benjamin nice to see you come in side."
Benjamin: " It is a little cold and rough out there."
Benjamin was referring to the weather.
Old man: " Have you been out there long."
Benjamin: " I have been walking for a few hours. And then this the weather."
Benjamin wipes his feet and continues. That he knew where he was so he thought he would pop in. The man calls to his maid telling her to get some towels and put the kettle on and get Benjamin some fresh clothes. Benjamin knew that he had got this one spot on.
Old man: " Bring my new friend something to drink, thank you."
Within a minute Benjamin was wishing that he could have been a little bit more honest.

As Benjamin drys his hair as the old man kindly let him take a shower. Benjamin half dressed in the mirror Benjamin was straight to the point of asking the man questions such as how did he make so much money the man insisted that he does not know and does not want to discuss it however on this occasion he would tell him but not he whole story. He claimed to Benjamin had he had inherited it through the property had been handed down through generation to generation and how it was his turn. That was all the man was willing to say. Maybe Benjamin thought perhaps it was all he could say. Benjamin had finished dryng off. He was then invited down stairs. The man looked at Benjamin in a coinfused way and Benjamin was looking at him if to say what. Benjamin changes the subject quickly and asks the man another quick question as he does so telling the old man he that he was sorry as he did not mean to interagate the poor fellow the question was as follows what did they do for a living Benjamin was referring to his family. The old mn says nothing Benjamin answers him back "nothing." That's right nothing.

After that Benjamin says nothing as that's right the old man says nothing.

Benjamin: " well er you have not put me off old chum."

Benjamin had leart a new word then it happened again.

Benjamin:"Old chap."

Benjamin grabs his mouth the old man answer him by saying that he was pivcking up te lingo. Benjamin looks at him strangly apologising smiling and telling the old man that he was just joking honestly it was just a joke. The man agrees as they both walk side down a long corridor bumping in to his maid.

Old man: " make sure that Benjamins bed is good for him. I gather that you would be staying the night."

Benjamin: “ Er am I welcome.” Benjamin again pretends agin to look surprised knowing that he was welcome but still acting like he did not know.
Old man: “ great yes why not. Good take a look around if you want.”
Benjamin: “Er no I am fine.”

Old man: “ that’s fine.”
Benjamin new clean clothes had been brought to him he is lead away form the old man by the maid. Benjamin is given his clothes for that evening he undresses giving the dirty clothes that he was wearing back to the maid. In return gives Benjamin some clean clothes She tells Benjamin that his normal clothes would be ready in the ,morning for him and that she would bring them to him. Benjamin agrees and she goes on her way only for her to be called back.
Benjamin whispers I do not kn ow how to say this and it might sound a little funny I’ve got trousers, jumper, shoes and socks. The maid looked wrieldy at Benjamin trying to thunk about what he was trying to say. Benjamin looks at her trying to say the words, he shouts undergarments. She looks at Benjamin and laughs as he points down wards. The made walks off only to come back a few moments later with the undergarments. As he does the old man walks back in shouting pants he needs pants she always forgets. The maid walks off laughing again the man apologises sorry old chum she always forgets. Pants that was what I was trying to say.

As the old man explains with a smile and it was quite hard for him to say, the man agrees telling benjmain she does that to me everytime she dresses me it like she is alurgic to those words. Benjamin smiles and everytime she runs off. Im sure that she does it on purpose. She should of learnt by now. The old man apologises for her benjmai insists that it did not matter and it ws not important. It was an easy mistake that she would forget they both agree. Once benjmain was probably dressed they met again in the mans study. Benjmain was slowly building a repour finding that himlsef and theold man had a lot in common and they were both about to find out as they were now aquianted and getting closer. A piece of cake the old man offers it to Benjamin he didi not want to eat but it seemed a lot better than food that was taken from out of a bin and on top of that it would seem rude so benjmain abliged. He thanks the old man again as he eats it. inafct benjamin thought it ws nice and asked the old man for some more, the old man agrees again and again Benjamin thanks the man. in fact Benjamin could not wait for the old man to offer him some more. The man was watching Benjmain carefully and benjmain could feel his eyes upon him. anybody would with benjmains current back ground. With his new relashioship they were both thinking the same. They both talk about experiencing and expressing great knowledge about relasionships and places they had been it was an interesting time Benjamin thought and it was a more than interesting conversation the old man thought, Benjamin agreed.

Benjamin had made a friend his other friends would have been impressed except Benjamin knew that the relasionship with the old man started woth a lye and at forst benjami was using him not knowing that there relasionship was going from Benjamin now he has to change his tune and tell the man the truth about his arrival. That some of the things he had said he had said and what the real reason that he was there was. And that he ws in his home for false persenses. As Benjamin explains the man calls for his maid the maid walks I to the room and tells Benjamin that he would see him tomorrow Benjamin says good night. The maid and the old man walk out leaving Benjamin alone he stands taking a good look at himself as for being welcomed he could have been himself. Benjamin believes that the relasionship with the old man was going to end. It was going to be a short relahionship if that at all. The only thought that would run through Benjamin's mind was that he would be leaving in the morning and then return a few days later as invited. He was happy and grateful. He wanted to return the favour and benjmain was thinking hard and agrees that it would have to be a small one finding the solution as he laid in bed. That was it he shouted not realizing where he was Benjamin was to invite the old man to the café a a favour as the old man gave him one. A place where he can meet everybody else. He could have free coffee and cakes like he gave me. It would work. I will just leave early and as soon as my clothes are ready and returned yes Benjamin thought that is it.

Benjamin believe that his plans for told man would work. He goes to sleep thinking about what he was thinking about only to be woken in he morning by the maid with his clothes at hand layng them down on the table near the bed on the other side of the room. Once Benjamin ws dressed he looks at the maid not knowing how to say good bye he asks her for a pen and paper the maid tells Benjamin what ever he ws going to right he should tell her she would remember. As Benjamin agrees and fills her information. He asks her to rewrite he aks her to recite it exactly as he had spoken it. she gets it first time. He explains to her that he has no money so there ewould be no house keeping tip, the maid removes her hand looking disappointed. Remember to tell him were Benjamin last words be fore he is dressed by her as she picks up his jacket and puts it on to him as he turns around Benjamin thanks her as he is shown the door he asks her again to remember, Benjamin goes on his way. They would meet so Benjamin will tell him the truth.

Benjamin believes that he is in luck as the gentleman that he had just met looked like he was rolling in it he had a lot of money. Benjamin was more for him Benjamin could not stop thinking about how did he make so much. Benjamin pushes the thought to the back of his mind hoping that he would forget and he would except Benjamin's invitation he wanted to get into a relasionship with the old man. and he wated to tell him the truth about his arrival. He wated to tell him that when they ahd first met he was using him. it was obvious hwy he was telling him this.a few days had past and the old man had not arrived Benjamin ais sat at his table looking miserable and frustrated. Rebecca walks in looking at Benjamin as he knows exactly what she was going to say,. Looking at him as she normally does but also with a look of concern. Benjamin was sitting down having a conversation with himself. Rebecca wants to join in. benjamin confession was that he did not think that the old man that he was trying to befriend was going to turn up. rebecca just looks at him. trying to figure out what Benjamin was thinking about. Benjamin leans forwards hands and arms in thee normal place looking as if he had lost something infact he ws sulkin and rebbeca catches on.
Rebecca: " you look sad, you look like a child that has lost it's toy."
Benjamin: " do I, what."
Rebecca: " You have been sitting there for hours you have said nothing."
Benjamin:" Infact it has been two."

He rasises his hand to his face and leans on it. Benjamin is tired of waiting and wants some fresh air as he stands up half smiling knowing that the apology was not going to be enough. He closes his eyes in shame and in desperation to concel his real feelings, as he walks out of the café. As rebbeca walks in with the tea that he had ordered, he calls out to her and tells her to leave it on the side he shouts to her telling her that he would be back later and that he was going out for some fresh air. Benjmain wanted to shout but he controls his feeling of being let down. The pain that he was in the emotional pain was like failing an exam or even worse failing the audition, miss placing something that you cannot find. Even though either way Benjamin was off to recollect his emotions Benjamin is walking to the bus stop. As he checks himself for his bus past not knowing he had left everything in his old jacket but is lucky enough to find an old ticket in date on the floor out side the bus shelter. After he pats himsloef down like a criminal and then double checks himself again. as he looks upwards the sky was close to tears the light blue again slowly turning in to that exciting horrible grey. As the clouds were drawing there picture and the storm ariseing was staring down upon him. with the city in congestion he could not hear the children or the people due to the voice of the traffic every car that past him s]had that ghostly whisper like a silent grave as the cars went by Benjamin was quite impressed as there was lots of different models now a days they were bigger and different better but yet again smaller they seemed to be a political side to everything.

Taking everything that benjmain had seen within the last few minutes he was happy that hehad not purcessed a car he ws happy just plodding a long infact he was not finaically comfortable he was on the bus either way and it was easy to jump on to one when they arrive on time. Benjmain already knew not to smoke on buses however the driver did not notuce and they always seemed to be concentrating on the journey rather than what was going on the bus. Makijg sure that he was taking the right route. This gave benjmain the upper hand he could have a qiuke sneaky smoke in the back seat. Benjmain pulls a smoke out of his back pocket in fact it was a cigar. He had required it from the old man whilst in his company. benjamin did not think at the time where it had come from as he pushes the extremely large end which was the start in to bis mouth and lights it. there was nobody around so there was nobody to complain. However half way through the bus driver didi say something it was something like I am watching you do not push it. benjmain knows that he has been caught and puts his lighter away.

Benjmain did not speak for a while until he realizes that he had missed the stop and missed his destination. He presses the button for the driver to stop it was luck that they were coming to a bus stop the bus stops and benjmain gets off not knowing hwere he was. As he looks for a sign he has no luck and just to make things worse the driver of the bus was no help and had driven off before benjmain hadb theb chance to ask him where he was. It looked like it was somewhere in the country side.

The hut that Benjamin had found was cold and wet but built enough to shield him from the weather Benjamin was out of the wind. Benjamin had stepped off the bus he ws in a wooded area. He was not scared he just did not like it. he needed somewhere where he would feel safe. This particular bus shelter made Benjamin feel uncomfortable. He was in the area that he intended and he would wait for the morning to continue his walk. As it was dark he headed off on his journey not caring in what direction he was heading in. again he finds himself walking through a apple orchard. Apple trees each side of him. No pathway's just muddy tractor tire marks. As Benjamin slips and slide s around in the mud his journey was practically impossible he slips over not once but twice and lands each time straight on to his back lucky it ws a soft landing s on both occasions saved by a bath of mud and water. His clothes were ruined both trouser and jacket totally cover in mud. He was really upset and the clothes that he was wearing were not country clothes. As Benjamin picks himself up only to slip again and again he fell on his back. As Benjamin gets up again he slips over again in the same spot. This was the for the time and this time he decides to stay down on the floor in the muddy pool of water as cold as it was Benjamin was on his knees crawling out of the farmers land on to a road.
Benjamin:" That was really hard work." Benjamin looks down at himself.
As he rolls over in gto a nearby bush, picking himself up looking for a gap in the hedges. Benjamin had enough and chose to stay for a while even though it was cold and it would be warmer walking. He takes the rest of the cigar out of his pocket and lights it up, the smell was a good one.

As Benjamin sits and trys to get over the old man that he wanted to meet, Benjamin smiles as he knows the frustration of wnaating to meet somebody normal had surpast. He was feeling a little better about himself. All he had to do now was find his way back home. he thought about trying to make the journey in the morning but however a good long walk would do him good and sttle his mind. With or with out a dog and knowing that he had not got one, Benjamin looks up at the sky it was a full moon. There were no clouds and no sound it was really quiet, it must have been late and Benjamin had no watch, it was clear to Benjamin that this particular journey was not a good one.
Benjamin is all muddy and wet he had ruiened his coat benjamin gets the same feeling agin unsure of where he was, which was proberly the cause. He remember s the watch as a gift and he looks in his jacket again then remembers that he ahd given it to Emma ha he says laughing as he had remembered. As he continues on his way past and over the stool and in to another field still not knowing where he was heading or what direction he was going in. and still in the darkness. Benjamin sees sense most of the time he was upset still as he walks disorientated in the country side. He was being honest to himself he just wanted to get home and back to the café.

Benjamin was looking for his watch it had not regesterd that it had gone all it would take now was that Benjamin would except it and of couse tell sophie lucy the truth Benjamin had re-preceived his journey he ws going to take himself off to a new place to dwell, not just for the sake of it but he was still upset about the relasioship with the gentleman. And now his watch. As he walks Benjamin is thunking about sophie Lucy and knows that she will be getting upset with Benjamin when he returns. It was like she was there with him as he paces along the road his steps getting larger and his fercesome style of putting his arms in motion to joins his steps. His pace becomes fastrer he is finally channling his anger in the right direction as he walks on he realizes the end of his cigar is waiting to be used and finished as he lights it up as he walks this was not a good idea when the heart rate is up and your doing around sixty steps a minute. Benjamin did not care. With old memories coming back and quickly disappearing, Benjamin believed what he was doing was good for him.

Not knowing his future and not knowing his destination. As Benjamin is now thinking about he man remembering that he had left him his address Benjamin was now thinking that it was a mistake he had become jealous. As benjmain walked not caring about the direction or where he was going.

As Benjamin is talking to himself about everything and anything just to keep himlsef awake so he didi not have to sleep in some bush. He puts himself in a mood he wakes up slightly off the path that he thought that he was on. He turens around and strtes in to the darkness his mood fitting in with his surroundings. With nothing tolisten to apeart form the wind.
He swears to himself turning around again this time facing south as west was his last direction that he was walking from not too. He looks up at the trees they were tall and large they ahd leaves on them and a whirling sound that seemed to whistle a song to him the wind was there blowing around the bottom of the trees but right at the top where ethe leafs were. Then the wind stops there s silent s everywhere but only for the moment and then more russeling then silence. With all of this Benjamin wanted to scream he was lost and the only way back would be to go back, to turn around. He looks at his feet he raises his head lookin forwards thinking slowly of which direction he should turn to. He did not want to go back on himself he looked at that idea as a bad one spiritual reasons it was a personal thought. He gave himself a chance and would return via the woods hoping that he would find a path and there might be a chance what he did not want to do was to double back on himself. He continues his journey.

As Benjamin walked the ground was changing form muddy soft to smooth then hard. The ground that Benjamin was walking on was getting better as it was turning from muddy to good to soft to hard. This part of the journey reminded Benjamin of him falling over it ws a tough time as for walking was concerned as he used the bushes to keep himsslef up right and baleanced on them occasionally. Benjamin had fallen six or maybe seven times on this particular part of his adventure. Benjamin and his snew surroundings where not getting on. It seemd completely senseless why would he even attempt walking at night time in the country at this time. When Benjamin finally comes out of the woods completely covered in prickles and leafs bits of bush and muddy shoes he looks around he was actually in another ally way it was modernand well built. And he could feel the floor as he stamps on it there was no sign of mud.

As he walks onwards he can see the streets light he was glad that he had made it as he approaches it not knowing the time, looking up at the sky it was dark still he nust of walked for more than three hours he had found a new town., a small town by the looks of it. different to all of the others. He was no longer interested where he was Benjamin voice and nose take over as the smell of food hits his nose as he walks off following it in it's direction.

Benjamin first thinks that the smell of food was coming from the nearby fish and chips shop infact it was coming form a party it was a babarque Benjamin prepares himself as it was in a garden there was some noise mixed with some cheers and lots of talking. The entrance was close by Benjamin walks in through the open gate some drunken people stumble out in to the ally way. Benjamin turns around to watch them as they had turned a full three hundread and sixty degrees and were now heading back in to Benjamin's direction. They weredrunk and on there way to a taxi, which could clearly be seen at the end of the ally way. In the garden there were a few more people it looked like Benjamin had missed al the partying and ended turning up at the end. There was still few people hanging around and a few people crashed out on the floor probably drunken. The barbarque was free there was nobody around Benjamin jumps at the chance of an approach to grab some food. Sauaages, beefburgers and chicken. Benjamin thinks he is dreaming and says to himself pinch me. as Benjamin is in a hurry as he fills his coat with the food looking over his shoulder knowing not to get caught. Not forgetting the fizzy drinks that would calm him down after he makes his get away. Benjamin leaves unnoticed it was like he was never there. As he stands a little to close to being still on the youngs mans property, The owner of the property walks out in to his garden, there was a loud shouting noise and words to follow in order. Benjamin leaves unnoticed. As Benjamin bites in to another burger leaning backwards perched against a wall the boy was still looking for the food and is shouting as Benjamin is listening close by where is all the food you greedy little gits. Benjamin has to smile and laughs a bit as he walks off down the ally way. Benjamin leaves te ally way he can hear the young man still ranting and shouting about who had nicked his food benjmain made his steps quicker as he thnks that the young man was going to follow him. Benjamin makes it to a bench it was close nearby. He sits himself down it suited Benjamin's appearance and it would look like he had been there all day. He sits up right legs crossed and feet pertuding out wards. There was a shop across the road Benjamin is noyiceing theses thing he smiles telling himself that there was only one bench. He bites in to the chicken then he continues to insult the village about having one bench. Only to spit out the food in his mouth as continues to talk. As the young man appears Benjamin is spiting the food out it was good timing. As the boy walks past him swearing then he disappears only to reappear and then to Benjamins surprise sits dowsn right next to him the boy is quite up set and within the half hour of there meeting he had told Benjamin everything the boy walks off as he had appeared. The boy comes back and the same thing happens again.

Boy: " where is my chicken."

Benjamin was thinking that he did not want the boy to noticed him. this time the boy sits down he is in tears Benjamin was trying not to take notice of te boy and pretending to be a sleep. The boy did not know that he was resting upon Benjamin's legs Benjamin was starting to feel the pain as he is wanting him to get off. But does not want to listen to the boy sob. The young man starts to speak again he end s the conversation finally after an half hour and gets up off Benjamin. The boy walks off and Benjamin is left to think about what he had done.

After the boy had left benjamin and Benjamin has stuffed the food and lots of it he was trying to think and understand some of the things that the boy had said. he decided to move from the bench to the pavement put side the small shop beside the shop there was another building and it looked a little bit more sheltred that the first two places. Benjamin makes sure tat he is well out of harms way. Nobody was in and the large doors of the building was pulling Benjamin. He had a choice to approach it but he changed his mind to pick some butts off the floor instead. As he makes his way down the street then back up to the top of the street making sure he didi not miss anything that he could use. On the way back down the street again it seemd darker than it actually was. When Benjamin gets there he is delighted it felt it was warm Benjamin looked around to see what the name of the building was. He would use this for future reference. The large doors to the building gave it an apperence, and statious the lare doorway with step to go with it. Benjamin approaches it taking a really good look at it he sits down on the the six large steps and settles down for the night. Knowing now that he have the company of the passer bys as for the large car parking infront of the building and himself. Benjamin content lift and pulls together the lapels of his jacket it was getting colder up to his face, this was to shield him form the wind. His face would be unseen and out of view of any people, his broken cold hands would be in his pockets and the taste of food in his mouth.

Benjamin was content on watching the people come and go infact he was becoming a bit of an expert in watching people. That particular day went fast the next day quite similar and the day sfter that was the same again as the first day. Benjamin had not spoken to anybody he had been watching and occasional he would see the same people over and this was making Benjamin feel nervous for what reason he did not know even though nobody had noticed him Benjamin was thinking he was the invisible one there was an old lady who seemed to appear to Benjamin a lot she would sue the post box occasionally there were some young boys too. They would stand outside the shop and play they would be there for a few hours each day. Until they could find some one to help then by going in to the shop for then for cigerettes and booze. I think it was cigarette's and then the shop owner deliverys once every week at eleven oclock. The girls fro the local school once everyday again for cigereetes. Once every so often, the grils and boys the ones that look like they are starving and poor and up to no good. It was good people being people I guess. Faking in to my mind my own actions. I could not say that I was any better. It all looked so complicated

Juggling and complimenting complicated situations each of them with there own reasons. Any way behaviour was not his specialist subject.

As for te next couple of days Benjamin was qiute settled down quickly up until the point that the old aged pensioners had spotted him. and there covesation was over heard and it went on from person to person form there. Benjamin had been caught it was not a crime but to be the talk of the village within a few hours he felt qiute upset. They were not particular nice old people you would expect the opposite you would expect hat tey would be polite infact on his occasion they were really rude using swear words and other things to describe Benjamin. The last things that were said forced Benjamin to move they were thinking about calling in the police. As Benjamin heard this they raised the sound of there voices knowing that he would hear them they wanted an reaction. He struggles to except what was said and struggles to settle down for the last time in the afternoon by that time the police turned up to move him along. Benjamin had nothing to worry about he was expecting it.

As Benjamin looks around for the time he gazes up into the sky he says to himself just after wakng up as he suffs the food that was left over trying not think about the boy whom he nicked it off taste for meat had enterd his soul. It took the police two hours to find benjamin and by hen he had moved not far but close enough to the shop. The problem was solved and benjain smiles he thinks that he sounds like an interlec, close to stupid as he sits down and continues to watch. He starts with the traffic watching some delivery guy complaining to him slf if he ahd parked his truck in the right place and how much confusion such a thing would make. And watching the customers slowly readying there lips as ten taking his mind back to the driver of the truck did he know that he aas that badly parked. That’s a ticket benjaian says quietly to himself. Benjamin smiles to himself knowing that he had seen the man before. This complimenting and judgeing the people went on all day. As for Benjamin over staying his welcome in the village the police did not turn up.

As the day goes on benjmain was happy that he had not seen the two old ladys go by. Benjmain was worried believing that his presents in the small village had worried them enough for them to not want to come out of the shop. Benjmain knows that his dress had always put people off. But his manors when they showed were perfect, nobody had ever approached him to tell him to smarten up or to speak polity. A part of thinking about that and it ws not easy fight controlling the thought as he trys to throw it out of his mind. Infact benjmain was considering leaving the village he felt strongly about it he was thinking and his consciousness was tellingbhim to stay he felt really up set about the two old ladys at the end of the day benmain still feels strogly about the subject. The two old ladys did not appear and when they did there was only one of them. benjmain had to look hard at the expression on her face she was disgused by her wrinkles on her face and the make up. benjmain had good eyes he could see clearly that the expression on herface was not one of a good nature she was not her self. Maybe it was that she was on her own she seemed different today. It wa sthursday and she was doing the same dropping a letter in to the post box. And then in to the small shop. To make things even worse and even harder to figure out as benjmain watches some thing ahd changed out of the blue aan ambalence drives ghostly past then a police car and then a crowd of people appear.

Somebody was missing in action and it was benjmain sphie lucy as benjmain renamed her as for not telling himher real name was in the café. The repairs for her celing were going on it was busy. While she was ordering her work men around whilst having a double conversation with her self. Rebbeca and the men as she gives them her instructions, rebbeca is ordered to make the work men some tea rebbeca makes the tea. As she looks around watching the men climb up the large ladder. Then sophie Lucy continues where is benjamin rebbeca tells her that she didi not know. Rebbeca stands close by watching the work men. Tea, tea, sophie lucy said.

Rebbeca:" how do tey like it."

Rebbeca repeats the question.

Rebbeca:" how do you like your tea."

That would be two sugars for me he says as he climbs back down the ladder.

Rebbeca :" milk."

Builder:" yes."

Another builder wlaks in sophie lucy begins I hope that he is ok. He just uped and left. I hate it when he does that. It really makes me feel worried rebecca walks in puuting the sups of tea down on the table.

Rebbeca: " tea. So benjamin hoe is he."

Sophie lucy: " I do not know I have not seen him for days I hope he is ok I bet he is hanging around some bench."

Her conversation continues.

Sophie lucy:" you know what I think he is playing hard to get."

Rebbeca: " why do you say that."

Sophie lucy:" have you seen his face evry time he sits down in that chair."

Rebbeca:" you mean the table."

Sophie lucy: “ table then.”
Rebbeca: “ No it is deeper than that he is quite a spiritual fellow.”
Sophie lucy: “ a spiritual fellow with no money and nothing.”
There is a pause.
Sophie lucy: “ No prospects.”
Rebbeca: “ I think you are fond of him.”
Sophie lucy: “ A little here and a little there he just makes me feel safe and he is funny at the same time I like him er hold on to the left a bit.”
Sophie lucy was ordering the work men to put the last piece of celing in. Before both of them had to clim the dodgey stair case to support the work mwn in fitting the bath and sink units. Lucky the toilet remained the same as it ws not bdamhged as the celing fell away. sophie lucy once they were done tells them that there job was not yet finished they both looked puzzled sophie lucy sends them back upstairs and tells them to double check the work that they had done.
Sophie lucy continues as they check again yelling at the top of her voice that it could only happen in old places right. Rebbeca does not answer her she was else where simply flirting with some work mate in her kitchen.

“Rebbeca” sophie Lucy shouts pulling her away pinches her telling her to wake up. rebbeca jumps.
Rebbeca:” so back to benjmain where do you think that he is.”
Sophie lucy laughs she knows that benjmai is fine.
Rebbeca:” your smilimg why? is it the thought of benjmain I think you have fallen for him come on tell me the truth.”
sophie lucy orders the builders again rebbeca downs her cup of tea wiping her mouth as she continues to question sophie Lucy. That was for the builders as rebbeca takes another gulp. Her eyes wide looking at sophie lucy she tells rebbca to go and get the cake as rebbeca understands as she puts the builders tea down. Only for sophie lucy to watch the builder who comes down the ladder to quick who slips on the floor and falls in to Sophie lucys arms.
Sophie lucy:Hello she says smiling,
Builser:” excuse me.”
the builder says is that for me knowing that rebbeca had drank from it. Top up sophie lucy insists.
Builder: “ Yes thank you we are nearly done.”
Sophie lucy:” How long im running a business.”
Builder: “ Oh er about an hour.”
Sophie lucy walks out of the room.

Mean time Benjamin is looking for his next meal, again everything that Benjamin's needs is right in front of him. that included bins. It was quite busy even so if Benjamin was hungry he was hungry. Far apart from the fresh cups of tea from the café Benjamin was slowly pushing his hand in a bin as he fidge its around as far as he can knowing what he is looking for was due as for tha fact that he had taught himself the feelin and the shape of things from previous meetings with the council bins. Such as buger cases, bottles and chip rapping paper. Picking things out of the bins had a skill it you woud not of thought it. Benjamin thinks he has perfected it. As Benjamin pulls a half eaten burger out of the bin. And gets the attention of some passer by. Pulling faces looking in disgust and distaste. Opening the closed box with out the care he bits in to the cold meat. He did not even think about what else could be in it. As he takes another bite he seemed to be enjoying it. as Benjamin finishes the food as he licks his fingers not caring about the audinec and the two young girls filming it on there mobile phones. As he slurps his finger s counting them as they go and out of his mouth now a drink Benjamin thought as he puts his hand back into the bin. There was a loud arhh as he pulls out a beaker half filled with cold tea. Benjamin has a smile on his face shouting to the on lookers especially to the girls that were fiming it if they would like a photograph.

It had been four days since Benjamin had spoken to anybody. in Benjamin's eyes due to his surrounding believing that it was not him but the people in the small village were not particaurly welcoming, Benjamin knew that he would have to leave son. Benjamin sits on te only bench still watching. It was now not to busy only for a young girl to approach him begging him to buy her some cigerttes. How old was she Benjamin was thinking she played a part in benjmains decision in the end Benjamin gave in and agreed they continued to chat and another dession was made and Benjamin ns had excepted her quarrel. She handed benjain ten pounds and she looked grateful. Benjamin entered the shop it was his first time the assistant was behind the counter. Benjamin continud and asks for the cigerttes as he hold s his breath trying not to tell him that he was buying them for a small girl who was outside. As he finally convinces the assistant that they were for him.
Benjamin knew why he was being questioned it was his dress. The assistant finally gives in and gives Benjamin the packet of cigerettes. Benjamin with a smile on his face gives the assistant the money and Benjamin takes the cigerettes.
As the girl jumps on Benjamin for his help and giving him loads of thanks before exchanging names Benjamin was also thank full even though he had no reason to be.
Benjamin: " No thank you."
Benjamin continued until the girl got back into her car Benjamin stands twenty meters behind her up te road and watches her.

Benjamin ws keft alone again he was feeling reasonable glad that he had company for a moment that the girl had driven off. He was hoping that he woud see her again. she seemed to be polite she was obvoisly not from the village. Benjamin crosses the road not looking both ways and gets abeep from a psser by and then some verbal abuse. It ws something like get off the road and a few more beeps. Probably teenagers as Benjamin thinks as he didi not see the actuall driver. They wer ebeing noisy with there music blaring out Benjamin at that point catches on as a flying bootle appears from nowhere just missing him obviously thrown for the car. The car passes by again and the passgers give Benjamin a good long stare Benjamin looks at the bottle it was exactly what he thought it was a rather large bottle of urine. Benjamin puts the bottle down back on the pathment where he had caught it.
still got the old magic as Benjamin sasy to himself, as he crosses the road once he had got to the other side he was feeling better he was happy that he was out of site The large door way and steps would do for him now he would hide nicely behind the parked cars until later until it gets dark and then he would go find his next meal.

It had started to rain Benjamin was just getting warm it was not a large storm but large enough to shift the wind in to Benjamins direction as bringing a little chill to Benjamin. He was not in a warm place as the wind with the rain it was pouring down he thought that he should move he was thinking that he would probably be better of under the shops hood although Benjamin calacalates that he would be dryer but colder if he moves Benjamin has to make a dession to stay put or to cross the road and bear the chill of the wind Benjamin hands were very cold he choses to stay put as the wind was getting worse and the rain did not stop Benjamin loses his temper and shouts looking upwards yelling out that I was supposed to summer like he was talking to god he was acting. As the clouds finally settled and Benjmain was left to listen to the remaining last drops of rain dripping off the roof on to the floor it was enough to drive you crazy as Benjamin continued to talk. As the storm starts over he is watching the lightening and listening to the thunder it was worse but more exciting the second time around. It was that sound that you could never ignore. Benjamin was wishing that he had not left the café and now was getting upate about relasionships even if they worked.

After the skys with the elements had settled down Benjamin only concern was getting warm. Again he approaches the shop which was empty, no customers this was better for Benjamin he creeps though the door not knowing that there was a door bell that gave the most anioing ringing sound. It ws too loud for one and it reached from one end of the dhop to the other. They were making sure that they could hera who ever ws entering there shop. Benjamin waits nobody came to te counter at that time Benjamin was tempered to steal for the first time but to have him wait there was a better frill as he ws in the warm. As he pretends to look around picking products up and putting them back down. Hoping that another customer would enter the shop to give him more time in the warm taking the attention off hm. The assistant ws there all the time he was under his desk. As the lady lifte herself up and appeared lie she had been put there she speaks can I help you Benjamin ignores her at first he was pretending that he could not hear her. In his mind he was thinking for a few minutes he knows he needs more time he asks the lady behind the till if she had a basket she points to them then says by the door. Benjamin looks around some more Benjamin starts to feel his fingers again and hurrys to the basket only to think that she was going to notice his fingers felt normal again as he could lift things and feel them fine. He looks at his face as he passes the refrigerator and sees his reflection he looked old and cold his cheaks red he was flustered and extremely cold.

Benjamin manages to put everything that he had put in to the basket back onto the shelves the lady behind the till looks onwards at him as if it ws a joke and it ws in Benjamin's mind as he walks out nice and warm in asense as he can feel his fingers again. he found hat his body was warmer too. Leaving the little lady thinking of what he was trying to do. He steps out of the shop back into the cold as the whole process atrts over again. he was happy with himself as he steps back onto the large steps across the road under the door way of the building. He sits down. Back against the wall his legs crossed he ws sitting that way to keep warm. He closes his eyes and does not wake until the morning. Waking up in a happy mood feeling hungry also it was the worst feeling being hungry in the morning it ws ok for some people as for benjmain he always felt hungry weather it was he morning or the afternoon. For some reason Benjamin did not feel himself and the feeling of hunger had left him. Benjamin was feeling worse as when he looked up and seeing that people were throwing there food in the bins right in front of him. Benjamin was not amused and thought that he could go back later as tehe thought past Benjamin thinks that he has fallen on some hard luck. As it was bin day Benjamin jumps up watching the danger appear the dust bin men. He calls out. There sa silence and then a loud what. Benjmai is on his feet as he watches the bin men take and empty the bin he shouts that's my food. He runs over the road and grabs the bin man who shoves him off

Benjamin snatches the bin bag that is mine he says to him in a angry voice. The bin man lets go looking at Benjamin. That's my food that's my food Benjamin says like he had been taken over by some beast. Benjamin looks down sorry full he should have been looking up. as he looks at the dust bin men who in return snatches the bag back from Benjamin n and throws it in to the dumper. Benjamin did not have much to say after that performance he crossed the road and sits back down under the doorway.

When the wather had finally changed again making things even easier on benjmain he ahs a smile on hs face because he was back in the warm, more people began to appear and the kids came back it looked like he was being entertain, the more people that turned up the better benjain was feeling. As Benjamin was watching a small group of teenagers with bikes and cigerettes and beer, as he watched them not to bis suoprise one of the boys was boasting he is holding something up it as shiney Benjamin thinks it is his watch and walks out from under the building and crosses the road getting a beep froma car as he narrowly avoids it. Benjamin had forgotten that he had iven the watch to Emma and approaches the boy who was boasting about his watch to his friends. he walks towards the group of teenagers and they could see him coming over towards them. he was no longer walking he was running. Running at them.

Benjamin:" Hay."

Boy: " whats up my brother."

Benjamin: " can I have a look at the watxh."

Boy:" whats up dude my brother."

Benjamin:" if you do not mind bro."

Boy2:" what is it man."

Benjamin is getting good as he gets agood looks at the watch and thinks that it is his.

Benjamin:" if you do not mind dude, bro where did you get the watch finding being he ultimaaate word."

The boy looks at Benjamin and Benjamin looks at the boy. The boy does not explain but shouts out loudly the word dad. Benjamin clearly knew now that the watch was not his it was not the watch that sophie lucy had given him. why he thought the boy had it on he could not explain.

There was no reason for the boy to ride off in such a hurry, the rest of the young men just stood there feeling amused another boy who looked quite normal spoke out you better watch out he gone to get his dad. Benjamin looked disgruntled for a moment believing that he had caused the problem as the boys makes jokes just to rub it in further. The fact that Benjamin had lost his watch however withina few minutes Benjamin was on the run the boy obviously told the truth as he came back with his dad.

Dad:" oh you."

Benjamin: " oh great a greeting of peace."

Dad:" have you been picking on my lad."

Benjamin:" I have just asked him a question about his watch I ahd lost my watch and it looked from adistance that your son had it then I remembered that I had left it with a friend, that all."

The father of the boy looks at Benjamin as he loos at he boy. Benjamin s gives them both an apology and the man seemed content. The boy cockly tells Benjamin that he told him so. Benjamin walks off knowing that it was all his fault. As the father and the boy walk off together.

Benjamin was not happy in the village.

While Benjamin had been busy believing that he had been losing things sophie lucy had totally refurbished her café, including the toilet that she had to do. It had taken her the whole day and the sewers up above and down below took most of the day they were looking like imposible to find some body to do the job. Any way sophie lucy ws glad that she found somebody to do te job. They were ready to re open her tea bar. Except Benjamin was not there and it did not seem right with out him. more so sophie lucy decides to wait.it was her special moment and she wanted Benjamin there. Sophie lucy speaks to Rebbeca as there is a good crowd out side some of them customers waiting she has to open looking around hoping that Benjamin would turn up. Sophie lucy is upset and has to lean on Rebbeca, she did not mind. Unfortunately Benjamin was not in that crowd he was in a different one. As sophie lucy looked at the crowd she makes a short speech telling her audience telling them that the work is done and there would be no more and we are open again in er a few hours. There was some signs of dispiontment but sophie Lucy wanted Benjamin there. she continued that the opening is postproned for now and due to that when she does open it free coffee and cakes for everyone. There sa small cheer as the public disperse. She puts the dates of the new opening times on the front of the glass window at then front of her cafe. Sophie Lucy was in tears and needed a big hug for her efforts.

Rebbeca could see clearly that sohie Lucy was upset and needed to comfort her. She welcomed her telling sophie Lucy not to worry Rebbeca offers sophie Lucy a cup of tea. Sophie Lucy says that a cup of tea would not be strong enough. Sophie Lucy was starting to smle again she wipes the tears of her face giving the small hanky back to Rebbeca. Sophie Lucy contiues in the klitchen parpering a cake.

Sophie Lucy:" Nothing seemed to work when Benjamin was not here. Have you noticed he really makes me feel good he is always happy and smiling like nothing bothers him. how do you lose your self. He will come back he is upset for not nakng friends with that guy you know that strange man."

Rebbeca: well he is a tramp and tramps do crazy things. We are his friends right."

Sophie Lucy:" yeah."

Rebbeca:" what kind of person just us and goes off for a walk in the middle of the night,"

Sophie Lucy: " that's just it that is Benjamin."

Rebbeca:" My thoughts exactly. Have you fallen for him."

There is silence then laughing sophie Lucy is now in a better mind and continued to say where ever Benjamin is he better come back. Benjamin was a couple of hundred miles down the road.

For the next day or so sophie Lucy was really thinking about Benjamin, hard. Everytime sme body came in to her shop she would jump hoping that it would be Benjamin. Every time it was the post man or a customer he was disappointed and to hide her anger she would sit in the dark and occasionally scream. Sophie lucy was so upset she would turn all her ligts off in disrespute. She sits down in benjamins chair. She was really missing him. she really believed that Benjamin was not coming back.

Emma: " Come on sophie Lucy this is not the end of the world. He will come back where else would he go."

Sophie Lucy:" I can not stand it any longer the thought of him hbis driving me crazy."

Rebbeca and Emma smile at each other.

Emma:" He will come back."

Rebbeca: " He is different."

Emma:" I bet as soon as you calm down he will walk through that door holding a big bunch of flowers."

Sophie Lucy:" That would be something."

When the night finally comes and village was nice and quite only for the odd car stopping for the shop Benjamin was back to being cold it was the feeling that now Benjamin would hate. The weather was slowly becoming Benjamin s demons every evening seemed like a fight and the early mornings did not help and the days were longer. Benjamin still in the most orcward of positions continues to watch on. He was right it was the only thing he could do. As he leans three hundred and sixty degrees around even what he could see was not a wall Benjamin laughs. Benjamin was watching more care fully as the village seemed to be bigger than he first thought. He was sure that there was a solution to what his mind was saying and what he was trying to work out he was making sure his mind was working. As he trys to calculate he fails for the first time. He tries again trying to keep focused it was something to do as the night was cold he could see the traffic lights he had not noticed them before and double checks why calcalting everything esle around him.

The next morning Benjamin decides that he would leave. He had finally had enough and was going back into town back to sophie Lucy and the café. He leaves straight away forgetting about breakfast, his journey starts quickly and there was going to be good weather if the sun would rise it would be warm enough to walk. He could just about see the sun as it wass gong to rise from behind him by lunch time it would be in front of him. as for now it had settle behind some grey clouds which look like volcano smoke they were moving slowly. Benjamin preferred to walk in the morning simply because of the weather. it wa actually quite deangerous walking down the country lanes he would be walking around corner for the next few hours. He would be dicing with death. He would always say a prayer before he left. Not that it really matter he was not too religious, he belived if your smoked your smoked. End of the conversation and definatly the end of the journey. The skys didi not change as he presumed the sun stayed hidden between the clouds Benjamin was worried that it was going to rain making his journey twice as treachious. Benjamin preferred dry ground and with that a strong pace. Having the feeling of his boots griping the ground. Benjamin says to himself tht he should of waited for the summer he knows it was just bad timing. As he slips and slides a bit as he walks. Black ice very dangerous. It was a short distance before Benjamin found some proper ground for walking no mud. Puddles the usual things like a badly pathed road.

The road finally gets good Benjamin makes it to the smoother road and gets some proper grip he can walk properly now. He was happy to be back on concrete again.

Benjamin knows he has a long journey ahead of him he is glad and happy that he had reached level ground with no ice he was able to walk better it was a lot easier on his mind and easier to concentrate as Benjamin walks and feels uncomfortable taking his shoe of realizing that the problem was in there as he had a stone in his shoe and there was a hole not a large one but big enough to cause him some discomfort which was threatening his journey. He did not know what to do he could only imagine what would happen if he ruiens his shoes before his joueny was finished Benjamin continues it was always the small things that upset Benjamin even so he continues the journey knowing now that he needed a new pair of shoes he stops and takes a second look. The view of the farm land was close and there was as few sheep out as there was people and cars the sheep gave Benjamin something to speak to as he walked along side there fields Benjamin thought that these animals were funny the way they would just stand there. even so a least they gave Benjamin some berearing knowing now that he ws walking in the right direction. There was bushes either side of him Benjamin was now keeping an eyes out occasionally stoping and thinking as he finds something that had been thrown out of a passing car on the road. on his occasion it ws a bottle of juice benjmain was tempted to pick it up but the thought that it might have been urinated in put him straight off. He looked a little bit further and foud an half eaten sandwich it was nothing speacail benjian had eaten worst. He did nt have to much of a choice at this moment in his situation it was also un usual for Benjamin to try and hitch a lift at this point of his journey and as a car pulled over he was temped to get in only to deine himself and the farmer his company. Although Benjamin did say thank you and continued walking.

As the road that benjmin was walking on seemed different, he had stoped to look around the long road had not convinced him that he was walking in the right direction. As for the traffic there was very little again making benjmain feel like he was lost. Benjamin often had to turn his back on the traffic that was there as for the weather the small road as in the width of it did not help the lorrys splashing water on to him from the left over puddles. After being forced in the bushes once to often benjmain forces his way back out when the traffic settled down through a large bush and through a fence in to a field another one, he found that after a minute of waiting it was just as bad as the muddy filed benjmain makes his way back to the road his clothes covered in mud he stamps in the floor to clear the mud off his shoes and pushes his wet, dirty hems of his jeans back into his socks. He continues his journey starting back on the road. benjamin is back in his element and he had started to smile as he walks along talking to things such as birds some well wishers drive past giving him a boost in comfidents but it was not like he needed it. the beeping of there horne actually put him off while he was in motion. Infact the last couple of driver s that past him gave him some verbal abuse, benjmain did not care but it was rude. He was in that good of an mood he chooses to ignore the insults but he would not forget them. benjmain checks again his where abouts he is still not sure that he is in the right place it wasa bridge he is confused at first then he remembers it he crosses over it there was nothing like an adventure he says to himself realizing that the sign post was on the other side of the road behind him.

Benjamin was feeling quite hungry and watching the sheep did not help he was thinking big roast dinner he was in adays walk of his destination including the evening before that Benjamin sighs saying to himself that he would just have to wait. Mind you he continued I guess it was something to look forwards to benjamin is now in the area that he knows the best he realizes a couple more hours and he would of reaced the farm and small village. This village was a very quiet one. It was peaceful and when Benjamin reahes it he smiles and with that look of surprise on his face like he had achived it. He is thirsty and he decides to wait out side the vilages post office. The weather was looking fare and the silence of the village echoed right through him and through the streets beside him. with posh houses either side of him. The roads were clean and there was a different smell in the air. The only sound that Benjamin couls hear was his own breathing, until it started to rain. The peacefulness of the village was about to be disrupted there seemed to be a storm on its way. Benjamin stayed put it had lasted an hour once it had finished the steam of the ground rose quickly. It was hotter than usual again Benjamin after percivering gets what he wanted as a man walks outside from inside of the post office offers Benjamin some chocolate, Benjamin had to except his offer. After a short conversation and a good bye. As the man grabs his paper folds it inhalf and cover s his head as another storm had started. The man disappears around the corner, Benjamin was thinking what a nice bloke. Benjamin stays out as the storm starts again leaving Benjamin with no place to go.

Benjamin is caught in two frmes of mind should he make the challenge and continue or should he stay put and sit it out. Benjamin sits down on the floor it wa sjusst enough celing to cover him and with his jacket off and over his head he had prepared himself for the on coming weather. As he frees himself of the thought of going home. He pulls on the lapels on his jacket closer to him lifting the jacket further towards him. he was wearing no hat, and there was still the wind to compete with, benjmains head was getting cold. The wind would bring the cold with it, there was some light but to much, infact now there was a mist on the grass and it was slowly rising. The air was chilled and cold.
Benjamin was quizzed himself it wa snt like he had not made the journey before. He kept telling himself that home was not to far over again. as he spoke of this it ws like he was having a chemical reaction to the cold weather the cold and having no food in side of him made things worse. At that point it was like everything ahd stoped there no sound , no traffic. no birds and no people. As Benjamin hold his tongue out in his state trying to taste the fresh air. Benjamin stops realizing that he was acting peculiar just for that moment. People do silly thing at times this was one of them.

Benjamin ahd thought that he ahd cracked up as he licked the air and pretended to eat food the cold air and the walking ahd finally got to Benjamin's head. He sits still for a moment talking to himself then didappears around the corner and then down a road. Benjamin stops at the end of the road it ws a short one he takes a large breath he knows some thing is not right as he takes another deep breath again he says to himself that it was cold he repeats this to himself three times it's the cold,c old , cold. He sits down again and unties his boots then takes his socks off Benjamin had found his problem his toes had gone cold. With that Benjamin knows that hee needs to finish his journey. There ws a bus stop near by. He looks at his toes they were all bright red, he covers them back up by putting his socks back on. Benjamin knows that he is stuck for the night. He had timed the whole journey it was a few days walk left he liked to be punchual and he expected to be on time. Even though nobody was going to meet him on the other end it was just his way. Knowing that sophie lucy, Emma and rebbeca would be at the café which was the place that Benjamin was trying to reach. Hope fully just in time for afternoon tea. With the thought of the girls gave Benjamin some thing to focus on. Whilst in pain he was telling himself that the journey was not far. Mind you with a little bit of frost bite Benjamin's journey was looking extremely long.

Sophie Lucy was about her business, she had decided that she would open the café with out Benjamin to her disappointment. She continued to rebbeca that it was to late even as much as she liked him while Benjamin is away the business comes first. Rebbeca in shock agrees, a small crowd out side gathered almost instantiuosly and with everything that was going on Sophie Lucy still ahd a smile on her face rebbeca was chosen to cut the ribbon.
Sophie Lucy did not wamt her own honours of the job rebbeca could see clearly that Sophie Lucy wa still up set with out Benjamin by her side and rebbeca jumped at the chanace as soon as it was mentioned. Her picture would be in the local paper along side Sophie Lucy and Emma. As she claps her hands and jumps around in excitement. Sophie Lucy takes the long piece of ribbon with the small tea tables and the chairs out side she adjusts all of them so that they would look perfect, as hse ties the ribbom up. Sophie Lucy takes one more look at it. Within a few minutes her café would be open again but with out Benjamin.
Rebbeca is ready and Sophie Lucy gives her the thumbs up to cut the ribbon, at that point the crowds exploded with cheers and clapping.
Rebbeca stands tall feeling really proud as Sophie Lucy ushers her away rebbeca she was surprised that it had happened so quickly it was over within a few seconds.

Toward sthe end of Benjamin's journey he was struggling the pain was to much but he was determined to fight it. he wanted to finish it he anted to win. It seemed he did not want to give in. he was taking his journey as a challenge even more so Sophie Lucy was at the end of it he closes his eyes visualizing the rest of his journey and telling himself that he was going to make it. As he opens his eyes the sun pears down wards he thinks its is a sign. It was Benjamin mind, all his negative thoughts through that thought brought more positive thoughts to him fro a dieing prospective. It was an weird situation to be in. Benjamin continues in pain. Each step a smaller stride. As he comes from around a corner of the road only to see the bus stop he was happier and smiling again he could ear the traffic in the distance. He knows his joueney was nearly over. As he watched from a beautiful view across the fields and being brought back to life it was now spring. Benjamin again could feel the change in the air he says to himself he looks on the floor and notices a couple of butts probably thrown form a car window he picks them up puts them in to his pocket. There was just enough to relax him. the only thing that worried Benjamin now was the taste of what he had to smoke. Benjamin trys to feel his feet he had only check an hour ago he was feeling more worried than before when he first looked at them. the last few miles he would walk in pain.

Rebbeca sits down in Benjamin seat fed up with all the customers of the day with one hand embeded in the side of her face talking to herself, sighing. Sophie Lucy on the other hand as just as happy as anybody else including Rebbeca. Rebbeca pours her self a cup of tea, sophie lucy wlaks in. rebbeca invites her to join her she agrees thanking her for the invite. They begin to talk and the subject ws still Benjamin. As theyb talk and laugh they both forget the time. Sopjie Lucy for the first time was a hour late in opening up again for lunch. She continued that it was ok it did not matter as she turns the closed sign to open. Then out of the blue whilst standing by the café doorway sophie lucy pulls a packet of cigerettes out of her pocket. Rebbeca could clearly see them. Sophie Lucy pulls one out of the packet Rebbeca stands there watching her in shock. Hesitating as she speaks sophie lucy jumps knowing that she had been caught. No I do not theses are for Benjamin he left them behind I was just looking after them for him and if you want to know why I am holding one I was just playing around Sophie Lucy throws the ciggertte up into he air and catches it in her mouth see she replys. She takes the cigarette out of her mouth does the trick again. Rebbeca smiles as they both laugh.

Taking in to account the events of the last couple of days Sophie Lucy does not think that Benjamin was going to return and she ofentells rebecea that she was missing him there was no letters or phone calls nothing. Although they were thunking about each other this must mean something sophie lucy checks her messages and nothing Sophie Lucy was sitting down in Benjamin's chair. As she pours herself a cup of tea and sighing in frustration Sophie Lucy spills the tea she was not concentrating her mind was else where. Straight after she does it again his time it ws not her cup but the salt and pepper. She was lucky that neither of them were hot. Rebbeca heard the crys of her shouting knowing exactly what she had done with out actually being there Sophie Lucy was in tears. She did not know how to comfort her this time around she just looked at her helplessly Sophie Lucy gets up saying nothing sophie lucy knew that Rebbeca could see that she ws hiding her tears. It had been another whole day and Benjamin had not returned and now rebbeca was at it where is Benjamin. May be he ahd left for good or maybe worse I will not say it any way it is not me that is missing him as she puts the cup in to the sink water and calmly says I am sure that he will return. As rebbeca walks out sophie lucy walks in with tears in her eyes they both say at the same time they hoped nothing had happened to bejmain sophie lucy says that they should call the police not thinking about benjain but thinking about Benjamin. No that ws not a good idea sophie Lucy jumps what about that mean that Benjamin wanted to befriend do youb thunk that he could be there no he would be to busy rebbeca reminds her it was Benjamin who was bowing out besides who would run the café and on top of that he could be anywhere sophie Lucy bursts in to tears again for a few minutes. Then rebbeca joins her. As they both lose control of ther feeling aboth in tears rebbeca says to sophie Lucy that they should wait. Sophie Lucy says what then another day then another Sophie Lucy agrees walking in and then out of the room clearly upset. As she picks up the used plates and cups. As she hands them to rebbecca to dry only to dump them back in to the sink for Sophie to wash them again, only to dry them again then handing them back to be washed again only for Sophie lucy to put them in the cubboard whilst slamming the doors unintentionaly of course, rebbeca would jump at all the slamming around and giggle afterwards. They continued the converstion ending in that they talks about him to much. It would makes things worse they both agree to sit it out. However it did not work within the hour they were talking about him again, and of course there was more tears. And there was still no sign of Benjamin.

Benjamin makes his way slowly back to the town with only a few miles to go a car pulls up Benjamin thinks he is in luck infact it was quite the opposite as Benjamin gets closer to the man behind the wheel believing that he was about to be offered a lift. The driver was looking side ways at Benjamin, Benjamin was about to pass out he was that tired and in pain. Benjamin slamming both hands on to the back of the car not acring about the pain the car drives of and Benjamin kept on saying that it was a nasty trick. Benjmain was upset for the first time. It did not take long for Benjamin to put the thought behind him out of his mind. Knowing that it could have been any body infact he was probably safer just walking the last few miles back on his own.
Even thougth he was going in Benjamin's direction. That upset benjain the most. Benjamin is struggling and the battle offighting the pain had begun. Benjamin was desperate he ws on his knees this did not work he felt stupid and it was just as painfull. As he crawls forcing his knees in to the ground this was only asking Benjamin feel worse. The only thing he could do was run and trust me it was not going to happen Benjamin was out of ideas. He continued the journey on his feet in pain again.

At this Point sophie lucy and rebbca had calmed down and were now laughing. Benjamin was not he was in pain as rebbeca continuation of her impressions of Benjamin was keeping her sslef and sophie Lucy happy.
Rebbeca: " The way he drinks his tea."
Sophie Lucy laughs with a smile to follow.
Sophie Lucy says to rebbeca that hse had not been the best of company and agrees that should have some fun she calms down only to burst out laughing again. she was sent all the way back to the beginning. As the night time came sophie Lucy closes up the café. She is on her own Emma and Rebbeca had gone home. she turns her shop sign over it wsa now saying closed. Sophie Lucy takes a seat sits down on it leaning with her arms stretched out wards on the tabke out side the café. With her head firmily down with them. with the thought of Benjamin arriving with the thought that he would just appear and knock on her door. She missed Benjamin teribley, sophie Lucy was a fighter if she wanted something she would know how to get most of the time. She waits in silence occasionally rasing her head. As for the paser bys as for the sound of Benjamin's footsteps she could reconise them anywhere.

Benjamin limping finally makes back into the town it had taken him thee hours it would have been sooner if he had not frozen his toes a normal forty five minutes benjmain had calculated and timed every step so he would know for future reference and the next time.
He appears mistiously from around the corner in to the high street. He is in extreme pain excruciating pain. He is now grunting as he walks and gritting his teeth he can feel the tears in his eyes but he was to manly to cry so he fights tears as well. As he walks he saying the words quietly help me. as he tells himself not to give in. as he makes it to the cafe doors and falls over on perpose lying down on his back. No longer thinking about the pain but thinking about Sophie Lucy. She had fallen asleep on the table while Benjamin lays outside not noticing that she was right next to him asleep. He calls her name out quietly to wake her by calling out her name Sophie Lucy sophie Lucy Benjamin was not sure if she could hear him. he gets up off the floor and trys again this time he whispers her name right in her ear Sophie Lucy. She does not move, knowing that she has good neighbours Benjamin is hesitant to shout any louder but in the end shouts at the top of his voice. Sophie Lucy jumps thinking that she is dreaming and goes to walk away as Benjamin calls her name out again she ignores it again and then opens the shop door just as she was going to close it she double checks then realizes that it was true Benjamin had come back sophie runs to throwing her arms around him and whsopers in his ear your back. Benjmain's reply was yes he was back. She continues I missed you. Sophie Lucy close the door leaving Benjamin outside she thinks that she is dreaming.

Benjmain is left outside in the cold he sits down in his chair slowly saying no repeatedly. Sophie lucy had no idea that he was there. as for the light being on benjmain picks up one of the chairs close to her door and places in front of him he moves closer to the door it was warmer there. he takes his socks of the wooly mess filled with mud and bits and soaking wet through wear. He looks at his topes no better or worse. It just looked sore how he was going to heal him self he did not know however sophie Lucy would know. Benjamin takes the blame he know knew that there was a cost for walking. This had happened to benjmain before but his time it was obvious that it was worse. He could not remember exactly but this time it was definatly worse. Even so benjamin was spending his last night on the street and out of the cold. He knew that he would have a better time tomorrow. He snuggles up in is big jacket under sophie Lucys café as usual he puts the sides of his collor up around his face. With that he lifts his legs up one by one pulling them towards his chest and closes his eyes and goes to sleep. As the night time slowly awakes and the people depart to there homes benjmain is left alone knowing that tomorrow he would be re in vited.

By the time the morning arose benjmain was already by the café door and waiting to surprise Sophie Lucy. Shivering with excitement but to cold to be able toshout out her name, to cold to press the door bell, which looked like it had frosted stuck. Benjamin waits, more people turn up. Mostly people that wanted there early morning coffee a fix. Benjmain was slowly pushed from the front of the que to the back. He did not know what to do Sophie Lucy had not noticed him yet. The que that benjmain was in was outside. Even more so as she opens her doors to let the customers in benjmain had a chance to get warm first he was cold. She still had not noticed benjmain most of the customer s had gone and as benjmain try s to speak to her his voice was tired and cold and he did not want to speak however on this occasion he raised his voice and shouted at the top of his voice. It was hardly the most romantic approach he would of prefered to appoched her nice and quietly susprising her at the coffee bar. Everybody in the café stops doing what they are doing sophie lucy looks up dropping the cup in her hand surprised with a big smile on her face as she takes her penny off running out on to the shop floor shouting benjamin benjmain your back. She throews her arms around benjmain come on lets get you warm your cold

Benjmain: " really freezing."

Sophie Lucy: " your back."

Sophie Lucy is grabbing him and hugging him as she pulls him through to her kitchen she shouts to Emma and rebbeca Benjamin is back he come home were have you been.

Benjamin:"Arhh that would be telling on an adventure."

Sophie Lucy: " Sit down."

Benjmain was expecting a short te,lling off but instead got a heros welcome with lots of cudling. Rebbeca walks in
Rebbeca:"whoooo who are you."
Benjamin: " my name is Benjamin."
Rebbeca: " oh your that guy I have heard a lot about you."
Emma knew him already and was just as surprised as everybody else and seeing him on his return shouts it is Benjamin he is back. Were have you been you old dog. As benjmain is welcomed with cheers and the early morning possie of people had gone he gets the chance to do some talking and is waiting for Sophie Lucy to come back out to the kitchen. She insisted before they stared talking about the adventure that benjmain should warm up and get washed and find some clean clothes. When benjamin was ready he begins rebbeca was listening close by doing the washing up and Sophie Lucy starts almost straight away, that he knew the protocol wash, change your clothe benjmain ws going for a nice long bath and afterwards he would tell them everything they would catch up afterwards.
Benjmain smiles and say nothing he was just glad to be back. Then sophie Lucy notices his toe she says nothing at first and benjmain was happy to ablige and tell her everything about it. he continiues to thank her as for having a new bath and he jokes that it is safe this time

He did not get a straight answer but hears Sophie Lucy joking and laughing in the back ground. Benjamin strips down, the water was nice and hot he does not get in it to soon instead sits on the side of the bath tub waving his hand in the water testing the temperature. As he sits waiting for his bath to cool.
Sophie Lucy:" are you desent."

Benjmain:" No."
Sophie Lucy:" Grab towel I want to talk to you."
Sophie lucy stands next to the door hiding her face and talking.
Sophie Lucy: " here is a towel and soap take it."
Benjamin: " Thank you."
Benjamin takes all the stuff that lucy had given him and puts it all on the bathroom floor he gets into the bath tub.

With a big ahh and an ohhh Benjamin sinks in to the bath tub. This was great he said totally relaxing himself his arms stretched out wards holding the side of the bath tub. Eventually Benjamin sits up again after congratulating Sophie Lucy for running him the perfect bath. Benjamin is feeling smooth as he begins to wash his dirty hands and fingers then his face until it had a shinny look to it. as for his hair it was long and when he had looked in the mirror he was in shock as it had grown considerabley. It looked whitish and a little grey Benjamin was surprised. This was all about to change as Sophie Lucy brings in the clipers with another bottle of shampoo. Benjamin looks up at her and tells her to bring it in she had no choice but to peek benjamin on the inside with out his clothes on was looking pretty sharp. He was skinny but seemed toned it looked like all the walking had paid off. Sophie Lucy is called back again this time she is in the bathroom as she puts one hand over her face taking the bottle of shampoo from Benjamin who was now washing his hair rebbeca walks in only to be pulled back out by Sophie Lucy by her arm. They both laugh Benjamin takes no notice from them and continues washing.

The End

www.ingramcontent.com/pod-product-compliance
Lightning Source LLC
Chambersburg PA
CBHW060537310726
48982CB00009B/1281/J

* 9 7 8 1 8 3 9 4 5 0 8 7 7 *